TWO TRUTHS

AND A

LIE

Suki van Dijk

First ebook edition October, 2022

ISBN: 9798356797132

www.sukivandijk.com

For Peter, who (lucky for me) inspired none of the guys in this book. I love you, baby. Always.

For Miranda and Jake, who inspire me every day.

For all the wonderful teachers I encountered in prep school: really, truly, none of this happened.

And my eternal gratitude to the Eagles for the Hotel California and Long Run albums.

Hiraeth: *a homesickness for a home you cannot return to or one that never was*

Two Truths and a Lie is a game played by children. One child tells three facts about her life. Two are true, one isn't. The other players win by figuring out which is which. The degree of difficulty in this game is greatly increased by familiarity. Because you already know everything there is to know about the people you know best.

Right?

Table of Contents

—⚬⚭⚬—

Derek

When I think of him now, I think of him doing those three-fingered push-ups over and over. As many as we both could stand. I'd walk down the hall, look into the weight room, and there he'd be, looking back at me in the mirror. He was this sixteen-year-old-bronze-and-golden-boy statue. I was fourteen, terrified that I couldn't catch my breath after he caught me looking at him.

I think of the way the veins in his arms stood out after those workouts. We'd go off to Mr. Hamori's photography class, and I'd trace the veins up his arms with my eyes. Up to where his shirt hid his skin. He'd look at me, and I'd look at him, and I couldn't breathe again, knowing he knew what I was thinking. And we'd always swear we were going to get some homework done. But there we'd be, in the darkroom. Alone. Again. We never did manage to learn a damn thing about photography in that class. But I learned a lot.

I think of him every time I hear "Stairway to Heaven." I feel his hands at the small of my back, my hands around the back of his neck, us swaying together, bodies pressed as tightly as we could get them. I can still smell the alchemy of his cologne and sweat and feel what that scent did to me. Even when the music sped up, we'd stay locked in our slow-dance embrace.

I see him coming off the lacrosse field, throwing that grin at me over his shoulder. I see those aviator sunglasses, the tip of a Visine bottle sticking out of his pocket. I see him smoking a butt at the Gazebo. I see him lying in the sun, on the hill going down to the Pond, eyes closed, singing Dead tunes softly to himself. I see him freezing his ass off that first winter, this too-cool California boy trying to stay warm while getting high in the New England woods.

I seem to mostly be able to summon his image back up only in pictures. Pictures I saw. Pictures I took. Pictures I meant to take but never got around to. Wholesome yearbook-type pictures taken for the grown-ups of the perfect prep school kids we were supposed to be. And then the glassy-eyed pictures of the way we really were, stoned and smiling, flashing peace signs, blissfully naïve.

I never see him falling-down drunk. I never see him mean. I never see him hurting people.

I suppose I stopped seeing things I don't wish to see a long, long time ago.

This Morning, Predawn

I'm back in the car, driving as fast as I can. This time I'm flying up the highway instead of the back roads. I've been in New York for twenty years, but I'm still a Massachusetts girl at heart, and I can make it from here to campus in two hours and fifty-seven minutes if I have to. Maybe in two forty-seven tonight. No stops and I can make it before sunrise. No distractions, all I do is drive and think—think about my life and the mess I have made of it all.

I have no idea how the hell this happened to me. How is it possible that I turned into just another one of those wan blondes this town is so full of? Every damn one of us, the same prettiest, smartest girl to come out of her stupid fucking backwater town. Every damn one of us, planted here like flowers or flags. Doing what is expected of flowers or flags, waving prettily in the breeze and not making any noise. Always put together, right hair, right nails, right clothes, decent tennis player, never an expressed opinion more contentious than white jeans before Memorial Day. Every damn one of us, making ourselves just a little bit smaller, every day, in every way.

That's not me. Not the me I know. When did I become someone so averse to conflict that I compromise before I'm even asked? When did I start believing the status quo was worth it, no matter the cost? When did

I stop listening to my own voice? How could I have let this happen to us?

As soon as I get off the highway, everything along the way looks so strange and so familiar in the near-dawn light, it's like I've taken a half step back in time. The Chinese restaurant where the hockey team got in so much trouble over busting it up after the tournament win is now a Mexican restaurant. But the packie they bought from is still there. Still standing proud. *Plus ça change*, right? I nearly have to stop the car to stop the tears so I can drive. But there is no time for that now. I can almost see her tiny body in the hospital bed. I yell out loud, at the shade I feel surrounding me, "She is mine. She has always been only mine. You can't have her. Go away."

Hang on baby, I'm nearly there. Damn, I wish I had listened to my sixth sense, gut, intuition, whatever you want to call it. Wish I had acted. That thought leads me straight into thinking about driving her up to Mansfield last week. It feels like it ought to have been so much longer ago.

Affluent Suburban Home

One Week Ago, 8 a.m.

The scraping noise and the sound of rock against metal isn't my first clue that our road trip isn't going to be as easy-breezy as I wanted it to be. But it's a doozy. It seemed like such a great plan when I made it. I'd drive Bree up to school the long way. Girls' road trip! We'd make a day of it. Now the day is here, and I have to go through with it.

I throw the car into park and get out to inspect the damage.

Fuck! I think.

"Fudge!" I say too loudly and brightly. I mostly say what I mean only in my own head these days.

Bree rolls her eyes at me. She's not at all concerned about my shiny new car. "I have heard the word before, you know, Mom. I'm nearly fifteen. I'm not a baby. You don't have to do that."

"Don't right now, Bree. Just don't." I'm not in the mood to listen to a list of my failings as a mother or as a driver. "We really need to get on the road. So, don't. And don't tell Daddy, OK?" I push my bangs away from my forehead and put my sunglasses up on top of my head as I run a hand over the paint to check the damage underneath.

"When would I possibly have the chance to tell Daddy? He is so busy. He's never around." She rolls her eyes at me again as she rolls up the car window.

I know sticking my expensive new sunglasses on top of my head isn't good for them, but I'm annoyed at myself for not being more careful with the car. So, I'm not careful with the sunglasses either. So what if I don't put them in their case like the saleslady said I was supposed to. Does anyone really do that? I'm the only one who worries about how much I spend on that kind of stuff anyway. He wouldn't think twice about the cost of a pair of sunglasses, even if he knew what they cost. I pay all the household bills anyway, so it isn't like my dear husband would ever know, or notice. Still, I feel a responsibility to take care of stuff. I like to treat things properly.

There's a good-size scrape along the rear quarter panel of the car. It's just barely deep enough to have gouged the paint. Standing in my own driveway, I can almost hear the fit my dad would have thrown. I start to rub my eyes, then remember that causes wrinkles and stop. My hand goes to my mouth instead as I try to stop chewing the inside of my cheeks, which is what I do to not bite my nails. Other people can see my nails.

Not for the first time, I'm glad I married someone so calm. He will just pick up the phone and call our insurance guy, with absolutely no drama. He'd much rather throw money at things than argue about them. I'll get a kiss on the top of the head and a casual "No big. That's what money is for, Kat."

This way of dealing with things is so diametrically opposed to the histrionics that would have followed the marring of a fancy new car in my new-to-the-middle-class family, it still catches me off guard even after all these years. My dad grew up desperately poor. He was a successful businessman by the time I showed up, but he never seemed secure that the money would last. He owned a chain of auto body shops and could have a car fixed with little effort or cost, but still he would have gone on at me for days about my responsibilities, my carelessness, and my wasting of money. The wasting of money through carelessness was super high on my father's list of sins. And it was one of my most common failings.

Even hearing it start in the back of my mind is too much for me. I need to squeeze my eyes shut tightly for a moment to block out the noise in my head. The quiet, softer cadences of my life now make me feel so much safer, so much more comfortable.

My mom, sensibly enough, dealt with these sorts of things with my dad by simply flat out lying. Faced with any scratch, any fender bender, she would just say someone must have hit her. Unless she was presented with irrefutable evidence of guilt—there was that time she got the car door impaled on a fire hydrant—it was clearly someone else's fault. I'm pretty sure she at least considered blaming the hydrant for hitting her, but even her remarkable verbal gymnastic skills couldn't pull that one off. Instead, she blamed me for distracting her while she was trying to park.

As steadfast as I am in my refusal to turn into my mother, in this case, I'll make an exception. Even though I know he couldn't be bothered to pitch a fit. I don't want to deal with it. When I get back, I'll tell him it was fine when I left it in the Friendly's parking lot. Someone must have hit me.

It's just so much easier. I don't want to argue. I don't want to worry that this is the moment he changes his mind and starts to be bothered by my carelessness. If someone else hit the car, then it can't be my fault. Peace and quiet continue their reign over our life. Sometimes, when this sort of thing happens, I honestly forget. Say something happened often enough and it's easy to believe it's actually true.

I try to brush the evidence of pale-blue paint off our stone wall, but the rough stone hurts my fingers. Bree and I should be on the road already, and he'll never notice anyway.

The morning had started off early with all sorts of yelling and recriminations. Bree and I are both nervous about this and both unwilling to admit to being nervous about anything. Honestly, both of us tend to be a little on the high-strung side on regular days, so we can verge on hysterical when we're wound up. My husband, who is usually quite a calming influence on us both, had to be away this weekend—some stupid hockey invitational. I know that's part of why I'm so flustered. I mean, it probably is easier for us to do this without him anyhow, but really, he couldn't have just skipped this one tournament?

Same Morning,
an Hour Earlier

Since Bree and I have the whole house to ourselves, we can yell at each other without interference or disapproval. I didn't grow up in this world of quiet; I yell. It's the people around me I prefer quiet. My darling daughter definitely got the yelling gene from my side of the family.

I have to drag her out of bed, even though I can hear her alarm blaring from my room at the other end of the house. As soon as she is awake enough to move her limbs, she starts her last-minute packing and complaining about everything I am doing to make her life more difficult. While she dashes around the house packing, I have to keep unpacking all of the stuff of mine that she is trying to take with her. I take two good belts, a black cashmere sweater, and my favorite hairbrush out of her overnight bag before I give up. Anything of mine I can't find when I get back, I'll just replace.

"Mom, where's my chamomile shampoo and my Terex? I told you I was almost out. Didn't you get any?" Her tone clearly states her belief that I am deliberately keeping hair products from her for my own nefarious purposes.

"Did you put it on the list?" I try to stay calm. "I need another cup of coffee," I mutter to myself.

"I told you, I can't go to school without them! My hair will be gross! Did you get me a new Airwrap?"

"If it wasn't on the list, I didn't get it." I put my hands into the yoga mudra for patience, palms up, thumbs touching middle fingers to make a circle, and take a few deep cleansing breaths. It helps. A little. Maybe. Sort of?

"Ugh, Mom, I can't believe you think you're the one who needs patience to deal with me! I'm totally taking your shampoo and conditioner. And your blow-dryer! Who knows what I'll be able to get in the hinterlands." She stomps off toward my room to take the nearly full containers of shampoo and conditioner from my shower—*me, I put things on the list*—and grabs my favorite hair dryer for good measure before returning to her packing.

"No problem, take mine," I say to the wall, as a flash of blond hair brushes by. I am trying to use a light tone to defuse the situation, but since I am at least as nervous about this as she is, it probably doesn't come out right. I probably sound sarcastic. I should know better; Bree is the only one in this house who is allowed to be sarcastic these days.

While she is in my bathroom, I pull another sweater of mine—*my favorite chocolate-brown cashmere cardi, damn it*—from the bottom of her bag and quickly stow it under her extra pillow. I make a mental note to come back in here and grab it when I get back and the house is empty but for the dogs and me.

We both refuse to eat any breakfast and, after letting the dogs out, decide to just get in the car and stop along the way. Which is about thirty seconds, before the scrape. My two-week-old car was a combination I-know-you're-unhappy-with-the-baby-going-away/sorry-I've-been-so-busy-lately/the-early-birthday-present-you've-always-wanted   bribe from the hubby. I know he understands on some level how conflicted I am about sending her away. My gut feeling is that I'm just not convinced that she is ready to live without our supervision yet. He thinks I'm being ridiculous. She'll be fine.

He so rarely catches me by surprise in any way, but I was honestly shocked when he turned up with my dream car in the driveway for me. He must be feeling very guilty to just go for such a total extravagance. September is stupid early for a December birthday present, but he said he wanted me to be able to enjoy the convertible while we still had some nice weather. *That makes sense, right?*

Baby—yes, I did name my new car Baby, Dr. Freud—is my forever fantasy-mobile. She's a silvery-blue Mercedes convertible. He knows that I've wanted one for the longest time. When Bree was five or six, she saw one on the way to the club and said, "Mummy! Look! That's the car for you! It's blue, it's a convertible, and it has a peace sign on the front! You should get one." The kid has always had great taste.

It took about ten years, but two weeks ago, the hubby made me close my eyes and come outside, and there she was. Baby. She was even wrapped up in a big navy blue bow. Every time I get in the car, even if it is just to go to the supermarket, the new-car smell fills me with joy. Baby is a dream to drive, and I love driving. It is entirely possible that I may have actually squealed with joy when I saw the tires had a different pressure rating for driving over 100 mph.

After the false start with the scrape, we finally get on the open road. I am looking forward to the driving part at least.

Back Roads, Heading North

8:45 a.m.

B ree looks over at me through hair that's being blown all around by the wind whipping past the car. I desperately wish she would put it up in a clip so her ends won't get all ragged since there is no decent place to get it trimmed up there, but at this moment everything is peaceful between us, so I keep my mouth shut. Her mood seems to improve the farther we get from the house. I wonder if she's excited to be starting a new phase of her life or just happy to be away from us. There is no good answer to that question. And I am smart enough not to ask it out loud.

It's a beautiful late-summer day, so our plan is to take the fun car and the scenic route, not the minivan and the interstate. Even with the bulk of her belongings sent ahead, Bree's carry-on luggage is taking up all of the space in the car not currently occupied by the two of us. I'm going to have to do a whole-house inventory when I get back to figure out what the hell else of my stuff she has taken with her.

When I imagined this drive, I had a vision of us having a freewheeling mother-daughter road trip. It's our last chance to be together until we go up for Parents' Weekend in October. Schools like to keep the parents away through September, to let the homesickness pass before the first visit. After that we won't see her until homecoming, which is the first weekend in November. Then she will be back home for four days for Thanksgiving and then for nearly four weeks at Christmas. The fall calendar is fully mapped out in my head.

Today I thought we could have a nice lunch and maybe stop in a little town along the way to shop and stretch our legs. Spend some girl time, just the two of us. I'm going to miss her so much. As much as she drives me crazy lately, I don't know what I'll do without her underfoot. What will I fill my days with, if they aren't spent on momming her?

We used to have so much fun together. Sometime in the last year or so though, my sweet little baby girl was replaced with an entirely different and surlier self. One day my little buddy went missing and a sneering changeling appeared in her place. I swear it was almost the very day she turned fourteen. These days, everything I say and do is wrong. Until she needs something, of course. Then I'm the best mom in the world again, at least for a few minutes, until I resume being an idiot.

It hurts my heart to think of her being away from me, so I've been doing my best not to.

I see her out of my peripheral vision as I drive the early part of the winding country road that will take us north toward Mansfield Academy. Our alma mater, *Mansfield, Mansfield, our noble school*, Bree's new school. My husband went there as well. We first met there as children. His dad went there too, as did his grandfather, at least one great-grandfather, his brother and sister, and nearly all of Bree's cousins. I'm the only alum from my side, until Bree graduates, of course. Collectively though, we're a Mansfield family.

It's some comfort for me to think that at the very least she knows the campus well. She won't be a lost little frosh, wandering around without a clue, like I was. It would make me so much happier still if she had some cousins there now, to look after her, but they're all older. Hubby's the youngest in the family. Bree will be there on her own.

There is always something about returning to school that makes me revert a little bit to the girl I was there. It happens to everyone going home, right? Returning to the scene of the crime, as it were. Our lives are so wrapped up in Mansfield, so maybe I feel it more than most. There's always one of us on the board or on an advisory committee or reunion committee, or whatever it is they need from us at any given moment. For all my involvement, it's still hard for me to wrap my head around going as a parent, not a student, or even as an alum.

There are days when I can't believe I've been out of school for almost twenty-five years. Hell, other times, I can't believe I'm more than twenty-five. But here sits my almost fifteen-year-old to prove it. So, it must be true.

Maybe it isn't just going back that returns me to my teenage self. Maybe none of us really grows out of our teenage selves. Maybe we just heap on layers that help us hide that part of us from the world most of the time.

The new car is a talisman of sorts, protecting me from being just a parent, a mom. It announces, fine, maybe I am a mom, but I'm also still one of the cool kids. I'm a cool mom with a hot car. Or maybe I'm a hot mom with a cool car? *Whatever,* I'll take whatever hotness or coolness I can get right now.

Bree seems happy enough too, and we will ride onto campus with the top down. She gets to make her entrance in a convertible that could plausibly be hers as a senior. The minivan definitely doesn't make that same kind of statement. At least I'm not the only one in the family who appreciates what a cool car can do for your image.

I know she has questions. She's been coming at me even harder, ever since her acceptance letter came. Not that it was more than a formality, but formalities must be kept up, right? Otherwise the whole system falls apart. I'm just not sure what the right way is to answer her. I want to keep her from making the same mistakes I made. Do I do that by telling her what those mistakes were? Or am I better off continuing to allow her to believe I never made any? Do I sugarcoat? Do I tell her the truth? Should I be more worried about her getting into trouble, like my parents were? Would my experiences even apply? Honestly, it was just such a different world back then.

I don't look over at her, using concentrating on the road as my tacit excuse. But it's as if she can hear what I'm thinking, because as soon as I think it, the questions start again.

"So, Mom, are you ever going to tell me anything interesting that happened when you were at Mansfield? Crushes? Boyfriends? Parties? Did you ever get in trouble? Did you ever even get a bad grade? You're always so lah-di-dah. Was there no dirt?" She pulls her hair back into a ponytail, sucks in her cheeks, and makes duck lips at the light-up mirror on the visor. "Were you fabulous and popular? Did you have a crush on Daddy? Did he have a crush on you? Come on, you can tell me if you thought he was a cool older boy. I won't tell him. I promise! He'll never be able to lord it over you."

* * *

I suppose I could just give in and tell her I was an above-average, self-absorbed stoner teenage brat. Weren't we all? I don't know if she is really looking for the truth from me, or if she just needs some reassurance that leaving home and all her friends won't be a total drag for her. What could

I possibly tell her about my time at Mansfield, with Derek, without giving anything away? Is this about her, about me, or about us?

Maybe I could just tell her my theory that every woman has a secret fantasy about going back to her old school, seeing her first love, and rubbing his nose in just how great she turned out. How do I tell her that theory when I know she thinks my first love was her dad?

It makes sense that she believes Hubby was my first and only one true love. I mean, we did meet at Mansfield. Not to mention, we are her parents, so her mental vision of our lives before her is probably pretty tame. Of course, she is going to assume he's the one I think of when I hear Van Morrison sing "Moondance." Will she be angry at me if I shatter her perfectly logically constructed image of our world? Will she hate me if I tell her the truth?

As I glance over, I wonder when she'll meet the boy who first makes her feel that way. I hope it isn't too soon. Let her grow up a little more first. She's so close to being the age I was when I met Derek.

It's not that I'm opposed to her having information about the dangers of the world. Bree has had piles of sex ed and drug ed classes at school. I guess I'm just opposed to her having any information about anything I did. How can I expect to maintain any discipline over her if she knew what I was like?

I'm adopted, so Bree is the only person I've ever met who I'm biologically related to. And she looks just like me. Which is indescribably incredible to me. The feeling that comes from being able to say "Hey, that's my nose" is appreciated very differently by those of us who have never experienced it before. Plus, looking at Bree reminds me how much fun it was to be young and beautiful.

Honestly, I'm not even sure she'd believe me if I told her what things were like at prep school in the eighties. Life is so different for these kids.

Schools are so much more clamped down now. Can she even conceive that I might have had any sort of interesting life prior to her existence? That I had fun? That her proper, rules-enforcing, image-curating mother was once a crazy, irresponsible, terrible teenager?

Besides, times really have changed. When I was in school, youthful indiscretions were treated as just that. Rarely, if ever, were they actionable. These days, kids are being thrown out of schools and sometimes even into the legal system for the kind of offenses that would have gotten us a stern talking-to. Maybe there would be a phone call home, or we would get boarded if we did something that bad. But the idea of our school calling the police? Baffling.

These poor kids don't even get close to the point that would have gotten us thrown out. They have so much less opportunity to make a few youthful mistakes. Now kids get booted at the first offense, or maybe the second, but I've not heard of anyone's kids getting a third chance. I suppose it could be possible that some of us would have been better off with the kind of toss-them-out, tough-love treatment that seems prevalent today, but I can't believe most of us would have had better lives for it. I know I wouldn't have. I just needed a little time to grow up. Like most of us did.

I know we agreed and all, but the closer we get to school, the more I am not all that sure about this. It's so far away. She won't be able to come home for weekends. I won't be there when all the confusing high school stuff happens. Even if she doesn't want me to be there for her anymore anyway.

Bree is a year older than I was when I started at Mansfield so I am pinning my hopes on her being a little wiser. Precisely a year—we share a birthday. December eighteenth, the two of us, and Keith Richards. She is the best birthday present I have ever gotten. She is the only birthday present I can think of that could possibly beat out the new car.

When I was a kid, the school year age cut-off followed the calendar year, if your fifth birthday came before the end of the calendar year, you went to Kindergarden. Especially if you were a girl, and double especially if you were a girl in the public schools. A handful of the November and December boys were held back, but not many, and that's how it was referred to—sotto voce—as they were being "held back." Now nursery school directors call it "being given the gift of a year" and there is nothing sotto voce about it. There was never any question of my being sent to school on time. Even as a mid-December baby, I was sent on ahead with my class, and I excelled.

There was nothing wrong with Bree, so I always intended to have her start kindergarten at the regular time, just like I did, but her nursery school strongly discouraged us. All our friends strongly discouraged us. People I barely knew, it seemed like even people who struck up a conversation in the line at the supermarket, strongly discouraged us. It was like we'd stumbled onto some weird suburban cult that existed only to enrich nursery schools with the "gift of another year."

Bree was only four, and yes, she was small, that is never going to change, but she certainly seemed ready for kindergarten to me. She could write her name, she could read basic words, she could count, she didn't bite. But then just about everyone we knew started giving us a hard time. And there was just so much advice. The advice came just short of calling us abusive parents. We were practically accused of being willing to risk scarring her for life, pushing her ahead for our own inexplicable reasons. We couldn't really possibly be thinking of sending her to kindergarten before her fifth birthday. Then my mother-in-law weighed in, and the decision was made. Bree was to spend another year at the world's priciest suburban preschool.

I didn't know then I would be so thankful for that year. That holding her back for another year of nursery school meant that I would get another year with her home with me before I had to send her off to Mansfield. Had I realized that this day would come so quickly I might have held her back for another year. I can't imagine how difficult it would have been for me to give her up a year ago, when she was still nice to me most of the time.

I know I sound just like my mother when I start with all the "when I was that age" stuff, but honestly, the holding-kids-back thing has just gotten out of control in the striver suburbs. We have kids in town now who are turning seven in kindergarten. Seven! I understand the inclination to give your child an edge and all, but it has just gotten ridiculous. And it will have real-life consequences when those kids get older. Bree will have friends who are able to drive as second-semester freshmen. That just can't be a good idea. I wasn't old enough to get a license until I was a senior. These kids are just learning how to handle themselves away from home. They certainly shouldn't be driving.

Maybe being a year older will give Bree the maturity advantage that I didn't have. Maybe she'll find scholarly joy in her schoolwork and won't get so caught up in the social whirl. I smile, since I can't even think this with a straight face.

Right. Bree? My Bree is the eye of the social hurricane.

I think her phone is permanently attached to her hand. She had to text seven friends from the dressing room of Nordstrom to weigh in on her dress choice for the eighth-grade-graduation dance. Her friends had to vote on pictures of her in each outfit. Lots of pictures, from all angles. Complete with the accessories for each outfit. Bree's social life is her entire life right now. They spend all day together at school. They go to Starbucks together every day after school. And still, they are never not texting! We had to implement a strict no-texting-at-the-table rule when Grammy and Gramps are over.

Bree's grades have always been very good, so we can't complain. It's not like being a social butterfly impedes her learning or anything. She's able to have fun with her friends and still be near the top of her class. In that way she is just like me.

Still, there is no way for me not to worry about the trouble she can get into being away from home, because I know exactly what kind of trouble she can get into being away from home. And even we can't ignore how different the prep school world is now.

There are schools now claiming that they no longer give up their in loco parentis rights to decide upon student conduct, even when the students' actual parents are present. One family we know had their twin girls thrown out because they posted pictures of a family trip to France. Good family. Great girls. The girls had wineglasses in front of them in some of the pictures. Both sixteen-year-olds, upon being questioned, admitted to school officials—taking the whole honor code thing way too far, evidently—that they had been served wine, at dinner, in France, with their parents, on summer vacation. Then, instead of being patted on their little blond heads for being so honest, the school decided that the girls had violated the rules and were therefore no longer welcome to matriculate. Boom, booted, done. No second chance. Gone.

Honestly, everyone I knew was agog.

Their parents threatened all sorts of legal action of course, but since they had signed the "zero tolerance" alcohol pledge along with their girls, they had no legal recourse. I still can't believe a school would treat a family that way. This story was a complete shocker to all of us who grew up with the understanding that our children and grandchildren would be well cared for by our schools. Frankly, there is no way that school's endowment won't suffer. Zero tolerance is an untenable fundraising strategy.

I'm sure Mansfield hasn't swung quite that far on the pendulum. There is no zero tolerance pledge to sign or anything. Our alums wouldn't stand for it. And of course, even if there were, our contributions to the life of the institution would still hold significant weight. We are pretty comfortable in the knowledge that Bree will be welcome as long as she doesn't light anything really important on fire.

Still, we can't totally ignore the facts. The tolerance line has moved well away from where we knew it to be. I'm not sure any of us are positive where the line between reasonable punishment and "please remove yourself, posthaste" is at this moment. And it's not exactly the sort of question you can ask. "By the way, Headmaster, would you mind delineating precisely which of our former misbehaviors might get our little darlings sent packing? Thanks awfully."

So, what if I was to tell Bree everything about all the kinds of things we did? And then what if she was to take that information as permission to do the same? What if she got in trouble and got thrown out? Honestly, what good could telling her the whole truth about me possibly do for her?

I am simultaneously terrified that she'll get caught and thrown out over some small little nothing thing and terrified that she won't get caught and she'll spiral into addiction because what she really needs is help. Will she be more like me, or more like the kids who couldn't handle it and never managed to grow out of their teenage lifestyles?

I mean, it's not as if it is something we don't have to consider, genetically. The best description I can come up with for my dear husband's parents would be functional alcoholics, or, you know,

WASPs. I mean, I love them to death, but even at their age, they can still pack away an impressive amount of booze. Their standard for judging restaurants is the amount of pour. "Tiny glasses, dreadful, darling. Just dreadful. Don't even bother." Alternatively, "Lovely place, yacht club pour" with their fingers stretched out to indicate a good six inches of drink.

There are times when I seem to forget a little that Bree isn't just a me clone. She has my face and my small frame, but she's naturally blonder, like her dad. She has her dad's bright blue eyes, not my green ones. And she has always been all sunshine and ease, just like the hubby. She is so much more secure than I was. Whereas I was the type of kid who calculated everything by how it would look to the right people. I still feel that twinge of unease at times. "Am I doing this right? Bread plate is on the left, water to the right. Right?" Sometimes I still make the BeD symbol with my hands - flat hands, facing the table, thumbs outstretched to touch, fingers long, B stands for bread on the left, D stands for drinks on the right - just to double-check. Bree is totally comfortable in her own skin. She would just laugh if she picked up the wrong glass.

I do worry though about how she'll react if she is ever made to feel like she's on the outside looking in somewhere. I don't think she has experienced it yet, but it's bound to happen sometime. I just hope she will be able to roll with it when does. I can't imagine it could happen at Mansfield though. Her family practically built the place. That sort of thing still means something.

I worry both that she won't find any friends at Mansfield and that she will find all the wrong friends. I worry about who will tell her to stop reading and go to bed, and will they make sure she actually does turn out the light? I worry about her not waking up for classes without me to drag her out of bed. I worry she won't eat right if I don't prod her. Then I circle back around again to worrying about who she'll sit with at lunch and what kinds of friends she will have. It's exhausting.

Of course, the hubby says I'm worrying over nothing, but he's not her mom. I understand that she hasn't ever gotten into any trouble or ever come home wasted from a night out with her friends, but some days we'll be having a nice time together, and all of a sudden, she'll give me the teenager stink eye, and I can almost see a flash of Derek-style rebellion in her face. I can usually calm myself down with the knowledge that it's just her showing normal teen behavior and what I'm really freaked out by is seeing a shadow of my own teenage rebellion peeking back at me from damn near my own face.

I'd probably think it was funny if it was happening to someone else.

In those moments I have great sympathy for my mother. I suppose that's how we all come to appreciate our parents, right? Maybe someday Bree will think the same thing about me. I hope we'll stay closer than that. My mom and I never had this kind of relationship. We never had fun. She was just in charge of everything.

I know I agreed to send Bree to Mansfield. It's a wonderful school and we want her to love the place and be part of it, like we are. I guess I just didn't expect it would come so quickly. And just because I agreed to something doesn't mean I have to be happy about it.

* * *

"Mom? Mom, I asked you a question. Hello! Anyone home?" Her voice brings me back to the car and out of my own head. Bree always uses an exaggerated Julia Child–like "Helloooooooo!" when she needs my attention.

"Of course I was fabulous and popular, Bree. How could it possibly be any other way? Have you seen how cute we are?" My answer is a feeble attempt to dodge. And she isn't buying it. I turn my head for a moment to beam a great big smile at my beautiful little girl. I am going to miss our girl time together so much. From here on in, it will just be me and the hubby and the dogs. And even our dogs are boys. Maybe the goldfish is a girl. I think I'll decide right now that she is. I need some female solidarity in my house.

"C'mon, Mom, tell me something interesting! Anything!" she pleads, brushing her hair with a tiny pink brush she pulled out of the side pocket of the door and admiring herself in the mirror. That girl gets a lot of mileage out of that little mirror. I realize that's where my purse brush has gotten to. I make a mental note to make sure she doesn't grab it for school when she gets out of the car.

"Really, Bree, I can promise you, nothing interesting happened, it was just school." I continue saying the same lines I've always said. It's a familiar dance. She needs to keep asking the same questions, and I need to keep fudging the answers. "We studied. We played sports. I played sports badly. You know I was in the drama department. I did a lot of plays. I studied Shakespeare. Daddy's older than me. Maybe he had a little crush on me, but he wasn't my boyfriend. We didn't date then. We didn't really even know each other all that well. I don't know what else you want me to say."

"I don't know, Mom, I just want to know what it was really like."

"I've already told you all my stories …"

"Only the boring ones."

I laugh at her pout. "Well, those are the only ones I'm telling you, baby girl. Besides, I expect your experience will be very different from mine. You're going in as a boarder. I was a day student. Grandma always wanted me home at night. I went to Mansfield a long time ago, as you keep ever-so-kindly pointing out. I can't begin to tell you what it's like now. Did you ever send an email to your cousin Lacey to ask her? She graduated not that long ago. She can probably give you much better dirt than I can."

"It's no big, Mom." Bree blows her hair out of her face by forcing air noisily out of her bottom lip up toward the top of her head. "Lacey's way too busy with college to text me back. God, Mom, no one emails people anymore! Lacey would think I was a weirdo if I sent her an email. I'll find out for myself soon enough anyway. I was just curious about what it was like at Mansfield back when dinosaurs roamed the earth and ice coated all the land."

"Charming." I give my standard reply to any of her minor misbehaviors and stick out my tongue at her.

"Double charming." She answers right back, giggles, and sticks her tongue out at me.

Bree fiddles with the radio and clicks it over to her favorite station. I swear they play the same fifteen songs in a row, day after day. I try my hardest not to say "That's not music. That's just noise," like my mom did. Some of the songs are OK, some I like, some really do just sound like noise.

Bree slumps back in the seat, closed off in her own thoughts. I wish she would sit up straight. But I don't say anything. I just set a good example. I keep my back straight and my eyes on the road, and before long I'm back to being closed off in my own thoughts. It's a good thing that I can pretty much do this drive with my eyes closed, because I pretty much do. I pay enough attention to the road to see brake lights in front of me, but that's about it. My thoughts are in the New England preppy world of the eighties.

I'm thinking about the story I would tell her if I did just tell her the truth.

Science Wing

October 6, 1980

My Mansfield story would start with Derek. So much about me does. The first time I met him I was knocked off my feet. Literally. I was running for class, late as usual, since I used the short time between assembly and first period to grab a smoke in the Gazebo and see who else was hanging out. I came careening around the corner, down the ramp to the science wing, and smashed headlong into the most beautiful human I had ever set eyes on. At least I was pretty sure he was human and not my teenage dream guy, brought to life. Crash, bang. I bounced right off his incredibly good-smelling, impossibly broad chest. Books flung everywhere. Blue-and-red Mansfield book bag contents strewn about. One clog lost off my foot. A loud expletive released from my lips. We had the whole meet-cute scenario. From our first moment, we were a school legend.

There are a lot of lovely buildings on Mansfield's campus, but the science wing isn't one of them. It had been wedged onto the left side of the stately main school building three years before I got there. A truly unfortunate example of modern classroom architecture, the science wing looks like a trailer and a half-trailer welded together. Its two most distinguishing features are ramps instead of stairs and an acrid, kidneylike smell that lingers near the labs. About the best thing I can say for the science wing is that you could get going pretty darn quickly down those ramps when you were late for classes.

When I looked up at Derek, it was like an electrical charge was running through my body. I had never felt anything like this before. I was breathless. I was light-headed. I wanted to run my hands through his shaggy blond hair. I wanted to feel his beautiful mouth crushing mine. *Oh my god, Kat! Snap out of it. What the hell is the matter with you?*

"Yuh OK?" were the first words he spoke to me. My running into him and bouncing off didn't seem to have moved him much. I blinked a couple of times and nodded, unable to make my voice work. He looked at me, grinned, and continued speaking. "I'm new here. I didn't know this place was so dangerous." He held out his hand to help me back to my feet. *Oh my god, we were touching!* I didn't want to let go, ever. I hoped my hands weren't sweaty. I felt very warm. My stomach was hovering somewhere between butterflies and barfing.

I attempted to regain the ability to form words and hoped he would attribute my being mute to my being knocked on my butt. "Hi, I'm Kat. Where'd ya come from?" *Breathe,* I said to myself. *Breathe and please don't say anything stupid.* I pulled my hands back and brushed them off on my jeans. I shoved my foot back into my errant clog. *Please don't let it smell like feet in the hallway.*

"I was in day school back home in California. My dad thought prep school might be better for me. Actually, my dad thought me being three thousand miles away from him might be better for him." He laughed, in a not-at-all-joking way.

This vision of teen-boy perfection was helping me pick up the detritus of my life when he saw my Marlboro Lights. "Sorry, jeez, I forgot to say, I'm Derek. Can I bum a smoke off of you? I'm out. I need to get to town, but I'm stuck in classes all day." He paused and looked around as if he was about to impart some great secret to me. Leaning down, he said in his low, slow, soft drawl, "I was a little scared at first that you were another one of those perfect preppies here."

His quiet, low voice and conspiratorial manner had an unfortunate effect on me. I giggled. "Definitely not!" *Oh my GOD! Do not giggle, you moron. You sound like an idiot.*

"Phew, because they scare me. They're like robots. It's like there's a factory somewhere spitting them out, all dressed in patchwork pants. Hey, wanna come with me to the Gazebo? Got anything more interesting than ciggies in the bag?" With that, he started poking his fingers around in my tote in an overly familiar way.

I grabbed my bag, feeling a little bit violated and not all that unhappy about it. I thought about ditching class. I really wanted to. I really, really, really wanted to. But I was already in the science wing. And I'd already been spotted by Dr. K when I came in. He yelled at me to slow down in the hallway, so he'd definitely remember I was here and wouldn't sign off on a late note. I was so happy I hadn't listened to him about slowing down. If I had, I wouldn't have met Derek. But I was stuck. There was no way I could blow off class without getting in trouble.

Besides, I was too cool a girl to just follow some new guy around like a puppy just because he asked me. I knew some things about boys. "Sorry, I'm already late. See you 'round." I was able to get my wobbly legs under enough control to walk away from him of my own volition. *Please don't trip, dummy,* was just about the only thought in my head as I walked away backward without breaking eye contact.

"OK then, yup, see you around." And then, I swear, he winked at me. *Who winks? What kind of freak winks? Seriously?* I was so smitten. I turned around and booked it the rest of the way to class.

Derek must have knocked the sense right out of me when I knocked right into him because from then on, I was never the same. It feels like I can pinpoint that as the exact moment I stopped being a child. I know my mom thinks it happened when the Shaun Cassidy poster came down and the turbaned Keith Richards picture went up, but really that was just the first volley of adulthood. This was real. After running into Derek, I no longer wanted to kiss Andy Gibb or Peter Frampton or any other pop star, not even Brian. I just wanted to run my body into Derek's again and again. I had no control over my thoughts or my body's tingling. I hated it. I loved it. It was the most confusing, exhilarating, terrifying feeling I'd ever experienced. *Maybe I hit my head or something when I ran into him.*

It wasn't like I was a complete novice in the boy department. I'd dated boys, even senior boys, freshman year. But I had never felt any real desire before that moment. Boys were trophies, boys were how you measured where you stood in the school's pecking order. The cooler the date, the higher your spot. Kissing boys was fun enough, but it was more about being one of the girls that the boys wanted to kiss than having any great longing for them. Until I ran into Derek. Then I finally understood what all the fuss was about.

I zoomed into biology and there was Mr. Burns, droning on and on about what we'd be covering this week and turning bright red at the word "organism." Why would that make him blush? It was so way creepy. My two bestie-best friends, Dots, née Dorothea, and L. B. pronounced Ellbee, Texan for Lizzie Beth, short for Elizabeth, were in Burnsie's bio class too, so I hissed "Have I got news!" as I leaned over to get my book out of my bag. As soon as we were set free, I pounced on them to find out if they had any scoop on the new boy. And to call dibs.

More Truths about Me

Freshman year isn't part of the story I'd tell Bree. She doesn't need it. She probably wouldn't even understand it. The ease she was born with was the very thing I worked so hard to learn how to fake during my freshman year. I came to Mansfield as a nerdy, bright thirteen-year-old Jewish girl with giant glasses, flyaway dishwater-brown hair, and a straight-A average at my so-so public school. My mom said I was pretty, called me shayna maidelah, in Yiddish, but I knew nothing about this new world. Except that I wanted to belong. Adopted children are in general very good at being chameleons. As a whole, we are quick studies at picking up the mores and social Qs of any new situation. I am especially gifted at this.

Freshman year, I discreetly studied the kids who had it right. I even took geeky *Harriet the Spy* type notes, which I later burned. It took me much of the first semester to figure out exactly what I should look like, what I should wear, what music I should listen to, how I should speak to be seen as I wanted to be. I knew what I needed to do, and I knew that it would work better with more time to create a little distance. I put my plan for Me 2.0 into action while Mansfield was on Christmas break.

I came back from break with contact lenses. I got up extra early to blow-dry my hair and put on makeup every morning. I bought and wore all the correct clothes, with the correct amount of careless abandon about them, and I positively reeked of Chanel Cristalle, my very sophisticated new signature scent. Having a signature scent was good, because it almost completely covered up my additional new scents of Marlboro Lights and marijuana.

Once I looked the part, I worked hard to get accepted by the right crowd, at turns caustic and obsequious, until I was in. That's it. That's the entirety of my freshman year story.

When I started at Mansfield, it was after thirteen years of not feeling like I quite fit in anywhere. I didn't look like the other girls at our synagogue. I knew my birth mother was Jewish; everyone else knew from looking at me that my birth father was not. When I was a little girl I had baby-fine light-blond hair, green eyes, and pale skin, although I was olive enough underneath so that I tanned like a champ. I felt conspicuously invisible in the sea of exotic-looking, thick-haired, dark-eyed beauties who attended Temple Emmanuel Israel Hebrew School with me.

I didn't look like anyone in my public elementary school either. Nothing like the French girls, who were mostly dark-haired and olive-skinned but so tall and a different kind of stick-insect skinny. They carried themselves with flair and somehow inherited the ability to tie a scarf with insouciance by age nine. I didn't look like the Irish girls either, with the cute little lines of freckles splayed across perky ski-jump noses and a seemingly never-ending supply of brothers and sisters. There was never any chance I was going to be able to pass myself off as one of the Greek girls; not only were they also darker, but they started developing while I was still scrawny.

Besides not looking like anyone else growing up, I was in a different economic stratum. I was a rich kid for my working-class town. Even if all our money came from auto body shops, we sure had plenty of it compared to everyone else. My mom drove a huge black Cadillac and had two fur coats. I would never know what it was like to come to school without having had dinner the night before.

I'm not entirely sure why my mother decided I needed to be educated out of district, but in seventh grade, she got it into her head that I was too smart for our local public high school and I'd be going a different route. One of her friends' kids got into Dana Hall, and if that was good enough for Florence Cohen's daughter, it was certainly good enough for me. Eighth grade became about looking at private schools within a fifteen-minute drive, ones that would accept day students. Where we lived that limited us to about twenty schools. I eliminated some for pure snootiness during the visit. Some eliminated me on my complete indifference to team sports. Still, as a full-tuition day student in a time of economic malaise, I would have my pick.

We had barely gotten out of the car on Mansfield's campus when I was greeted by an overenthusiastic, enormous, hairy, beautiful golden retriever. Mr. Summers's dog Scout, wearing a blue-and-red Mansfield-logoed bandanna, bounded over to me to be petted. I felt welcomed. I felt home. I was covered in dog hair I was allergic to, but I was home. Allergy shots seemed a small price to pay for all that doggie love.

Before I started, I was a little scared I'd be labeled a blue-collar kid from the wrong type of town. Or as a day student, I'd be left out of things. But the preppy world with its roof rule—we all exist under the same metaphorical roof, so we're all of equal social standing—was not only welcoming, it was the first place I had ever been that seemed orderly and logical to me. People stopped asking me, "What are you?" They just accepted me; I was there, ergo, I belonged. Mansfield was the first place I could easily fit myself into. With only a few minor adjustments, I could look like everyone else. I could sound like everyone else. I could be any one of them. For the first time in my life, I could blend.

By the beginning of my sophomore year, I'd figured out fitting in, and I was ready to stand out. The best way to hide any insecurity about being an outsider is to act like an insider. By sophomore year, I was ready for people to look to me to see what to wear, what to listen to, what to sound like, who to be. That's when I really came into my own. That's where my life as me really begins.

I met Derek two weeks later.

I was nearly fifteen, all of five feet tall, and maybe ninety-nine pounds after a very large meal. I thought I knew everything about my world. I knew that I knew lots more than my parents, who still steadfastly refused to let me board this year even though it was ruining my life, and I hated it at home and could have gotten lots more work done if they had just let me stay at school like normal people did. They never listened to me about anything.

I was never going to be one of the rich kids who had it all at Mansfield, but I was pretty, I was fun to be around, and I was smart. I was someone people wanted to be seen with. I was the very picture of a stoner preppy. I had my pack of Marlboro Lights and a beautiful white roach stone, lavishly hand-decorated with a flying Pegasus, in my Mansfield tote. I knew where everyone would be hanging out between classes and after. I knew who I'd be with, what we'd all be wearing, and who we'd be talking about. I knew everything that was worthwhile knowing.

I laugh to think that, although it would horrify Bree, teenager fashions haven't really changed all that much in the intervening years. She wears jeans nearly every day. I wore jeans nearly every day. My favorites were those soak-to-fit Levi's 501s. You washed them, then put them on wet, and then hung around in wet pants until they dried to your shape. It was horribly uncomfortable and made a mess of the house, since it was literally impossible for me to stay in the bathroom while waiting for my dripping-wet jeans to dry because the phone cord didn't reach that far. Bree prefers Hudsons, but they're still jeans. Our jeans were usually topped off with an alligator shirt or a polo, a turtleneck, a button-down, a Fair Isle sweater, or all of them layered together if it was really freezing cold out. There's a look I'm glad has run its course. Bree doesn't layer to that degree. She seems to only wear Free People shirts or my cashmere sweaters. It's certainly a more streamlined look, but it's not wholly unfamiliar.

On my feet were either my beloved Dansko clogs, the cool new white Nikes with the red swoosh, Frye boots, or hiking boots. Bree rarely wears anything but flip-flops. She isn't any taller than I am, so I don't know why she doesn't wear something to give her a little height, but she doesn't listen. In the winter she's mostly in Uggs or Sorels. For us, winter weather meant we were wearing those clunky tan suede Swiss hiking boots with the big fat red laces. Everyone wore them, boys and girls. I will never understand why—those boots weighed a ton, left huge blisters on your feet, and were ugly. But we all wore them without question.

When I hear my conversations in my head from back in those days, I hear them in the broadest New England accent that possibly exists. The word "loser" is pronounced *loooooooooooooooooooooozah* with the stress on the *ooooo*. We used this word with great frequency and almost always to indicate great admiration. It took me a very long time and a lot of hard work to lose that accent, but I remember it fondly. At least, as long as those sounds stay in my mind and aren't coming out of my mouth.

Once I left New England for college in New York, I worked very hard to leave everything about my then-self behind. I picture myself jettisoning things at the border. Religion? Out the window. Accent? See ya. Preppy clothes? Buh-bye! I'm a New Yorker now, time to dress all in black. I think pretty much the only thing I kept from my former life as a Massachusetts girl is my lead-footed driving style. I don't tailgate and I don't weave in and out, but if you are in the left lane, you had better want to drive faster than I do, or you need to get the hell out of my way.

The accent was the hardest thing for me to change. I practiced for hours so I could speak without betraying my origins. I was planning to be an actress, not a Kennedy, so the dulcet tones of my childhood needed to go. The silly phrases from prep school lasted a bit of the way into college, but they too were eventually sacrificed to a more conventional speaking style. Still, occasionally, even now, when I get off the phone with Dots, I realize that I've lost all my r sounds and started speaking about 'zas. Dots stayed in New England, but even she has had to modulate in her high-powered legal job. It's only when we're drinking wine and gabbing that we let the old style flow back in.

Back then, I didn't know that I had an accent to people outside of New England, or that I sprinkled my speech with ridiculous made-up words. I have to laugh when I think of how we must have sounded. Unlike some of the moms who get annoyed when their kids use their silly teenager language, I think it's adorable and fun.

Bree used to appreciate my good humor about it all, but not now and especially not if I butt into her conversations or dare use any of their words. I'm supposed to be seen when they need a ride or something but not heard if any of her friends are around. If I make an attempt at their patois, I get cut off with a glare, a short sigh, and an "Um, no, Mom, fail."

Our preppy world truly was beautifully reflected in *The Official Preppy Handbook*. We thought it was a great book, just right enough to be hilarious and just wrong enough to keep all our secrets safe. We really did say things like 'za for pizza, "Gag me with a spoon" for yuck, and "Put a massive crankage on the tuneage" for "Could you please turn up the volume on the radio, Dad?" Yeah, he loved that one, especially after writing a big tuition check. When you wanted something passed to you, you would request it by naming the item and adding "me." "Please pass me the salt" became "Salt me," and of course, "Might I please have one of your cigarettes?" was "Butt me."

Also, the word is pronounced *Bimmer*. Bimmer is huge. None of us would ever say Beemer to refer to a BMW. That word pegs you as NOKD—not our kind, dear. There are piles of other shibboleths, little bits of trivia, pronunciations, monogram locations, you name it. Gross stereotype it may well be, but no actual preppy would ever be caught dead wearing docksiders with socks. If it's that damn cold out, put your ugly boots on. It is perfectly acceptable for you to wear socks under those. Two pairs, if necessary.

These were all part of a code that set us apart from the rest of the world and convinced us we were better. Just reading the handbook wasn't enough to get it quite right. That's why the book was fun and not a betrayal. It let out enough secrets to easily point out anyone who might be a poser. Hilariously, it still does every once in a while.

At a dinner party a few years ago, I mentioned something about going to prep school and a woman replied, "Oh, where did you prep?" I'm a polite grown-up now, so I kept my face neutral and managed to not say "Um, no, Heather, fail," at least not out loud. If anyone is ever faced with this situation, please just ask the person where they went to school. Trust me. Feel free to ask them where they summered but not where they prepped.

Mansfield Academy sits just over the border in New Hampshire. It was named for the Mansfield family. They gave us our first five headmasters and donated the land and original buildings in 1789. That also makes us one of the oldest schools, which is a point of great pride in our world. Relatives of our Mansfields founded the town of Mansfield in Massachusetts, far to the south. Knowing where Mansfield Academy is located is one of our major tells. Anyone who attended another prep school knows where we're located.

Other norms are different. One of the starkest differences is in the names of kids going to prep school. In the eighties, the boys still almost all had the same few names. William was Will, not Bill; Robert, Rob, not Bob; John all called Jack; and Charles, Chucks, to the man, mostly for the funny rhyme factor. Since most of them were named for ancestors and had siblings and or cousins matriculating at the same time, they often had close to identical names. Those boys were therefore identified by a variety of nicknames and full name combinations.

So in a school of only three hundred kids, I knew four Trips, nickname for III; five Chips, nickname for Junior; and an inordinate number of Wills, Willies, and even a Wally, whose real name, I found out at graduation, somehow was Robert. It could have been a parody if any one of us had been self-aware enough to be joking.

Although the girls' given names were equally uniform as the boys', we strove much harder for individuality within the bounds of conformity. It wasn't like you could have two girls at school with the exact same name. So our chosen names veered even further toward parody. We didn't have any Muffys at Mansfield, but we did have a Buffy, a Bunny, a Binky, and a Babe. Sometimes the nickname corresponded to the given name with a letter or a sound, sometimes it was a favorite item, color, or a piece of family lore. I knew a Froggy, a Blue, two Kittys, and even one girl who everyone called Moo—but in our defense, she was sort of bovine.

There were only two types of kids at school who had unusual given names. The largest cohort of them came from other countries. We had a sizable international population back then, especially of Iranian kids. They flooded our schools after the fall of the Shah. The international kids pretty much instantly Anglicized their names, so they were familiar if not always exactly right. The other kids were the Prep for Prep kids, smart, poor kids from inner cities who were whisked away to be educated in our rarefied air. Those were the kids we found to be actually "exotic." They were Black and brown kids with names we'd never heard before, like Aricella and Lincoln.

It is entirely possible that those kids may not have felt the preppy roof rule applied quite as strongly to them as it did to the middle-class Jews and Catholics who found acceptance as part of the Eastern elite in the cash crunch of the late seventies and eighties.

Lots of norms were undergoing transitions during my tenure at Mansfield. Everyone always thinks *après moi, le déluge*, right? Before me, Bitsy, after me, Brittney. The kids that were older than me were much more constrained by the preppy establishment. The younger ones were more like the kids in the outside world. The classes after me seemed more adventurous, freer. Of course, it is all complete nonsense. We are all completely tied to the preppy establishment. Whatever ways we chose to rebel at school, we grew up to live the lives they expected us to.

Mansfield sits in the bucolic middle part of New England. It is surrounded by gentlemen's farms and the occasional apple orchard. These gracious farms are nothing like the hardworking farms that spatter some other bits of New England. Our farms are toys for the wealthy, not ways to feed the masses. The neighboring towns are filled with other prep schools for us to play sports against and socialize with. Preppy kids don't interact much with the townie kids anywhere. While the various schools may have long-running rivalries, it is us and them when it comes to townies. Townies don't much want to associate with us either. They think we're stuck-up. We think they're stupid.

* * *

The back roads on the drive to school are charming and fun to drive. The sun feels great on my face. Fortunately, I put on enough sunscreen this morning so I can enjoy the feel of sun on skin and not worry about what it's doing to my forehead lines. I love the way this car feels as it takes curves and goes up and down hills. I love the feeling of control. I love always knowing what's about to be on the road ahead.

Since I spent most of my time at Mansfield trying to find out how much pot one small girl can smoke, actual memory isn't really one of my strong points anyway. So honestly, even if I did want to tell Bree some of my stories, most of the stories I could tell are just what I can piece together from fuzzy recollections and other people's words.

Memory is such a strange process for us all. None of it is really true. None of it is really untrue. It only lives in our heads. So, it probably all falls somewhere in between. And if memory is just a story that we tell ourselves about what happened, then how should I decide what story I should tell my little girl? If other people know us only from what we let them see, what parts should I be showing her? I can't see any benefit to showing her the unpleasant stuff.

Except, I worry, what if she isn't like me? What if she begins to show signs of alcoholism or she gets addicted to drugs? If I'm not there, who will catch it in time to make sure that she is OK? Who knows her well enough to know what that would look like? Should I warn her? How? What if she meets a boy like Derek?

Not for the first time today, I wish I'd never agreed to send her away. We had just been married; we loved the place so much. It made so much sense at that point to say "Of course she will go to Mansfield." I made that promise all those years ago and I'm sticking to it. But the closer we get, the less sure I am that it's the right thing. My gut keeps telling me that she isn't ready.

Hallway

"OK, so who the hell is he? Why is he here so late? We're over two weeks into term. Spill," I whispered, as we walked three across down the bright blue hallway to our next classes—bright colors make your brain work better being the prevailing theory of the time. We had three minutes to get down the hallway, up the ramp, past the lockers, up two flights of stairs, and down one more long hallway where we each had a class. Most important, we had three minutes to talk.

"So, alls I know is that he got here this weekend." This came from my second-best friend Ellbee and was accompanied, as always, by her left hand flipping up and down dismissively as she spoke. "I heard he got thrown out of school for drinking and fighting and that he was sent here to straighten out his life. His dad was worried that he had fallen in with the wrong crowd."

Ellbee McCreedy was a tall, blond Farrah-haired girl from somewhere near Houston, Texas, whose oilman father had recently bought a nearby five-acre farm in our middle-of-nowhere New England town as a semi-retirement place. Since they were local, Ellbee was also a day student. Her mom was originally from Boston, but her dad couldn't stand living in a city. This was their compromise. In addition to pretend-farming, Mr. McCreedy was investing in a couple of companies that made personal computers. He was convinced they were going to be in every home sometime soon. In his words, "Boy howdy, did I call that one or what?" Ellbee still lives off of those funds quite nicely.

Ellbee and I became best friends the first day of freshman year when we were both innocent day students, but we were currently moving in very different directions. Ellbee smoked, but only cigarettes, didn't drink, didn't do drugs, and didn't think very kindly of the waste products who did. By the beginning of our sophomore year, our friendship was becoming strained and wasn't going to hold together much longer. I was quickly becoming one of "the wrong crowd." Her pointing this out about Derek was a rebuke, not an accident.

The idea that people sent their kids to prep school to straighten them out was hilarious. We knew better. We knew we had better drugs and easier access than the kids in public school. We could afford more. We knew that as long as we managed to appear to be OK, no one was going to look too hard into what we were really doing. It was called "having your snap." If you could snap your fingers and do a passable impression of a sober person whenever an adult spoke to you, you were golden.

"He is completely fab! I can't believe you smacked into him. Oh my god, Kat, you are such a loser." She meant that as a term of great affection. Dots gave me the universal salute, holding her right thumb and forefinger up on her forehead in an L.

Dots is still my very best friend in the whole world and one of the closest people in my life. She's Bree's godmother and the first person I think of when I need anything. Dots is the only person who knows exactly how conflicted I am about letting Bree go, and most everything else that's going on. We may live a couple hundred miles apart, but we're never very far away from each other.

In 1980, she was a tiny, curvy brunette. She is currently a tiny, curvy, brunette. I bet she can, and I bet she does, still wear some of her preppy classics from school. Dots had a serious hourglass figure by the time she was fifteen, big boobs, teensy waist, great smile, and hips that annoyed her no end. She could have been one of the illustration pages in *The Official Preppy Handbook*. From her matching Pappagallo headbands and Bermuda bags down to her Tretorn-shod feet, she was always a study in preppy perfection.

At least Dots was a khaki-and-navy preppy, not a pink-and-green one, because at that age, I don't think I'd have been able to look past those colors to the great girl underneath. Dots was a boarder who let me sleep on her floor whenever my parents would allow it. She was a fairly recent refugee from an all-girls education, so she still found boys to be a bit of an alien species. "He's gotta be six feet tall. And all that hair! He is so blond. Oh my god! Kit-Kat, your mother will have a cow and a half if you go out with him!"

My mother chose to refer to my boyfriends at Mansfield as the Hitler Youth Brigade. It was one of our very favorites from her repertoire of desperate ploys to point out that I should be dating the kind of nice Jewish boys she envisioned as right for me. Her nagging was such a consistent drumbeat that it became part of the shorthand of our group. NJB meant boy your mother would approve of. None of us wanted that. Not even Ellbee, who was the most parent-pleasing of us all.

I went in the other direction from Ellbee, going for the biggest, blondest, bluest-eyed boys I could find. It was an excellent way to torture my mother. She was forever telling me that she was going to cut me out of the will if I married someone who wasn't Jewish. It didn't worry me. I knew a bluff when I heard one. Also, frankly, marriage wasn't really a primary concern in high school.

She never understood how different I was. I was an all-American hybrid: a Jewish American Princess–New England preppy. My given name was Katherine Anne Tarkoff. Hebrew name, Channa. Preppy name, Kat—my initials. No simpering, preppy-approved "Kitty" for me. Dots often called me Kit-Kat because I couldn't resist them and she thought it was funny.

I was part of an actual shift in the preppy world, but the shift was invisible to me. My class and the couple before me were full of the usual complement of WASP kids but also included Jews and Catholics. It was a huge difference from less than ten years before, when only the occasional very rich Catholic was allowed in and then still only into certain schools. I can honestly say that I never saw anyone teased or treated differently for their ethnicity. I vaguely knew "ethnics" were a recent addition to the prep school world; I didn't know that I was considered one of them. In my mind, "ethnic" meant Iranian, Indian, or Chinese, or a Prep for Prep kid—someone "exotic."

But I did get some strange questions sometimes.

"Did you have a bar matzoh?"

"A what?"

"The Jewish kid thing, you know, with presents. A bar matzoh?"

"Oh, a bar mitzvah. Of course I did. I mean, no, because I'm a girl and girls have bat mitzvahs. Matzoh is what you eat on Passover."

"Oh."

Stuff like that, but the questions weren't rude, just curious. The bigger differences between us seemed to be between the haves and the have-way-mores. We all went on nice summer vacations. They flew first class. We all had cars. Theirs were brand-new. We all asked our parents for spending money. We got twenties. They got hundreds. They were a world apart, even in our world.

I imagine though that the Prep for Prep kids saw it differently and lumped us all together. I can't really say I knew any of those kids well enough to know how they felt. Which I guess illustrates their probable point. I suppose it's true that some of us were more equal than others.

Also, if I am being honest, I'm glad that Bree is going into Mansfield as one of the have-way-mores. Thanks to the hubby's family, Bree goes in as part of the group that has run the place forever. She's not part of a social experiment or there because, after the economic malaise of the seventies, schools needed the money we "ethnics" could provide. She never has to pass to belong. She will never have to think about what could happen if the tide turns.

By the time I started at Mansfield, my family had been in New England long enough to be regular people on the outside, but they were still Eastern European villagers inside. My parents spoke Yiddish to each other at home, but never out in public. Their discomfort in the wider world manifested itself in a strict adherence to social niceties and in jewelry. My mother referred to the earrings they got me for my bat mitzvah as training diamonds. She had real, substantial jewelry. Mine was good, never junk, but not over-the-top. That wouldn't be appropriate for a young girl and my mother is huge on appropriate. She always made an appropriate entrance with the car my friends called the Yom Kipper Clipper. It had little antennae that stuck up from near the front wheels so that she could find the curb to park. They didn't help her all that much. My dad had an old truck he used for work. He wasn't as interested in demonstrating our worth as my mom was, and he didn't want the employees thinking he was doing so well they could ask for a raise.

Jewelry is portable, concealable, and easily converted to cash. Even after generations, the shtetl mentality dies hard. Once I passed my driving test, I lobbied like crazy for a convertible for my seventeenth birthday. Even though I knew my dad would probably get me an old clunker to drive to school and something gold, since seventeen was one of the lesser birthdays and didn't warrant stones. He gave me a 1974 Oldsmobile Delta 88. It was mostly pale blue until I begged him to at least paint it all one color. Then it was navy. In the cold weather, the battery terminals had leaks that corroded the connections, so I'd have to whack them with the wrench I kept in the glove compartment for that purpose before the car would start. We had a lot of fun in that car. At least I could fit a lot of friends in it. I also got a nice gold rope bracelet for my birthday, which I still occasionally wear. Well, that is, if Bree didn't pack it.

I don't have any of the cars he bought me, but I still have most of the jewelry, so maybe he was right. I can track the American economy and the fortunes of my family every December of my life by seeing how good the jewelry I got was.

My family was so firmly entrenched in the upper-middle class that we rated no scholarship money from Mansfield. Yet my parents never really felt secure. They were the product of generations of deprivation. Each was the first of their families to be middle-class. They were each the first to live in a "mixed" neighborhood, not in the Jewish part of town.

Looking back from this vantage point, I can see that they were very conflicted about what kind of life they wanted for me. They wanted me to be comfortable in the larger world. They wanted me to have all the benefits of a great education and then bring that knowledge back home to our tribe. What was confusing to them was that I thought of my tribe as the people I went to Mansfield with, not my Hebrew school class. My parents were happy that I was seeing a wider world than just the Jewish neighborhoods they had grown up in. They wanted me to make new friends, of all kinds. They just really wished I wouldn't date them. I think they really didn't understand why I would want to. To their minds, we couldn't possibly have a future, so why bother?

I don't think they ever recognized that the future I saw for myself wasn't anything like the one they had set out for me.

* * *

Oh my god, Kat!" Dots squealed, as a couple of freshman boys looked over at us with undisguised longing. We returned their looks with undisguised disdain. "Do you know who Derek looks just like? He looks just like Brian! It's almost freaky. He really does totally look just like Brian. Do you think he could be one of the kids? Or maybe, maybe, he really is Brian. Maybe he's finally come back from the dead for you." She made ghostly *whoo-whoo* sounds and waved her hands in front of my face. I couldn't help but notice her sailor bracelet from the summer was still hanging on her wrist. I wished it would fall off already. It was dingy gray and kind of gross, but I had to admit, when it moved, her tan line did look really cool under it.

To be clear, we didn't really believe my dead-rock-star/guardian-angel had come back from the dead to claim me. But we also weren't ready to completely rule out the possibility. Stranger things have happened, right? So even though we knew that it wasn't reality—we were stoners, not psychos—it was still a fun thought to play with. So much fun that we kept the subject going for years. Especially once Derek really went off the deep end. It was so much easier to blame his bad behavior on his being possessed by a dead rock star than accept the truth.

Brian

Yes, I realize the Brian thing was weird. Even for us. And yes, we did know so, even at the time. It was like one of those group hallucination things. Something we dismissed as fantasy and yet deeply believed, simultaneously. Reading *The Crucible* made us deeply uncomfortable.

Brian needed no last name. We talked about him as if he had just left the room, even though he'd been dead since we were babies. Brian was Brian Jones, late of the Rolling Stones, my dead-rock-star/guardian-angel. I first saw him in an early Stones photo and found him gorgeous. Then I found out that I had almost drowned on the very day he died from drowning, and our mystical connection was sealed. It was through-the-looking-glass clear that we were tied together in some sort of cosmic way. I was sure he had somehow given his life to protect me. Or something like that. The details weren't important. The romance of the idea of that kind of cosmic connection was all that mattered.

Music was a huge part of our lives at Mansfield. We were little hedonists, and we created the gods we wanted to worship in our image. Like everyone else's gods, even if we couldn't see them, we knew they were there. They lived through us—the Beatles, the Dead, the Doors, the Stones, Queen, Bob Marley, Led Zep . . . everyone had their band, the one that spoke to them. Every newspaper article, every album, every photo was an opportunity for communion, a chance to find secret messages from them, revealed only to the true believers.

We all worshipped our favorite rock stars. Sure, it's possible that maybe I might have taken it a bit further than most. I had pictures of Brian all over my room. I lit candles in front of them. I talked to him every night before I went to bed. I bought every book and album and watched every TV clip I could find. I was too old for an imaginary friend. I wasn't interested in religion. I had a dead-rock-star/guardian-angel instead. And all my friends eagerly agreed we were intertwined and participated in my delusion.

If you were going to choose a dead-rock-star/guardian-angel (or have one choose you), Brian was perfect. He was one of the musical greats. A talented musician and the founder and the soul of the Rolling Stones. He wasn't as well-known a figure as Janis or Jimi, so choosing him marked you as someone in the know. Not some fluffy bunny, new to the rock pantheon. Those girls always gravitated toward Jim Morrison and his Lizard King hips.

Brian pushed the sex and drugs and rock and roll envelope to the ultimate limit. He was known to have at least six children scattered all about the globe. Before he was in the Stones, as a teenager, he was run out of more than one town by more than one jealous husband. There were dark stories about him as well, wasting his talent on drugs, beating girlfriends, and all sorts of cruelties. But on Brian's death certificate, his death was listed as "death by misadventure" and that was just about the most romantic-sounding thing I had ever encountered.

My friends and I would take the bus into Cambridge to see film festivals featuring old Stones movies and British TV appearances. Early sophomore year, we were hot on the trail of the holy grail of Stones films, the unreleased *Rock and Roll Circus*, which, according to rumor, was secretly exhibited once a year in Boston. You just needed to know who to call. We knew we'd find it someday.

When we were in school, listening to music was a communal activity, not the solitary headphoned cocoon of today. Stereo speakers were pointed out dorm windows toward the quad. Boom boxes brought along to any gathering. In any kind of nice weather, we'd spread out on the grass in front of one of the dorms, leaning on each other in a great big boy-girl puppy pile, books and notebooks in front of our eyes, our heads resting atop each other's bodies.

Our number one radio station was WBCN, out of Boston. Radio wasn't as segmented at the time. BCN played everything we loved, old stuff, new stuff, rock, soft, hard, they played it all—as long as it wasn't disco. Radio is so programmatic now, there's no room for personality.

From Charles Laquidera to Darell Martinie (aka the Cosmic Muffin) to Oedipus and Duane Ingles Glasscock, our DJs had no shortage of personality. Now there aren't any DJs picking out songs they feel like hearing. There aren't any DJs at all. Just numbers and demographics. Radio is soulless and boring. That is another thing I miss about those days.

Most of the music we worshipped was from the sixties and early seventies. Albums that predated the disco era. All these years later, hearing those first few notes to "Stairway" still brings a warmth to my body, and if I shut my eyes I can feel strong arms around me, warm lips on mine, and get a whiff of Eau Sauvage. We loved old music because much of the current top-forty music was dreadful. "You Light Up My Life" by Debby Boone was a huge hit. Punk may have been starting to rage into the public consciousness in London and New York, but early 1980s rural New England was not yet aware of its power.

My band was the Stones. Dots had the Beatles. Ellbee was a Who fanatic. Derek loved the Stones too, but because he was Californian, he was labeled a Deadhead. That suited him just fine. He always cultivated an air of not noticing or caring about anything other people said about him. If other people decided he was a Deadhead, whatever. He was too cool to correct them. The Dead were cool too.

New wave was beginning to trickle in. For the first time, we saw real bands fronted by women. Debbie Harry, Ann and Nancy Wilson, Joan Jett, Chrissie Hynde - those women made it possible for us to think about being the front man for a band, not just sleeping with one. Country rock had its fans. We had a reggae crowd and a smattering of heavy metal fanatics. Preferring one genre wouldn't prevent you from enjoying others. Bruce Springsteen was a huge hit with nearly everyone. "Born to Run" got everyone out on the dance floor.

The greatest constant in our music was that it was intertwined with drug use. Most of our favorite bands had at least one dead member, almost always from drug or alcohol abuse, most often, but not exclusively, the drummer. Hubby and I went to a concert in Connecticut recently and saw Jonathan Edwards. Before he sang "Lay Around the Shanty Mama," he told the audience that it still reigns as the unofficial song of the preppy world. That song has the perfect preppy-stoner vibe.

I suppose if Bree comes back from first semester humming "Shanty," then I'll know what she's been up to. And I'll have to move my pot to a better hiding spot.

Derek did look quite a bit like Brian Jones, with those pouty lips and turned-down-at-the-corner stoner eyes, and he knew it. He did everything possible to play up the resemblance. He kept his hair in the same sort of disheveled blond shag that Brian sported. Derek's hair was more important to him than he ever would have admitted. Even when the rest of the lacrosse team shaved their heads for the finals, Derek refused and stayed shaggy. He also affected the same sort of laconic speaking style Brian was famous for. At least he didn't attempt a British accent.

It definitely wasn't like Dots was the first one in his life to notice the resemblance. Derek came to school not only going out of his way to push the similarities, but also to push the mystique of kinship with Brian, even hinting broadly that his dad Jack, might not really be his dad. That it was just possible that he might have a far more exotic provenance than being some rich Marin County businessman's kid.

Derek's mom was dead, so no one could ever flat out ask him, that would be beyond the pale. Obviously, went the whispers, that was the reason his dad was so mean to him. Derek was a constant reminder of his mom's infidelity. Again, the line between reality and fantasy isn't the solidest when teenage girls and rumors are involved.

Upstairs Classroom

My next class was English Lit with Mr. Summers, the teacher all the girls mooned over. He was handsome with thick dark hair and dark-blue eyes, and older but not old—he was probably all of thirty-two. And he made us feel like adults. He read Shakespeare and Chaucer aloud to us, making us love them as he did. Allowing us to hear the words as they should sound. He'd point out all the dirty jokes to us, not treat us like little children who shouldn't be exposed to that sort of thing.

I loved Mr. Summers. It is entirely possible I might have even used the word "dreamy" to describe him. He seemed to enjoy the effect he had on all of us. Mr. Summers was the teacher who would sit a little too close when explaining a Shakespearean sonnet and stare into your eyes a little too intensely. He was *le sigh*. However, on that morning in October, Derek Wilkeson joined our English Literature class, and from then on poor Mr. Summers, who one moment before had all my attention, ceased to exist. Poof.

Derek and I left class together, without a word acknowledging we were walking together, and made our way across the quad, halfway to the dining hall. The early-October breeze rattled the brown leaves left on the oak trees. Derek had to lean down a little to talk to me, he was so tall, and I so wasn't. All I wanted was for him to lean down a little further and kiss me. The middle of the quad was the middle of the universe as far as I was concerned. The eyes of the school were upon us, and I wanted to be claimed right then and there.

Instead of being kissed, I heard, "I'm going over to the dining hall for lunch. Maybe I'll see you after E period at the Gazebo? I've got soccer tryouts later. I guess my dad talked to them and they agreed to give me a look, even if the team's already set." Forget a kiss, I wasn't even being asked to lunch.

"Maybe." With my one-word answer, I was trying to appear cool and uninterested. I tend to babble when I'm nervous, so I tried to keep my words to a minimum, hoping not to sound like an idiot. I was hoping that I didn't actually look like I was slack-jawed and drooling as I watched him walk away, his perfectly tight Levi's swaggering down the path and his jean jacket thrown over one shoulder, male-model style. *Damn, I think he knows he's got me.* He never looked back to see if I was looking at him. I headed right to the library instead of following him straight ahead to lunch.

Campus has barely changed at all since we attended. Really, other than the addition of the ugly science wing and the student center called Doc, it has barely changed since Bree's grandfather attended. Probably not much even since her great-grandfather attended. Continuity of experience is very much prized. Most changes are things you can't really see or wouldn't really notice. Better heating equipment and new lampposts. A blue-light campus security system, like the kind that colleges have. We don't really need it in the middle of nowhere, but everyone has one now. It makes the parents feel like the kids are safer. The staff offices have been moved out of dorms. A couple of new buildings have been built for them on the outskirts of campus, but the core remains the same. A picture of the quad from the early days of photography would look much the same as a picture taken today.

Campus is beautifully planted with mature trees, some of them as old as the school itself. Bree's ancestors have all walked underneath their branches, some of them climbing up to be sheltered in them. I was always too scared, but Bree is a climber. She loves climbing up those trees, disappearing into the high branches. When she was little, I was forever having to close my eyes to not watch her. She'd yell for me to look up when she reached the top and wave, happy as anything. I tried to not yell at her to keep both hands on the tree. My heart was always in my throat until she returned to terra firma.

Mansfield is spectacular in the fall. We have sugar maples, red maples, oaks, and birch and beech trees. The reds, yellows, oranges, and browns of the leaves seem to enhance the blue of the sky and make the brick buildings and white dorms stand out.

It's so easy for me to get lost in my past there. It should be making me deliriously happy that Bree is finally going to get to go. But I want so much more for her. I want her to know she can be whatever she wants to be and isn't beholden to anyone's expectations. I don't want her to ever feel like that.

The center of campus is oriented around a quad. Later building additions spread out from that central spoke. The classroom building Derek and I came out of is the head of the quad, at the crest of a small hill that plateaus across to the dining hall. The classroom building is neoclassical, in red brick. It isn't original to the school; our first one was wooden and burned down in the 1830s. Still, it is old enough to have developed the kind of patina that makes people rhapsodize about its quirks. I remember its heating system as notoriously uneven, but they swear they've fixed that. It has four floors of classrooms. The headmaster's and dean of students' offices are on the first floor, along with a large auditorium that's used for daily assembly and major testing periods. It also has a couple of big classrooms, boys' and girls' bathrooms, and a teacher lounge. The now-not-so-new, but forever called new, science wing sticks out of the school building's lower left side like a cowlick. Not much we can really do short of razing it. We are working on a capital campaign to build a state-of-the-art science center and restore the classroom building to its unsullied state. The second and top floors are all classrooms with a few teacher office spaces. In the basement where the ground slopes down behind the building is the school store, day-student lockers, the bigger student bathrooms, and a couple more stray classrooms. The back of the headmaster's house is directly behind that entrance.

The oldest boys' dorm stands to the right as you're leaving the headmaster's office. Charles Mansfield Hall is named after our first headmaster. It was originally the Mansfield family home and is one of the oldest buildings in town. The mid-1700s white two-story wooden structure has stood since the very beginning of Mansfield Academy and the school is very protective of it. There is zero leeway to the open-flame rule in Chuck—which is what everyone calls the dorm. Chuck is the most public dorm on campus. It has always been known as the good kids' dorm. I don't think I ever dated anyone in Chuck.

When I was there, Chuck also housed the nurse's office and the alumni affairs office, but those rooms have been refitted and taken over by the dorm master and his family. The nurse's office now sits down the hill farther to the right, and the alumni office is off to the left side with a beautiful view of the chapel.

Directly across the quad from the school building is the Blackstone Building. It's also made of red brick with a white cupola and houses our cafeteria and sports center. Mandatory monthly kitchen duty for every student is still in effect. It "builds character," according to every administration that has ever been. The ability to pay a scholarship kid a few dollars to take over your mandatory kitchen duty, which builds an understanding of the way the world really works, is also still in effect. The cafeteria is on the upper level of Blackstone; its lower level holds the sports offices, the boys' and girls' main locker rooms, and the weight room, as well as a pair of squash courts. Back during most of my time there, we had a great TV room with cozy couches next to the girls' locker room. Now that space has treadmills and other machines with individual TVs. The sports center leads out to the football field and the Pond and to Doc, the student center.

The final building on the quad is my beloved Anderson Mansfield Library and Performing Arts Center. It's an elegant nineteenth-century red brick building with white Ionic columns framing a wide patio at its front. It houses a good-size library and our art and theater spaces. It was my haven.

Bree took her first steps in front of that building. We were up at Mansfield for some event, and she was about a year old. We were all standing on the patio and chatting. Bree was holding both my hands through the fabric mitts of her snowsuit. She wanted to get to her dad and was making little grunting sounds to get him to notice her, but he was engrossed in a conversation and didn't hear her. He wasn't very far, but he was out of her reach. She pulled her hands away and instead of dropping down to crawl, took five unsteady but enthusiastic little running-steps over and grabbed his legs. She turned around and gave me a great grin of triumph. He hoisted her up onto his shoulders and proudly announced to the entirety of the company that his good little girl was already trying to get into the library to study, just like her mama. We all laughed.

Our library building was donated by the classes of 1860–1870 to commemorate Anderson Mansfield. He was the last of the Mansfields to be headmaster and died in the Civil War. The library is beautiful, with double-height floor-to-ceiling windows that illuminate the interior, filling the stacks with light. It's also completely peaceful; no one could bug you in there without a harsh reprimand from Mrs. Chase, the librarian/dragon. You were always safe there.

The quad is the highest point of campus, so the ground slopes down at the back of the library building as well. The basement holds our theater and dressing rooms, to one side. Music rooms and painting and photography studios are on the other. I spent some of my favorite hours in that building. I hope Bree will too.

Down the hill, in opposite directions from the quad are Westford and Holden, which are the coolest boy and girl dorms, respectively. Of course, the student legend is that they keep those kids as far apart physically as the campus allows. Three other boys' dorms and two for girls are sprinkled in between. Each dorm has its own character, reputation, and place in the hierarchy.

Bree has been assigned to Colby. We could have asked for a single, but I thought she might be lonely. She's in the best double, on the second floor, with a good roommate, from a good family. Colby will probably be host to a few other children of our classmates. I haven't gotten the full list yet. Colby is top-notch and solid, smart, not too party-hearty, not too study-study, old-money families important to the life of the school. The administration clearly puts a lot of thought into placement. We were pleased.

Gazebo

2:45 That Same Day

Derek didn't show up at the Gazebo after classes got out. He completely blew me off. I was totally devastated. To ignore my misery, I talked to Willie Hooks and a couple of the other boys in a wanton effort to suck up to some of the cooler juniors. I twirled my hair and smiled. Willie was super cute, all curly blond hair and pretty blue eyes, wearing his awesome Bob Marley jacket, and he was always so nice to me. He wasn't at all hard to smile at. His mom had had an artist paint a tricolor Bob Marley portrait on the back of his favorite denim jacket for his birthday. It was from a poster or an album cover or something, I wasn't sure, but he loved it and wore it everywhere. It was an unbelievably cool present. I'm not sure if I'd ever even heard of a mom getting someone a cool birthday present before. And he looked so cute in it.

Cool birthday presents didn't come from moms. Moms got you the stuff you needed and maybe if you were lucky a Walkman as well. But Willie's family was different. They were old Mayflower blue bloods, and they lived in New York City, which automatically made them way cooler than anyone in New England. I was totally intrigued by the lives I imagined they lived. They had the kind of money and social standing that allowed them to laugh at convention whenever, if ever, it suited them. That sounded like an unimaginably perfect life to me.

Willie gave me a joint for later. I hid it in the change purse part of my wallet, thinking that maybe if I saw Derek after practice, he might like to spark up with me. I was also thinking, *Look at me, I am a very cool girl. I have my own pot. I don't need some boy to give me pot. Well, OK, technically, I did just need Willie Hooks to give me pot. Whatever. I think Willie might like me. He's so nice, and he keeps giving me pot. I like it when he smiles at me. He has a very cute smile.*

The Gazebo was our premiere on-campus place to hang out. It is a good-sized white lattice structure. It seats about twelve on benches, some on laps, a few more on the floor. The wood inside is covered with carved names and graffiti we found hilarious. *Latin is a dead language, as dead as dead can be. It killed off all the Romans, and now it's killing me.* Back then, it was ceded over for the kids to use as one of our smoking spots. That alone shows just how long ago my school days were. What were they thinking? I can't imagine letting Bree go to someplace anyone can smoke, much less one that would allow children to.

Mansfield is now a completely smoke-free campus. Had that been the rule in our day, most of the teachers would have been having nic fits alongside the kids. Back then, the teachers were allowed to smoke indoors. We had to freeze our butts off outside.

The Gazebo was the primo place to smoke, chill out, and figure out our social lives. It's tucked into a little glen about halfway up the gentle hill to the front of campus. And it's far enough away from all the school buildings to be a refuge from prying eyes. From there you could see Cooper House, where the head of the Athletic Department lived, and Halifax House, which was home to the head of the English Department, and to the side, at the midpoint of the hill, the back door to the main school building and the back of the headmaster's house. We had another small smoking area behind the school building, but you only went there if you were desperate for a quick butt in between classes. It put you right outside the headmaster's back door, which was a little too close for comfort. You didn't want to say anything there that could be overheard. Also, you'd often have to deal with his uber-preppy kids. They actually wore those patchwork tiny-whaled wide-wale cords. Once Derek put the image in my head, I always thought of them sewing late at night in their little rooms on the top floor. The image of their preppy indentured servitude made me giggle.

Dots and Ellbee joined me, eager to hear what had happened, since everyone had seen Derek and me walking across the quad after English. We moved a little out of the crowd, onto the stone pavers in front of the Gazebo, careful to remain within the smoking area so as not to make ourselves vulnerable to being busted by an errant teacher. On the pavers we could have a modicum of privacy from the other smokers. We huddled close together and kept our voices low.

I told them about my conversation with Derek as quickly and quietly as I could.

"So then," said Ellbee, "where is the new wonder boy?" She smiled at me wanly and pulled out a silver Zippo and a Virginia Slims. At least if she was using one hand to hold her cigarette in her mouth and the other to light it, she couldn't flap her hands about. Her Texas drawl became more exaggerated when she was being a jerk.

"Shut up," I replied, inhaling deeply. I wasn't about to admit to Ellbee that I thought Derek was blowing me off.

"Zip it! He's here," Dots hiss-whispered.

I didn't turn around. Instead, I smiled broadly, just in case my mouth was currently in anyone's field of vision. Then I stubbed out my butt under my clog, put my Mansfield-logoed notebook into my Mansfield tote bag, and headed on out of the Gazebo area, all the while keeping my gaze steadfastly forward. "Later, guys," I said perfectly casually, as if I didn't know he was coming up behind me.

"Kat? Is that you?" I heard Derek's soft voice coming from where I had just stood. "Hey, I thought that was you. Wait up a sec?" My friends didn't even pretend not to watch us walking down the path toward the Barkers' house. If they had had popcorn, we would have been the perfect afternoon entertainment.

Yes! I think I've got him, too. If he was willing to delay his chance to have a smoke to talk to me, he was obviously interested. I continued feigning nonchalance. "Oh hey, Derek, right?" *As if I wasn't sure of his name!* "What's up? How was your first day? Have you met the Hulk yet?"

Dean Heinemann, or the Hulk as we called him when we were sure he wasn't lurking about, was the single most feared presence on campus. He was a former Marine and the dean of students, which meant he was the one responsible for meting out punishments. The Hulk determined if you got study hall, kitchen duty, or both. He signed the board notices. He decided if you would stay or go. His was the last face you saw if you got booted. We used to mock him mercilessly behind his back, quoting David Banner: "Don't make me angry. You wouldn't like me when I'm angry." But in reality, we were all actually terrified of him.

Over the course of my freshman year, the Hulk threw out three of my boyfriends for drug violations. Trip Gunderson got caught at a party mid bong hit in late January. Will Jennings made so much noise crashing into the ice on the Pond just before Miniterm, they drug-tested him and sent him to McLean. And Jack Nathan was hiding more than a hundred and fifty hits of acid in his fireplace, in early April, evidently not very well, because the cleaning lady found them and narked. It was bad. There was a point that winter where I was afraid to go home for the weekend because I knew I'd probably have to find a new boyfriend when I got back on Monday.

From second semester of freshman year on, when I started going to good parties, I had the reputation for being an excellent party barometer. I always left any party five minutes before it got busted. I was way more afraid of facing my mother if I got thrown out of school than anything else. I knew if I got thrown out there'd be no other prep schools for me, just public high school and months, probably years, of lectures on what a disappointment I was.

I stayed out of trouble out of self-preservation. I got good grades, was polite to the grown-ups, spoke up in class, turned in all my work on time, and booked it if I felt any hint of a tingle on the back of my neck that we might soon be getting busted. I lost twenty-five friends over the course of four years, but I never once got caught. I always had my snap.

My friends attributed my party-barometer prowess to my possession of a sixth sense, which I heartily encouraged. Soon, if I left a party, other people started melting off too. If it was any kind of sixth sense, I hope it's something Bree inherited. The ability to stay out of trouble is vastly underrated as a skill. Especially if she is going to go to the kind of parties we had.

The only thing I ever got in real trouble for at Mansfield was being at Gus's Pizzeria during class hours. I tried to argue with the Hulk that since the school handbook said "We want you to consider all of town your campus," I wasn't technically in violation of the off-campus rule, but it didn't work. I got three days of kitchen duty. And my name, crime, and punishment were all posted on the board.

Being "boarded" was preppy humiliation at its finest. People would gather around the board, in the hallway just off the rotunda, at the beginning of every day to see who the latest miscreants were and what they were in for.

Worst of all, you weren't allowed to pay anyone to do the kitchen duty you got for being boarded. So I had to do those three days myself instead of paying Cathy Carroll or one of the other scholarship kids, which is what I usually did when I had kitchen duty. It was gross and horribly unfair. The plates and glasses were so hot when they came out of the industrial dishwasher that they burned your fingers, and you couldn't wait for them to cool. You needed to clear them quickly to get to the next load. Or the kitchen lady would yell at you. It was epically unfun.

"Nah, I haven't met the Hulk yet. Actually, I'm kinda hoping to not even see him until he puts us onto the buses for Logan at Christmas." Derek laughed. "Maybe I can make an entire year in this place. Um, hey, I was wondering, could you show me how to get to the Cave? I hear it's really cool, but I haven't been there yet and wouldn't want to get lost." He had the most exaggeratedly innocent look on his face I'd ever seen. He was always the best at that.

I laughed right at that look, flattered but not fooled, and pointed. "You walk down that way, stay straight on the road, keep going down the hill, and then keep walking until you run into some railroad tracks. Then you cross the tracks and follow them left until you see some big rocks. There's a small overhang, that's the Cave. You can't miss it, there is a stone fire circle in front. Don't go to the right or you'll end up behind crazy old Mr. Pepper's house, and he shoots at people who are on his land. I'm not kidding. Really, we are totally in the boonies here. He shoots buckshot."

If Derek wanted me to go to the Cave with him, he was going to have to ask me to go with him, not ask me to be his tour guide. *OK, he is super gorge and all, and fine, my heart is beating at about four times its normal speed, but I haven't completely lost my mind. Boys like a challenge.*

The Cave was our most favorite spot to go get high. Not our run-of-the-mill got-to-make-it-through-the-first-few-periods high, or even our after-lunch-mellow-out-for-afternoon-classes high, but the all-out classes-are-over, no-homework, no-practice, smoking-doobies-in-the-woods-for-hours totally high. The Cave was the Garden of Eden. Nothing bad could ever happen there.

"It only takes a couple minutes to get there, but this morning didn't you say you had tryouts today? So you won't have much time there if you go now."

"Shit! I spaced. Oh my god, Kat, you totally saved my ass. You are amazing! Thank you! My dad would have been so pissed if he set these up and I spaced them. He would have fucking killed me! I totally owe you one. My dad is expecting me to make varsity soccer. And hockey, and lacrosse. I think he'd be OK if I chose wrestling or tennis though, but I dunno. My dad's kind of a drag. I better motor. But anyway, hey, what time do you go to dinner? Maybe we could eat?"

"No dinner for me tonight, sorry. I'm a day student. My mom comes at five thirty most weeknights. Sometimes they let me stay over with Dots and even pony up for the overnight fees if I'm here for a few days, but it's rare. I can't wait till I can have my own car. It's such a drag to have to be driven around like a kid."

"Yeah, I had to leave my car at home, but my dad says if I make through till Christmas OK, he'll send it in January. I'll take you for a ride. It's totally bitchen. It's a Spider Veloce. Red." He leaned down toward me as he spoke.

Damn, he even has a cool car! "Nice," I said, hoping my voice was expressing admiration for the car, nothing more. "You already have a car? Wow. When do you get your license in California?"

"Sixteen. I was sixteen over the summer."

"Oh. I'm still only fourteen. I mean, I'm practically fifteen. I'll be fifteen in December. December eighteenth, same as Keith Richards. I mean, not like he'll be fifteen or anything. That's just stupid. He's much older than that. Anyway, my dad says I can have a car if I keep an A-minus or higher. But I won't be old enough to get my permit until June next year though, so it'll have to be senior year anyway. Even though school says you can have it on campus, as long as you make honor roll or above." I was rambling. *Shut up Kat, stop talking, shut up!*

"Fuck, forget grades. Honor roll? My dad just wants me to not get thrown out. This is my third school. He'll work something out with the school or rent a space for me in town if I can't have the car on campus. Your parents expect A-minus or *higher*? How is that possible? Are you sure you aren't one of those perfect preppies in disguise?"

"Do I look like a perfect preppy to you?" I raised my open palms to shoulder height in a mock question as I turned slowly around for his benefit. I was pretty darn confident about the view. Recently all of my girlfriends had discovered that we could make boys do just about anything we wanted just by walking around sans brassieres. I'd stash mine in my book bag when I got to school and change into it again before I got picked up to go home. Being able to find an excuse to giggle and jump up and down a bit evidently made boys completely willing to do our bidding. We didn't care why it worked, and really didn't want to think about it. We were just enjoying the balance-of-power shift while we had it.

That day, I was wearing perfectly broken-in Levi's 501s embellished with a rainbow I'd embroidered across the back pockets, a red webbed Mansfield belt monogrammed in blue (KAT), a snug black popped-collar polo with a purple pony, and my embroidered denim jacket. I had on long peacock feather earrings that came down to graze my shoulders and way too much black eyeliner for a fourteen-year-old girl. On my feet were burgundy kiltie clogs with three-inch stacked heels. Is it any wonder I can walk in anything? I spent my formative years clomping around fields in wildly inappropriate footwear.

I love heels. I dread the day I become too old to wear heels. If I have my way, I'll be buried in my black patent Louboutin boots. Bree might have something to say about that though. She's the same size. I always thought that she would hesitate at taking them right off my cold dead feet, but after this morning, I'm not so sure.

OK, I did look pretty preppy, just not in the little-green-whales-on-blue-corduroy manner that was popular with the kids we derided as preppy-preppy. My crowd's version was stoner-prep. Unlike the girls whose Bean barn jackets were adorned with enamel Pappagallo pins of their favorite animals, my denim jacket was festooned with buttons that said things like "Question Authority" and "Lizzie Borden was Framed," and it was embroidered across the back with a palm tree beach scene complete with multicolored waves and a dolphin pair in the distance. It took me weeks to do, and I was insanely proud of it.

"Yup." His voice lowered a bit, and he bent down further. "But you still look pretty good to me." Then he bent down just a little more and brushed my lips with his. At first it was a gentle hint of a kiss. Then more, stronger. A bit more pressure, a little lick. Finally, I felt his tongue in my mouth. It felt really right, not gross at all. I wasn't scared of how he made me feel. I was on top of the damn world. I was kissing Derek

Wilkeson on the path to the Gazebo. And if Froggy Ferguson was still at the Gazebo, the entire school would know about it before dinner. *Oh, yikes, and if Willie Hooks was still there, he probably wouldn't be giving me any more pot for a while.*

"Actually, you know who I think you look like?" he said when we came up for air. "Have you ever heard of Anita Pallenberg? I think you kinda look like her."

I was gobsmacked. *Did he just come up with that? Did someone tell him?* There was no higher compliment in the universe. You could have compared me to Cleopatra, Christie Brinkley, and Nastassja Kinski all rolled into one and it wouldn't have approached those heights. Anita Pallenberg was Brian's one true love, the one who left him for Keith Richards and caused the rift that sent him to his grave. She was Circe. She was a witch and a temptress. She was everything I aspired to be. I longed to think of myself as looking like her. Of being as all-powerful as her. *Derek didn't just see me; he saw me as I so desperately wanted to be seen.*

The same way we believed it was possible that Derek was related to Brian, we also believed it was possible that I was actually Anita's child. After all, I was adopted. So that meant, technically, it was possible. Much like everyone who discovers a previous incarnation finds that they were a historical figure of note—notwithstanding the inordinate number of dead peasants in world history—nearly every adopted child fantasizes about their famous parentage. My fantasy mother was Anita; all of my friends lived that fantasy with me. We were both short and had pointy chins. It was possible.

"Really?" I reverted back to hair twirling while I thought about how incredible it was that Derek could see our resemblance.

"Yeah. I do. You have the same lips." And he leaned down to kiss me again.

I was still thinking about what he'd said when we pulled ourselves apart so he could head to the soccer field. "That's so weird that you said that. I love her. She is so amazingly cool. You know, in an evil kind of way." I laughed. "I almost cut my bangs like hers over last weekend, but then I was sort of wasted, so I thought maybe it wasn't a good idea to have scissors near my eyes." I giggled again. "Maybe I'll try it tonight."

"Shit, really do gotta motor. Tryouts. See you after?"

"Maybe. Or I'll see you tomorrow."

My mom came by at five thirty on the nose and picked me up outside the library, where I was supposed to be studying, so I didn't get to see Derek that night. It wasn't the first time I wished I wasn't a day student. But it was one of the strongest times I ever made that wish. I wanted to live on campus more than ever.

But every single time I brought it up, my mom would say, "We only live fifteen minutes away. Besides, you'll be off to college soon enough. I want my baby home with me." And my dad would say, "And it's too expensive." And that would be that. As the years went on, I spent so many nights on Dots's floor that I kept a sleeping bag, pillow, clothes, and toothbrush there. I may as well have been a boarder. Sometimes the dorm mistress would notice, and my parents would get charged the sleepover fees, but usually they wouldn't even bother to do a room check.

Once I got home that night, I called Dots, and we went over every moment, every syllable in the conversation I had with Derek, even though she'd watched the whole thing from only a few feet away. While we chatted, I cut my bangs into a rough approximation of Anita's fringe. I thought I looked dangerously rock and roll.

I totally forgot about what I'd done to my hair until I went in to kiss my mother goodnight. She completely lost it. She said it was an uneven mess and insisted on getting me an emergency appointment with Manuel at Bloomingdale's on Saturday. It just wasn't worth arguing with her. You had to agree or she'd keep at it until she wore you down. I could be myself when I was out of sight, but when I was with her, I did as I was told. Otherwise, it was just too exhausting.

As I like to say, *plus ça change.*

The Cave

The origins of the Cave as a Mansfield hangout are lost to the mists of time. As far back as any known student lore reaches, the Cave has been our paradise, our escape hatch. To get there you walk past Westford House, off campus, and past town.

Westford House has always been the coolest boys' dorm. I mostly only dated Westford boys from sophomore year on. I'd probably be a bit concerned if I found out Bree was dating someone from Westford. Then again, I'd probably also be a bit concerned if she never dates someone from Westford. Like she's not good enough? It is a no-win situation inside my head at times.

Mansfield acquired Westford House from the neighbors in an expansion that took place in the 1890s. It's a beautiful white Federalist homestead with blue-painted shutters and doors. The shutters are so old, and the paint on them is so thick, that you can't see any of the grain of the wood underneath. The door sticks like mad in any kind of humidity, and it creaks ominously when you push it open. When you walk by Westford to go to town, you see a haphazard fieldstone walkway leading up to a wide-planked front porch. Now the boys' rooms are upstairs with only common rooms and a dorm master suite below. In my time there was one dorm room downstairs—coveted for its nonworking but still cool fireplace and easy access to the outdoors. It's since been repurposed as teacher office space, so none of the kids have a window that's relatively easy to climb into or out of. That was Derek's room.

The boys used to keep a spittoon in the front parlor under one of the windows. The trick was to make sure not to climb in through that one. Using the door took all the sport out of it. They would move it around to try to get each other to land in it. Chewing tobacco is no longer allowed, but for all I know they could be using that spittoon as a chamber pot now, and that would be even worse. Times may change, but I don't think the grossness of boys does.

Past Westford House, a right on Main Street takes you into town. A left puts you back toward the highway and brings you to Jensen's Ice Cream, about a half mile past the old graveyard and the two golf courses. Jensen's has the best frappes on planet earth, and they let you go out back to the cow barn to say thank you to the cows for the delicious ice cream. Occasionally I'll still dream about the famous Jensen Triple—cheeseburger, fries, and a coffee frappe. The best.

If you go neither left nor right onto Main Street, but stay straight—yes, we did think that was hilarious—you run right into the path to the Cave. The Cave was an overhang in an outcrop of rock, a bit past a lightly used set of railroad tracks, just big enough to make invisible a small clearing in the surrounding woods. The path to the Cave, blazed by only god knows how many Mansfield students before you, was a welcoming spot where kids could light a bonfire and be together without attracting any adult attention.

As far as I know, the Cave has never been raided.

More often than not, by the time we got to our special clearing, someone would be there already, bong or spliff handy. If it was cold out, there would be a fire going by three fifteen for the kids not doing a sport that semester. Kids who had practice would join us just after five.

Sometimes, during the fleeting spring weeks when it was warm, the girls would venture closer to the railroad tracks and smoke pot and sunbathe topless, to the delight of the conductors who occasionally passed by. If any of the boys tried to join us, we'd all squeal and grab our shirts for cover, but the men traveling by on trains and hooting at us never concerned us at all. We didn't know them, so they didn't count. They were the transient version of townies.

Often before we headed out to the Cave, we'd stop in town for supplies. Town was five stores in a shopping center along Main Street. The town has grown a bit over the years, but it's still hardly a bustling metropolis. I think Bree will suffer pretty much the same shopping conditions that I did.

Town had a small drugstore where we shoplifted eye makeup, a Cumberland Farms convenience store where we bought cigarettes and "supplies" to ward off the munchies, an insurance agency, which existed for no good reason we could tell, an old-fashioned barber shop, also useless except just before Parents' Weekend, and a pizzeria where we spent many happy hours soaking grease off the top of the cheese with white paper napkins before consuming the most perfect delicacy in the world. Gus's Pizzeria had an excellent jukebox and a Star Wars pinball machine. If we weren't in class and weren't outside, we were sitting in a booth at Gus's.

Within a day of that first kiss at the Gazebo, Derek and I were a thing. We were at Gus's nearly every day. Wednesday and Friday were game days, so those were out. Other than that, we'd finish classes, finish practice, then head out to the Cave to see how high we could get. After that, we'd head to Gus's to get some 'za.

The first time Derek and I were together at Gus's it was as if I had walked on to a movie set. The colors appeared brighter, the Cokes fizzier, the pizza even more delicious. We were early and the first Mansfield kids in there. I grabbed an empty booth by the window, and Derek snuggled in next to me. He leaned way over so he could rest his head on my shoulder and put his feet up on the bench on the other side. My whole world was perfect.

"They're gonna yell at us unless we order something," I said, and pushed his hair away from tickling my nose. His hair smelled like baby shampoo, and I wondered if that could be what he still used.

"It's OK, they know me here. What do you want me to get you?"

He felt so good snuggled up next to me, all I wanted was for him to stay there. But I was kind of hungry too. "I'll just have a bite of yours if you're getting a slice. I'm not that hungry. And a Dr Pepper, please."

"I'll get two slices just in case you change your mind. Your Dr Pepper thing is just weird, Kat-Kat. Don't people drink Cokes here?"

"People do. But I don't. I do what I want. And I like being a Pepper." I felt like if I were to get any happier, I might burst.

He kissed me as if he'd be gone for a week and got up to order. While he was ordering I saw him making sure Gus saw him pushing a twenty into the tip jar.

When he sauntered to the counter, I got to watch him walk away. *Damn,* I thought, *I wonder if he wears boxers or briefs?* I felt the heat come up in my face. I was terrified I'd be blushing bright red still when he got back to our booth and he'd know what I was thinking about.

He stopped on the way back to play the jukebox, and I had some time to pull it together. A126: "Give It to Me" by J. Geils. He came back and folded himself in next to me again, and the baby shampoo smell was back. I turned my head and breathed in the comforting scent.

"I love this song!" And I began to booth-dance and sing along.

"Me too. Boston bands rock. This should be our song." He drummed on the table, crooning *"Come on baby, please."*

Instead of hearing "Order up!" when our pizza was ready, Gus's son Chris brought the slices and drinks to our table on a tray. "Told ya they know me here." Derek preened. "You want some?"

"Thanks, Chris." I nodded to the boy who couldn't be more than a few years older than me and who had never brought anything to my table before.

"Just a bite," I said to Derek. And I ate the bottom quarter of each of his slices. I only like the pointy part of a piece of pizza. It's softer. The rest is too bready and saucy for me. And who needs all those carbs.

"Just the tip, huh?" he said and grinned at me.

The way he said it, I knew it was supposed to be dirty, like "That's what she said." But I was so naïve that I didn't know what it meant until I called Dots later, and she explained it to me. I'm glad I didn't know when Derek said it, because I would have turned bright red again. When Dots explained it, I turned crimson. In the moment I just smiled back as if I had a clue.

"I've gotta say, Kat. That is a very odd way to eat 'za. Next time I'll order you a whole pie and a pizza cutter and you can just go to town. A giant Dr Pepper too, if that's what you want. I live to please you, Kat-Kat." He laughed, and I laughed along with him. I was cool enough to be able to laugh at my own weirdness.

Derek sat up to eat but ate with his left hand so he could keep his right arm draped across my shoulders. I loved the feeling that he was staking his claim. When we were finished eating, he got up to play pinball, and I watched. He was a really good player, and it made me feel all funny inside to watch him jam his hips into the game and hear all the bells and whistles go off.

He placed two more quarters on the side of the machine and told me it was my turn.

"I want to watch you play, Kat-Kat. Maybe I can even help out your technique a little." Our table sat unmolested while we played. The plates were cleared, but the drinks were left as a sign that we were still occupying the space. Gus didn't even seem to mind. Usually, once you finished eating, he'd yell at you to bring your drinks near the machine so someone else could sit. Not this time.

I put the quarters in and pulled the plunger handle. I had some pinball skills I could show him. But I didn't get the chance. Derek enveloped me from behind, putting his hands over mine to work the flippers and pressing his hips up against me. He didn't lean into me as hard as he had into the machine when he was playing, but he leaned into me hard enough for me to know something was going on back there. I couldn't control myself from wanting to push back into him. It felt so good to have my body surrounded by his.

Gus's was our Rick's Café American; eventually, everyone came in.

Dots would stop by our table with her man of the moment. At this moment, Chuck Donner. Yes, we called him Donner Party—wouldn't you? For the first couple of weeks that Derek and I were together, Ellbee still came over to say hi. But soon she was over on the other side of Gus's, sitting at the good kids' table, shooting us looks of disgust at how sloppy and high and stupid we all were.

Rob Whent and Robbie Penner were always around. Rob and Robbie were Derek's guys. They did everything he did, followed him everywhere. God only knows how they glommed on to him so quickly, but they were a pack by the time we were a couple. Looking back, those two had at least as big a thing for Derek as I did. They hated me. It was mutual. I hated them too. Even so, we all spent most of our time together, eating lunch at the big round oak tables in the cafeteria, smoking cigarettes at the Gazebo, smoking dope in the Cave, and having our late afternoon snack at Gus's. A few weeks into first semester sophomore year, my mom relented a little and let me stay until six thirty. I was nearly always that late for pickup anyway, and she had better things to do than wait around for me. Six thirty was when dinnertime started in the cafeteria. My mother expected me home for family dinner.

Freshman year she wasn't at all comfortable with me being on campus overnight or on the weekends unless there was something special going on. She eased up some by sophomore year, but still, unless I was in a school play, or said I was working on a project in the library, or there was a dance or a game, I was home. She said she didn't mind picking me up late at night. Better that I was in my own bed.

I missed out on so many things when I just couldn't come up with a plausible enough excuse for being there after the library closed. Sometimes it bummed me out, but the self-preservation side of me kind of liked it. In many ways it was the best of all possible worlds. I got to complain about how horrible my parents were for not letting me hang out, and I also got to go home, come down a little bit, and take a break.

So I wasn't there those first weekends when Derek and his friends managed to get themselves covered in bruises by Monday morning. It wasn't even hockey season yet. I never understood why the boys needed to pummel each other, but as long as it wasn't in front of me, I didn't want to think about it. They'd all get drunk and get into fights in ways that pot just doesn't encourage.

Derek said they got into fights because there was nothing else to do in this stupid little town. I'd kiss all his bumps and bruises and glare at Rob and Robbie, certain that they were the main culprits. Even though they mostly got the worst of it. Derek was a good bit bigger than either of them, and they definitely weren't smart or brave enough to gang up on him. No one ever ended up really hurt or anything, so I didn't really think it was that big a deal. They were just blowing off steam. I figured once hockey started, they could whale on people as much as they wanted, with the full blessing of our league conference. Maybe they'd even win us a championship this year.

There are times when I wonder what might have been. If I had done something at that earliest point, when there were those first hints that Derek's anger issue was different from run-of-the-mill teen emotional off-gassing. What if I had insisted right then that he get help? Could I have gotten Derek to go see a shrink? Maybe. Should I have called his father and told him what was going on? I don't know. At that point in my life there was no way I was brave enough to do anything like that. I'm not sure I am even now. It would have been inconceivable to me that I might call a grown-up I didn't know to nark on the boy I loved. It was contradictory to everything I held dear. And besides, we all knew everyone grows out of it.

In the Car

One Week Ago

The sound of my phone ringing startles me back into the present. "No Woman, No Cry" by Bob Marley—dear hubby's idea of a cute ringtone for him. The stupid Bluetooth hasn't worked properly since I dropped my phone on the stone terrace at his parents' place in the Hamptons last July. I needed to get to the mall and get a new phone, but I've just been so busy I keep forgetting. The screen isn't cracked or anything, so it's hard to remember when I'm not in the car.

"Sweetie, that's Daddy. Can you please answer it? Tell him I'm driving." I always try to set a good example when she is in the car, so I don't pick up my phone.

Bree digs the phone out of the bottom of my purse and answers it with the big smile she always has for him.

"Hi, Daddy!" Daddy being the happiest word in the English language. "Do you want it on speaker?" she says to me.

I shake my head and say no a little too sharply. That seems harsh, so I explain, "The speaker isn't working right either, sweetie. I need a new phone. I'm sorry, baby girl, just tell him we're on the road and ask if he needs me to pick up anything for him before I get back tonight." I really don't want to talk to him right now, but she doesn't need to know that. I take my eyes off the road for a moment to see if Bree has noticed my tension over the call. She shows no sign that she has.

"We're on the road and Mom wants to know if you need her to pick up anything for you before she heads home tonight. Her phone isn't working right," Bree parrots for me. I hear only her half of the conversation, but it's as if I can hear his words in my head.

You're sure you don't mind, sweetheart? You know if it weren't for this tournament and all the stuff happening at work ...

"No, Daddy, it's OK. I know, it's important. I hope you win! I'll see you visiting day."

I love you, little baby girl. You be good. And let us know if you need anything, OK?

"I love you too, Daddy. Of course I'll be good. Aren't I always?"

Make sure your mother gives you money before she turns around. Right?

"Daddy, I have plenty of cash. Mummy already took care of it. And she's already set up accounts at the bookstore and at the bank. There isn't any Starbucks for like a million miles, so what would I spend it on anyway?"

I break in briefly to ask her to ask him if he thinks he'll be home tonight, too. I'm very adept at keeping my voice steady and emotionless. It's just a question.

"Mom, Daddy says he doesn't know yet. He'll have to see what the day brings." I tell her to relay that I'll call him before heading home, and she does so before hanging up. We're always very polite and courteous toward each other. We always set a good example.

Homecoming

Football Field Bleachers

Sophomore year homecoming was going to be the best night of my life. Derek and I sat at the bonfire before the game, cuddled up against the chill. We had been dating for over a month. It was just a few weeks before my fifteenth birthday. Everything was going exactly the way it should. I had the cutest boyfriend in the school. My face wasn't broken out at all. My hair looked great. My outfit looked great. I was wearing Derek's soccer letter jacket, a black turtleneck, skintight jeans, and black clogs. My class won the cheer-off for the loudest class again, making us the class to beat since we'd won the year before, even as freshmen. My class ended up winning all four years, a feat not matched before or since. Bree loves the story of our triumph and likes to tease that I'm solely responsible for the loudness. It's the only thing I've ever told her about homecoming.

It was a gorgeous New England night, with just the right amount of chill in the air. As we walked, the leaves crunching underfoot sounded and smelled like the end of fall. If Mansfield had elected a homecoming king and queen, it would have been us. Unanimously. OK, maybe not by Rob and Robbie and a few stupid jealous girls, but close to unanimously. Except, of course, we didn't have those kinds of trashy townie king-and-queen rituals. Even without the public acknowledgment of our special status, everything was perfect.

Pot was very easy to get at Mansfield, but booze was difficult to obtain. I knew lots of kids who were getting shoebox packages of weed from their friends at home regularly. Those packages were shipped UPS instead of regular mail because sending drugs through the mail is a federal crime. We may have been high as kites most of the time, but we weren't morons. It was a great business model. They'd smoke some, sell some, and invest the money they made by sending back for more. Pre-Amazon, I can't imagine why the admin didn't find it suspicious that people were getting so many shoeboxes from UPS with such surprising regularity, but no one ever got caught.

Booze was a different story. It was too heavy and too distinctive sounding to get shipped to you. Busted once, you were given a warning and a week of extra kitchen duty. Twice and you were on probation. Third time, you were out. Expelled. "On your way to Spaulding." Spaulding Prep was the school you went to when you got thrown out of your original prep school. South Kensington was for after you got thrown out of Spaulding. I'm not sure what happened if you got thrown out of South Ken, Military school maybe?

So we smoked pot every day, often many times a day, but booze was a special occasion drug. There were no State Liquor Stores anywhere near us in New Hampshire, and just the one off the highway in Mass. Everywhere in Mass. carded like crazy. Occasionally, someone who lived nearby would have a house party and their parents would provide a keg, but that was a pretty rare thing. Other times, someone would return from a weekend home with a bottle or two. With enough cash, anything was possible, but it took more doing than our usual stoner paradise did.

Not being very big, I was never that big a drinker. Drinking was never really a thing in my family. Outside of the Seder, I don't think my parents ever drank wine. An occasional mixed drink on a friend's porch after a summer afternoon at the beach was about the extent of it. It was the same with all their close friends and our relatives. Drinking wasn't part of the culture I grew up in. That was very different from the culture I live in now. The wealthy suburbs may be the wettest place on earth.

I found out pretty quickly that beer made me throw up almost immediately; it turns out I'm allergic to hops. So beer was out. When vodka was available, I'd drink that mixed with lots of orange juice. And I'd always mix my own drinks. After one or two, I'd just pretend to put in the vodka. Even drinking super-light screwdrivers, I still didn't love the way it made me feel. Drinking made me feel all dizzy and barfy, with a horrible headache the next day. Not like pot. Pot was mellow and joyful. And never gave me aftereffects.

Plus, my parents would always bust me for drinking, but they never knew when I was high. If I came in from a night with anyone even near me drinking, my mom would say I smelled "like a brewery," and I'd have to sit through an endless lecture on the evils of drink before I could slink off into my own room. But even when I was stupendously high, they'd never know. I don't know why they didn't smell smoke the same way they did booze. I'd just tell them my contact lenses were acting up and go to bed. I'm not sure why they didn't take me back to the eye doctor, since my contacts must have been really ill-fitting to bother me so often. But it was glorious to have an excuse to just be left alone.

In the month we'd been together, I'd never seen Derek drunk before. I think he'd been careful not to drink around me, because he was definitely able to score booze on the weekends when I wasn't there. I thought the stories I'd heard about him when he was drunk were wildly exaggerated. How bad could it possibly be? I heard the same kinds of things, over and over. He'd start fights with Rob and Robbie. He'd start fights with any townies who ventured near campus or search them out in their local hangouts. It became sort of a joke around campus; people laughed and said he'd start fights with the shrubbery when he was drinking. But I never saw him like that. He was my happy-go-lucky gorgeous stoner California boy.

When Derek was high, he was the sweetest boy in the world. He'd be all crooked little smile, singing romantic songs, eager to make out in unused corners of campus, cuddly. We'd eat gross junk food and pretend we were hippies. He'd paint smiley faces and rainbows on my cheeks with stage makeup and let me paint hearts on his. We'd walk everywhere together with our hands in each other's back pockets. He loved the way my haircut made me look even more like Anita. He was such a talented photographer. He'd take pictures of us that were homages to pictures of Brian and Anita. He loved taking pictures of me. He was the perfect boyfriend.

Before homecoming, Derek traded with a townie and got a fifth of Smirnoff for a good ounce of Humboldt. He hid it in the fireplace—well-hidden, I guess, since he had the same room Jack did before him—but not before mixing up a liter bottle of vodka and Coke to bring with us to the game.

There we were, way up high in the football field bleachers. Enjoying the game and the freedom of snuggling in the dark. Then, in a very short time span, the booze was all gone. I sure didn't drink any; even the thought of vodka and Coke is revolting! And I was suddenly dealing with a whole new boyfriend. Gone was my sweet stoner boy who sang off-key tunes to me while I rested my head in his lap. This Derek was an angry mess. Raging at his father for sending him away. Raging at his mother for dying and leaving him all alone. He was rambling and so angry. He didn't even make any sense half the time.

I sat next to him, listening to him, completely confused, bolted to my spot. I had never seen him like that before. I had never seen anybody like that before. I was a nice little preppy Jewish girl from Massachusetts. People in my world didn't all of a sudden become raging, angry drunks. I didn't know what to do or what to say. What the hell was wrong with him? I didn't know why he was so mad. Or what I could do to fix it.

I adjusted my position, leaning my small body up next to his. I had my feet curled up underneath me and to the right on the bench. I was hoping he could feel the love and support emanating from my being. It didn't seem like smiling was appropriate, so I tried to keep my eyes on the game and my expression neutral. I wanted to tell him it would be OK, but I wasn't sure that was what he wanted to hear, so I didn't say anything. I just leaned on him.

He stopped ranting about his family, then put his arm around me and asked, "So whaddya want for your birthday?" The way he asked the question, it somehow came out sounding funny. His normal soft voice had an odd, rough edge to it and was all slurry.

"I dunno. There's a Stones bootleg out of Germany that sounds really good. It's on pink vinyl! So cool. Flowers, candy, those are all nice." As off as things were, I still had a good buzz going from the pot we smoked earlier, before the bonfire. I was hoping to lighten things up. Maybe I could just change the subject entirely, and then he would be OK. He sounded so weird. I was anxious and off-balance.

"I know what I'd like to give you for your birthday." It felt like Derek was overwhelming me, not enveloping me like normal. His usual grin was replaced with a tight grimace. He wrapped his other arm around me, making a big circle with his arms, and with my feet tucked up underneath me, I felt like I was in a straitjacket.

"Not gonna happen, baby. I'm only turning fifteen." I moved my shoulders to try to shrug his arms off a little and relieve some of the pressure. I was still trying to joke him out of his mood. Derek had tried to go too far a couple of times before, but always relented when I moved his hands back to the outside of my clothing. I just wasn't ready to do more yet. We'd only been together a short time. Besides, I knew what happened to the girls who gave in after falling for some boy's begging. I heard the kind of names those girls were called. I had even joined in on the name-calling a time or two myself. I wasn't about to let that happen to me.

Sophomore year there were only a few girls known to not be virgins. And despite what the boys tried to have us believe, not a lot of them had lost it yet either. It didn't seem like Derek was in that camp. He seemed to know what he was doing, but what did I know? The classes after us were a whole different story. The image of the eighties is of the Reagan years, the Gordon Gecko "greed is good" decade, but this was before all that. Nineteen-eighty was really still the seventies, Carter was President, John Lennon was alive, and Franco was still dead, as Saturday Night Live told us. AIDS wasn't yet on the radar.

There was a big societal change that happened during my four years at Mansfield. Even our cloistered old-school world wasn't immune. By the time I graduated, my hippie stoner jeans were replaced by Calvins, to which I had meticulously attached hundreds of tiny gold safety pins running the length of each leg. By senior year, my favorite new bands were The Clash and the Dead Kennedys. Pot was replaced by coke. The baby boomers were replaced by Generation X. But back in 1980, while we may have been saying we "did" when singing along to the Knack's "Good Girls Don't," all we were doing was singing.

"Yeah, and fifteen will get you twenty, right?" He let his left arm fall away from my shoulders, no longer encircling me. But then he grabbed both my wrists with his free left hand, his right arm still circling me, but draping down from my shoulder. His hand worked under my open jacket. His fingers grasped roughly at my breast. His thumb rubbed at my nipple hard, through my shirt. I felt my body spring to attention, betraying me by reacting to this strange type of touch with desire. "I could make you, you know." He didn't sound like himself. He sounded scary. I was scared. He wasn't joking.

"Yeah, but you won't. Baby, that hurts my hands. Come on, seriously. I mean it. Let go." I was starting to get angry as well as scared. I shifted my weight so I could put my feet down on the bleachers. Derek held on to my wrists even tighter as I wriggled to free them. I was going to have bruises tomorrow.

"I could just drag you down to the woods behind Westford right now and get it over with. Everyone is here. No one would even hear you scream." His eyes were full of anger, not the usual desire. I didn't know what to do. I thought he actually might decide to pick me up and caveman-carry me down the bleachers to the cheers of the crowd. They'd all laugh, and I'd die of embarrassment.

"Not cool, Derek. You're scaring me and you're hurting me. I mean it. Really. Stop it. It's nine o'clock. My dad's coming in a couple of minutes. I gotta motor out to the quad. He'll have a cow if he has to come up and get me from the bleachers. And you definitely don't want to have him see us like this."

He whispered in singsong right up next to my ear. "If I make you, then it wouldn't be your fault, and then we could do it all the time. I can make you like it, Kat." His left hand was still tightly curled around my wrists. His other hand now reached down my back and was tucked into the waistband of my jeans.

"But you won't. Because that's not how you want me. Right?" I asked gently. I was trying to figure out what sort of voice to use to get out of this. I was in way over my head. I'd already said I wasn't ready to sleep with him, but if he wanted to press it, there wasn't much I could do to stop him. The term date rape hadn't even been invented yet, and he was my boyfriend. Plus, he was twice my size. If he actually did throw me over his shoulder and carry me out of the stadium everybody would think it was hilarious, not a crime. They would probably think it was romantic, and applaud.

It was a common attitude at the time. When Luke and Laura became *General Hospital*'s super couple, their rape story was changed to a forced seduction story, whatever "forced seduction" is supposed to possibly mean. "He loved her so much he just couldn't help himself" was their PR blitz. But I remembered the menace of the scene when it first aired. I thought it was terrifying, not romantic. Being with Derek up in the bleachers felt the same.

I don't know what switch flipped in his head, but I am eternally grateful that in that one moment, Derek seemed to slip back into himself again. "Course not, I'm waiting for you to beg me." He dropped my wrists, put his arm back lightly around my shoulder, and that easy smile of his was back and all was forgotten. Snap. I kissed him and he walked me over to the school building, then left me to wait for my dad alone. I tried to never let my parents talk to any of my boyfriends.

Except, of course, it wasn't really forgotten. He scared me in a way that I had never been scared before. I was scared of Derek. I was scared he would hurt me. And that threat of violence lodged itself in my brain, ever after, no matter how sweet any subsequent interaction was. Derek was no longer the boy I knew. He wasn't the boy I wanted him to be. I couldn't have articulated it then, but I also knew he never would be. Homecoming was the beginning of the end for us.

Derek and I had a few perfect weeks together. A few perfect hours here and there. Everything else between us was a long, slow, inexorable slide toward an inevitable end.

So why didn't I just walk away from that relationship right then, after what I saw in him that night? I don't know. I never ask that question of other women. They stay because they don't know what else to do. They stay because the good times are good, and because no one wants to think about the bad times. They stay even if they don't know why.

Maybe I thought that if I loved him enough, I could fix him. I could make him better. Maybe there was something I could change about me to make him OK. If I did everything right, there wouldn't be any bad times to have to think about. Mostly, I just didn't know what to do, so I did nothing. Which does seem to be my default setting. Whatever my rationale, I never looked at him again without the knowledge that he might suddenly turn on me. On our good days, I could push it away, I could pretend that everything was perfect. But it was always lurking in the background. *Plus ça change, indeed.*

And the truth is, I was perfectly safe that night. He stopped. Nothing happened. But something did happen. That biochemical pull I'd felt toward him from the first moment we met was still there, but ever after it was tempered by fear. The sound of his voice that night stayed with me long after the bruises around my wrist bones healed.

For a very long time after homecoming, Derek didn't drink around me at all. His booze binges were all saved for the nights when I was safely at home. And I decided to believe that whatever he was up to when

I wasn't around wasn't my problem. And he obviously didn't have a drinking problem, since he could not drink whenever he wanted to. Occasionally, he'd be grumpy with a wicked hangover, or I'd find a huge pile of empties near one of our favorite spots, but mostly things went back to normal.

We continued to have the common teenage negotiations about having sex, but it became shtick, part of our running couple's commentary. He didn't really push me. Early on, right after homecoming, I was wary, wondering if he might threaten to rape me again. But the longer that didn't happen, the easier it was to push those thoughts away. He was drunk, he just made a mistake. He didn't mean it. Nothing happened.

There were always rumors. People liked to talk about Derek. He was beautiful, rich, melancholy, and aloof. People made stuff up, all the time. And yeah, there were rumors about him sleeping with other girls, but he was still my boyfriend, so it was easy to dismiss those rumors as stupid jealous gossip. That biochemical pull I felt wasn't only on my side. He felt as strongly pulled toward me as I did toward him. He did whatever it took to keep me his girlfriend.

We went back to being our happy stoner selves, spending hours making out, walking all over campus with our limbs intertwined. We bundled up more as winter settled in and spent more time indoors, in between smokes and joints. I could act like my life was perfect. And sometimes, I could even believe it.

It's not like we didn't have any happy times together after homecoming. We had lots of them. Derek would always make sure the whole school knew that I was his. I'd be in the hallway and he'd come up behind me and very, very slowly lift up my hair from the side of my neck with one hand while the other nestled into my jeans pocket. He'd lean down, even more slowly, and the hairs on my neck would stand up as his warm breath hit them, a literal shiver running down my spine. Then he'd plant a trail of kisses, some short, some lingering, from the base of my ear all the way down to my collarbone, where he'd leave just the tiniest of claiming marks, just below my shirt collar. It made my toes curl. We had lots of good times together, even as we were coming apart.

The Pond, the Manse, and Cow Tipping

One of the great joys about going to school in rural New England was the amount of trouble you could get up to outside. In addition to the Cave, there was an idyllic farm right next to school. Called Bright Star Ranch, it was owned by a pair of New York City escapees. They had about twenty head of cattle, which they kept in a pasture directly across the road from our football field.

The Pond, just past the football field, is a true-to-life cow runoff pond. I'm sure the security at Bright Star is much tighter now. Like they probably have some.

Our Pond had spectacular algae blooms each spring thanks to their cows. It was perfectly nasty, covered in green slime, and smelled like skunk cabbage. Of course, it was against the rules, but we were always challenging each other to figure out a way to ford it. We tried to float across on makeshift rafts. That never once worked. We tried to swing across, Tarzan-style, on ropes hung from trees near the edge. Nope. We tried to walk across it when it wasn't frozen solidly enough. I went in up to one thigh that way one time. Hard to believe that being covered in wet, smelly slime is a fond memory, but we really did have so much fun.

Across the road, uphill from the Pond, were the actual cows. And behind those cows were some ruins we called the Manse. They were the remains of the original stone farmhouse on the property. One wall was intact up to the second story, and you could climb up, finding hand- and footholds in the stones, and sit on the glassless slab windowsills. There was a fireplace on a huge rock slab on the ground floor. We'd get high, consume delicious Drake's cakes and the rest of our "supplies," and just enjoy being in such a cool place.

The Manse was an otherworldly spot. It seemed like sunset there lasted for hours. It was always golden hour, when the light hits everything just right and the whole world is perfectly lit. Sitting there in Derek's lap, his arms wrapped around me, the sunshine on my face, and a soft breeze tickling my skin, is just about as perfect as a memory could be.

The only hitch to our enjoyment was the Manse's security system, the cows. To get to the Manse, you had to sneak around the cows. Usually, the cows didn't care. They'd look at you, keep chewing, and let you go on by, as long as you didn't come up too close. It was technically possible to jump over the fence and make your way through a narrow, fenced-in passageway back to the Manse without being inside the cow enclosure. Or you could try and run through the cows to see if this was the day the cows didn't want you around. Guess which route we almost always took?

I have heard some unfounded rumors calling cow tipping an urban (shouldn't that be rural?) myth. I have no idea why this has become a topic du jour, but I am here to attest that cow tipping most certainly exists. I even tried to call in to NPR while they were having a segment on cow tipping, but fortunately, I couldn't get through. And neither could anyone else with any personal cow tipping knowledge, evidently.

Because everyone who got through said it was fake. Solo cow tipping is certainly a myth—cows are very heavy animals—but group cow tipping is an absolute reality. And after they fall over, cows are so not happy campers. A bazillion pounds of angry cow coming at you will really get the adrenaline going, but you do have the time it takes for them to stand back up working in your favor.

The way we did it was to get four or five kids, mostly hockey players, lined up by a napping cow. They sleep standing up. The cows, not the hockey players. On the count of three, everyone pushes in the same direction. The person at the front has the distinction of making sure the head goes down first, because the cow will definitely follow her nose. Once she hits the ground, you needed to run as fast as humanly possible, so you are far away when she regains her feet.

One time, we'd spent most of that afternoon up at the Manse. Derek and I, Rob and Robbie, and Dots and Skip Foreskin (his last name was Foresman) were sitting up in the Manse windows when Robbie decided it was time to tip some cows. Normally when the boys went on their own, they would try for more than one, but Dots and I thought that was just lunacy. Clearly that was the part about this that was crazy. This time we all agreed to head back to campus after just one little cow was tipped.

I was wearing a brand-new bright red wool jacket that my mom had just gotten for me. My denim jacket was my favorite fashion statement. I'd add a down vest when the jacket was too light to block the wind. But when it got just too cold or the jacket needed washing, I'd give in and wear something else, usually something my mom thought was "more becoming" on me. This was one of those times.

My new jacket looked sort of like a beefier version of a blazer, dark red, somewhere between crimson and cranberry, with a wide belt across the back. My mom adored it. It was "a classic that would last forever," so it was worth the price. I thought it was totally uncool, but I didn't have a winter coat yet and both my down vests were in the wash.

So of course, I wore it to go cow tipping. I imagine anyone would. Especially if they'd just been forced to sit through a lecture that very morning about how expensive their clothes were and how they really ought to take better care of them. With a "who knows how you manage to do these sorts of things, young lady" big finish.

The cow tipping itself went smoothly, but when I jumped over the fence with an angry cow coming up behind me, I snagged the trailing sleeve jacket on a piece of wire, which left a big gash on the upper part of the right arm. Everyone else was in hysterics, probably from the look on my face, but they weren't going to have to deal with my mother when I got home. I can't remember what cockamamie story I came up with, but I did learn that tailors have a thing called invisible thread and that is what they use to fix those kinds of things.

That was the end of cow tipping for me, it just wasn't worth it.

* * *

I could probably tell Bree the cow tipping story when we stop for lunch, if I edit it some. She loves stories that pit me against my mother. Especially when I'm the one who's wrong. My mother and Bree love to gang up on me. That story will make her happy. And all I want is for her to be happy with me before she leaves me.

Millbrook Diner

One Week Ago

After almost two hours of being in the car, I've had about all the Hits One radio station I can take. I look over at Bree, and she's mouthing the words to a song she thinks I don't understand. I swear, one day I'm going to play "Starfucker" by the Stones for her and completely blow her mind. When I was her age, it was one of my favorite songs. It was also one of the songs I would leap over couches and chairs to pull the needle off the record if my mother came home unexpectedly. I'm pretty sure I still have that record somewhere in the cartons of albums I keep near our wine cellar. I bet I have it on a tape or two too, tucked away in some memory box. Hah, maybe playing that would be a good way to get her to see me as I was.

Bree is doing her car dance, fingers snapping, hair flying. I think she looks adorable, a sentiment that would horrify her if I said it out loud. She's barely said one word to me since the phone call. Or maybe she has and I just haven't noticed. I've been completely lost in 1980.

"Millbrook Diner for brunch?" I ask, knowing what the answer will be.

"Yummo!" She answers in her best Rachel Ray.

The Millbrook Diner is the quintessential old-fashioned luncheonette. It has red vinyl booths, spinning stools, and waitresses who call you "hon." It's one of our go-to stops whenever we head north. I'm feeling so good with the sun on my face and the wind in my hair, I'm thinking I might even carb-splurge and eat some french fries. *I haven't had fries for a year.* This thought takes me back to thinking about when I could eat anything I wanted and not think about it. Which leads me back again to Mansfield, and I decide I will tell Bree the cow-tipping story over lunch.

And I'm relieved to think that since I know what I'm going to order, I won't have to pull out my reading glasses to look at the menu. I hate those stupid glasses. I keep buying them in all sorts of shapes and colors, but they all look the same. Old. I try to tell myself that reading glasses are really hot right now, everyone is wearing them. But even I don't believe me.

We pull into the gas station before the diner, and I wait for the pimply kid pumping gas to say something about two pretty blondes and a convertible, but he doesn't. He just smiles at Bree as he leans over her side to wash the windshield. He doesn't seem to notice me at all.

I can feel myself becoming more and more invisible as Bree gets older. Every day there is some new embarrassment telling me I'm no longer the one who garners the attention. Every day brings another petty humiliation, a small betrayal by my eyes, my ears, or my skin. Every night as I slather my face up with retinol, I search it for signs that I ought to be doing more. I mean, I can still pass for early thirties, but the problem is that the girls in their early thirties can pass for being in their twenties. And the boobs on those twentysomething girls? I don't even want to look at them in the gym locker room. It's too depressing to think I once looked like that. I'm petrified that I'll be someone who looks good for my age instead of just looking good. Or worse, I'll suddenly start being described as a "handsome" woman, instead of pretty. "Handsome" is what happens when the slackening jowls start to appear. Is that about to happen to me?

I allow myself a brief flash of annoyance toward this teen, who completely ignores me and is still trying to catch my daughter's eye. Then I just feel embarrassed. I am not some sex-crazed cougar wandering the byways of New England trolling for boys. Why the hell would I care if he finds me attractive? I am an adult. I don't need validation by a child. Plenty of people still think I'm hot. People who can drive themselves to the movies.

My thoughts get ahead of my ability to control them again. I'm perfectly happy with my perfect life. Why am I spending so much time thinking about an unattainable old love? Obsessing over the few stubborn extra pounds I can't seem to run off? Unwilling to put on the reading glasses I now need? Finding a new wrinkle every time I look in the mirror? Obviously, I'm not old enough to be having an actual midlife crisis. I'm only forty-two. Still, I often feel lately like I'm hovering somewhere in between the old ladies in purple wearing their stupid red hats and the new baby moms in town in their Frame and James Perse.

OK, fine, so what if I am having a midlife crisis?

Maybe I should parlay this ridiculous not-really-a-midlife-crisis into a little surgery for my birthday present. Go in for the full mommy-job: tummy tuck, lipo, just a little bit of filler in my face. Without Bree to drive around, I'll have plenty of recovery time. It'll just be the two of us. No drama.

The car is supposed to be my birthday present and all, but by the time my actual birthday comes around, Hubby will be so guilt-ridden over working all those extra hours and leaving me alone so much. He won't mind if I do something for myself. Besides, it's as much a present for him as it is for me. He gets to have Wife 2.0 without the trade-in costs. I go back to being perfect-Kat, not the dinged-up version.

Maybe that is exactly what I should do. I should just give him my mommy-job surgery for Christmas. Go in for a full overhaul. Maybe even add in a little eyelid work and get it all done before it all gets any worse.

This is crazy. I am being crazy. I need to get a grip. I don't need surgery. I still look like me. Why would I do something so drastic that I don't need? I don't even like the way surgery looks on people most of the time.

I must be losing my marbles. Like am I really only minutes away from a horrible case of trout pout and that deer-in-the-headlights, permanently stuck, surprised-eyebrows look? I don't want to look like the woman we call Duchess Duck Lips or Lady Saint Boobsalot from yoga class. She of the tiny spaghetti-strap tops and the gravity-defying balloon boobs. Yuck. But maybe what if I just got a little tummy tuck and a really good facial? I don't want to look like I'm trying too hard. But I don't want to look like I've given up either.

Christ, what on earth is wrong with me? I sound insane. Even to myself.

I suddenly flash on being at the gym last week, exchanging pleasantries with an acquaintance from town. She's in great shape, ten or fifteen years older than me, I'd guess, but looks fabulous. I was just about finishing my forty-five minutes on the treadmill, and she was about to start hers.

"I'm so jealous, you're almost done," she said before plugging in her headphones, a half-smile on her pretty and open face.

"Ugh, I know, it was so hard to get here today," I replied, panting a bit. "But you know, you have to do it." And put my hand to my heart as a symbol of good health.

"Yeah, I know. You have to." And she pulled some skin on her stomach away from her thin frame, as if to grab some fat. "I wish I didn't."

I smiled in solidarity, put my headphones back in, and went back to my cooldown, but it stuck. This woman was a huge success, she'd raised four kids through college, three Ivy Leaguers, and her littlest one just graduated from Sarah Lawrence. She's beautiful, not a line on her face, beautiful house, beautiful family, but she sounded exhausted, just beat. I wanted to cry. When does it stop? If she can't stop, in her fifties, where does that leave me? Will I have to be on this daily treadmill, literally, every day until the day I die?

I cannot think about this now. I shake it off and come back to the car and to my Bree.

I get my credit card back from the kid. Glare at him for eyeballing my baby. We do the "lucky park, lucky park, lucky park" chant, which works its magic once again. The perfect parking spot appears right in front of the Millbrook Diner. Bree and I high-five each other and go in.

As we eat — bacon cheeseburger with fries and mayonnaise for her, chef salad for me — I steal three fries off her plate. I tell Bree about my adventures in cow tipping, leaving out only the parts about pot smoking. I'm not entirely sure the story even makes any sense without the pot smoking, but I forge on ahead anyway. Bree doesn't seem to notice anything missing. She laughs at my idiocy and sides with my mother over my jacket.

"You'd kill me if I did anything like that!" Bree emphasizes her point with a french fry feint toward my face.

Our waitress brings over our check and directs us to pay at the front counter "whenever you're ready, hon." From the look on her face, I think we'd better be ready soon. The lunch crowd is beginning to file in. We aren't regulars, and we've held on to the table long enough. I put a twenty down on the table. Always overtipping is a great life skill.

"Don't be silly, Bree. It was just a jacket."

"Oh yeah? Remember when I got grape soda all over the front of my brand-new baby blue North Face? My ears still hurt." She smiles in great victory over my hypocrisy.

"Fine, but that was just carelessness." I cover my mouth with my hands as the words escape from my mouth. I laugh too and say, "Oh my god! I am turning into my mother!"

"I'll save you, Mom!" And she throws her arms around me dramatically as we stand in the cashier line to pay. For a minute we're having the kind of silly fun we always used to.

I spy her gazing at the register. She wiggles her fingers involuntarily toward it and I know she's trying not to reach out and touch it. When Bree was little, the old-fashioned heavily gilded cash register at this place used to fascinate her. It's nice to see it's still here. And nicer still to see that expression on her face, that joy, at the clunky buttons and clanging sounds. I swear she can smell the metal. I pay with cash so they'll use the old register and Bree can watch it come to life. I choke back the tears and try to just be happy for these moments we have together.

We get back on the road, and I claim driver's privileges. I need a break from her radio station. If I have to listen to it any longer, I'll start singing the songs myself. It's musical Stockholm Syndrome. I put on the Eagles' *Long Run* CD and click through to the fifth track. The first notes of "Heartache Tonight" send me right back in time.

Winter Social

We had socials one Saturday night each month. Everyone went to every one of them. They were held in the big lounge near the cafeteria. Chairs and couches got moved out of their normal cozy groupings in the middle of the room to line the walls. The stage was a plywood platform at the front just big enough for a band. The Winter Social was the first weekend of December. There must have been an endless supply of cover bands roaming the New England countryside in those days, because we almost always had live music, and I don't think the same band ever played twice.

I have no idea what the band for the Winter Social was called, but they were great fun. They played passable covers of everything we wanted to hear, Stones, Doors, Zep, Springsteen … and the lead guitarist was good-looking in a skinny, shaggy, Keith Richards-circa-1967 way. Which, at the time, I thought was very good-looking indeed.

The girls normally all danced together for most of the songs, while the boys sat it out on the sides and tried to look uninterested. We'd drape ourselves on our boyfriends for slow dances, but for most songs, we just wanted to jump around together. And they were too cool to jump around with us.

Dots and I were dancing in front of the band in a manner that would generally be agreed upon by reasonable adults as provocative. So were all the other girls. We were just having some fun. No one meant anything by it. And the band must have been thrilled. Get paid to play music and watch preppy girls bounce around in front of them? Great!

We were all dressed up for the dance in our finest rock and roll outfits or at least what we thought passed for such. Urban Cowboy had just come out, so there were boots and fringed shirts mixed in with the Pappagallos and wide-wales.

The realization of the type of hold we could have over the boys was still kind of a novelty to us. So yes, we were absolutely exploring that power. It was fun. I was dressed in tight Gloria Vanderbilt jeans, an even tighter ribbed fuchsia turtleneck, and black lizard cowboy boots. I don't remember what Dots was wearing, but I'm pretty sure it was preppier. I mean, I don't know what Dots is wearing right now either, but I'm pretty sure it's preppier.

Dots and I could tell by the way the band played right to us that they were having a great time being onstage and watching us dance. We made them feel like rock stars. They made us feel like groupies. Everyone was happy in their own little fantasy worlds, but never was that twain going to cross. At the end of the second set, the band invited us to go back to their bus and get high. We saw this as a total validation of our hotness and were totally psyched to be asked. But of course, we didn't go with them. Being invited was what we were after, not actually making out with third-rate musicians in a smelly VW Vanagon. They were essentially townies.

Still, Derek saw just the invitation as proof that I was essentially cheating on him. He stood over me, both hands leaning against the wall, at about my shoulder height. Trapping me in. He leaned forward in a perverse sort of wall push-up, "I can't believe I actually fell for someone who pretends to be so virginal but then is such a fucking slut. Do you really need to do the whole band, Kat?"

I was totally confused. I had been expecting him to lean over to ask if I wanted to sneak out behind the building and make out before the band came back for the last set. It took me a second to register the words. I just stood there trapped between his arms. I tried to come up with a smart-ass retort, but he continued, "I think you should take them up on their offer because we're done. There's no way I'd touch you now. You are damaged goods."

I looked up and hoped my face was showing anger instead of sadness. I was not going to cry in front of him no matter what kind of mean things he said. "What the fuck are you on about, Derek? I was just having a good time dancing. I didn't do anything! You wanna be done? Fine. We are done! You are a no-fun crazy person and I say we're done."

"No. We're done when I say we're done." And he took one of his hands down to let me out. "Go ahead, whore. The band's waiting for you."

I flipped him the bird and walked away.

I had no idea why he got so mad all of a sudden. I was just enjoying all the attention I was getting from the band. And from the other kids watching the band watch me. It wasn't like I would really go off in a van with a bunch of guys I didn't even know. *Who would do that?* I spent the rest of the dance hiding in the girls' locker room downstairs, alternating between crying and cursing. Mostly I was just hoping no one would come down and find me.

The Winter Social breakup set our pattern. He'd get mad about something, real or imagined, curse at me, and say horrible things. I'd get mad at him for being ridiculous, curse back at him, then hide and cry where no one could see me. We'd briefly date other people. Days, weeks, whatever, would go by and then we'd get back together, unable to move on from each other. Lather, rinse, repeat, ad nauseam. The particulars of each breakup were different but the results the same. After a while it was what passed for normal. It was what we did. It was who we were. We were one of those volatile, passionate couples. Like Brian and Anita. It meant we cared.

Battle Plan

The Winter Social breakup was our first big breakup, so I didn't know yet that breaking up and making up was our pattern. I was truly heartbroken. I cried for the whole rest of the weekend. I was so sad, my mom tried to cheer me up with shopping, but even a trip to the mall didn't lift my spirits. It wasn't like I was going to talk to her about what was really going on. It was nice that she wanted to make me feel better, but not much was going to do that, I just needed to cry myself out. By Monday morning, I had done just that. I wasn't still just sad, I was also angry at being treated that way. *How dare he treat me like that?* Angry and ready to find a new boyfriend, I'd show Derek who the loser was.

As much as I loved Derek and all, school was still about my reputation and standing more than anything else. Besides, it just wasn't like me to let anyone appear to have the upper hand. I wasn't about to show up Monday morning all mopey and disheveled. If I was anything, I was a girl determined to always look like I was the victor in any contest.

Most of the time, I didn't really care enough about things to have an opinion, so why wouldn't I just let my friends' opinions decide? Fashion, music, drugs, I would just do what all the cool kids did. The thing that really mattered to me was being cool. And since that was set by how other people saw me, I did what I had to for them to recognize my coolness. Before Derek, it was never really the boy I wanted to have as a boyfriend. What I craved was the standing of being the type of girl who always had a boyfriend.

Showing weakness in a pool of teenage girls is pretty much exactly the same as showing weakness in a pool of sharks. Sharks are probably less dangerous, since you can always just punch them in the nose and get away. I know Bree will soon find that out if she hasn't already. Girl-world hasn't changed that much. I don't know how I could possibly find the words to warn her, but she's lived through middle school, so she must know. She seems like she's getting through it OK. She's never mentioned anything about mean girls or about other stuff happening. Of course, I never said anything about it to my mother either.

Monday morning, I got the word out quickly that I was the one who dumped Derek because he was an unreasonable jerk. No matter what people had heard from Rob and Robbie on Sunday. Everyone knew Rob and Robbie's opinion of me, so my side of the story was completely believable. And since I had a network of girls to back me up, I won the PR war almost immediately. We only made up one-quarter of the student body, but we were far more efficient at passing along information than the boys were and, as an oppressed minority, tended to stick together on things like this. At the very least, I could count on most girls, even the ones lining up to be my successor, to repeat that I was the dumper and not the dumpee. This was almost as important as choosing the right boy to be my next beau, so I concentrated all my efforts Monday morning on shaping the story.

By the time classes ended at two forty-five, I was the clear victor. After that it was time to move to Phase II: determining the new boyfriend. Winning Phase I would only hold for a short while; if I let it go too long, I could still come out looking bad. Especially if Derek already had a new girlfriend. I don't believe there are any military strategists in the world that have anything on teenage girls.

One of the luxuries of being so outnumbered at Mansfield was that boyfriends were easily replaced. The old standby—boys are like buses, if you miss one, there's another one coming along in a few minutes— was pretty accurate. Dots was by my side to help me vet candidates, as always. Ellbee had long since drifted away. She made it clear she thought Derek was a bad guy, so she wasn't going to come around to make me feel better. And I didn't want her fake sympathy making me feel worse. But Dots was right there with me, helping me choose my rebound guy. She is my forever bestie. If I needed someone right this minute to help me figure out my life, Dots would be my first call. I haven't had the time to tell her everything that's going on right now, but I will. She's just been so busy at work, and I haven't sorted things out enough in my own head to talk to anyone else about it anyway.

That December day, Dots and I reviewed possibilities for the open boyfriend position, starting with the boys we already knew liked me. It would be quicker than starting from scratch with someone. We held our strategy session in the TV lounge next to the girls' locker room. *General Hospital* blared in the background. Luke and Laura shared a tearful scene as a few freshman girls huddled by the screen. Their little mouths hung open in anticipation of what would happen next. They looked like the Pond peepers. I wanted to scream at them—OK, I wanted to scream, and they were there—"You morons, Luke and Laura will break up, get back together, and repeat until February sweeps, then they will go on the lam. How do you not know how this works?" Stupid freshmen. Dots and I spoke softly but were secure in the knowledge that no boys would violate the soap opera sanctuary, even if the TV room was supposed to be for everyone.

Dots pushed her thick, dark-brown hair behind her ears with a madras-plaid plastic headband. Bree has the same one in her luggage. I just hope it's not literally the exact same one. Preppy high style also includes never throwing anything away. And Dots would absolutely give Bree the headband off her head if Bree admired it. At least Bree doesn't have the matching plaid-print cover for her Bermuda bag. Although she does have the dark-blue corduroy one with her initials embroidered in light blue that was one of Dots's faves. I think Dots sent her that and the corresponding headband as a birthday present last year. Along with a very nice check in the bag and an invite to go shopping to spend it together. She sent Bree one exactly like hers but with Bree's initials. Without any kids of her own, Dots tends to treat Bree as her protégé in all things preppy. Bree loves it, especially as I've long since shed whatever preppy veneer stuck to me at Mansfield.

Jack Sinclair was the name Dots opened with.

"Jack? Come on. Seriously, Dots? He's literally my height. He comes up to Derek's solar plexus."

"OK, but he is really good-looking and a complete one-eighty. Dark-haired, dark-eyed … clearly a very different type."

"Yeah—munchkin," I mumbled unkindly.

"What about Willie?"

"Hooks, Williams, or Zeets?"

"Hooks. He's always had a thing for you. Even when you were a tiny little frosh munchkin yourself." Dots hadn't missed my snark and wasn't going to let it go without comment. She had recently been convinced by a paperback that the secret to life was being kind and positive, and she was determined to show the rest of us that it would work and drag us along with her. It was completely annoying, and everyone hoped she'd be back to normal bitchery soon. We sabotaged her positivity whenever possible.

"He's cute, but I heard he left the dance with Jennifer on Saturday. I think they were sucking face until curfew."

"Stupid Jennifer?" she asked then clamped her hand over her mouth after realizing Jennifer's common modifier wasn't positive or kind.

"Yep. Um-I-dunno, Stupid Jennifer." I was in the mood to be mean to everyone, but Dots did call her Stupid Jennifer first. Also, that was what everyone called her. She might even have answered to it. She really was that stupid. In a world history class, her first week, she was asked to name one world-shaping event from the 1930s. Her several-second pause, gum-chewing, staring at the ceiling, twirling her braid end before finally answering "Um, I dunno?" in a questioning little-girl squeak was a school legend, and the one that forever earned her the moniker Stupid Jennifer.

It was nearly impossible to be one of the cool kids at Mansfield and be dumb. The cool kids got mostly As, but we weren't geeks about it. The geeks were different; they weren't as good-looking or socially adept as we were, so it didn't matter that they were smart. Cool was a tough standard. You had to look good and maintain a high average while usually high and while not doing any work that anyone could see, except in the couple of weeks before exams. Then it was perfectly acceptable to geek out and spend hours in the library cramming. That was the easiest part for me in becoming one of the cool kids. I always did well in school without having to do any work.

"You wanna really get to Derek?" Dots asked, tapping the front of her teeth with a pencil end and raising one eyebrow—badly in need of plucking, I noticed. I was going to have to attack her with tweezers after this.

"You know it. I want to make his head spin. How dare he treat me like that? I never cheated on him, I never kissed anyone else. I was the perfect girlfriend."

"You should go out with Rob or Robbie."

"Ew! No way. Ick! Gross. No. No. No. Gross. I'm sorry, but I only date within my species. That is gross. Ugh. No, I don't care how much it would bug him. The idea of cuddling up with either of those two makes me want to retch. Seriously, ew! You are a sick woman, Dots. Sick!"

"Yeah, I didn't think you'd go for it. But it would drive him mental, though. The whole Brian/Keith/Anita thing." She paused her pencil-tapping. "You know what, never mind. I'm wrong. I'm totally wrong. I bet that's exactly what he expects you to do. Don't do it. Don't let him think he's right. Confuse him. Pick someone completely out of left field. Kit-Kat, I'm really sorry but I've got to motor. I've got a guitar lesson in like three, and I told Trip I'd meet him after practice. Are you still going down to Gus's?"

"Hell yeah. It was my place before it was his. I'm going to mellow out a bit first.," I mimed toking on a joint. "But I'll be there by four."

"K, see you later, loser."

"Not if I see you first, loser."

We hugged goodbye and went our separate ways. Bree and her friends still do the same dramatic girl-hug, as if they've suddenly encountered long-lost friends, every time they see each other outside of school. Sure, it's a little silly at Starbucks a half hour after classes get out, but we certainly had weirder tics. To the best of my knowledge, Bree doesn't even have a dead-rock-star/guardian-angel, much less long, heartfelt conversations with him every night before bed. As far as I can tell, her overly effusive hugging habit doesn't involve any communion at all with the Great Beyond.

Gazebo

By the time I walked from the TV lounge over to the Gazebo, I wasn't sure I was going to be able to keep up the "I don't give a shit" act. I was glad at least the Gazebo was momentarily empty in the winter's chill. My lower lip was trembling as I lit the cigarette that I'd earlier emptied the front bit out of and filled back up with pot. We called these "halfsies." I inhaled deeply and held the smoke in as long as I could. I hadn't made eye contact with Derek since we broke up. What was I going to say if he spoke to me at Gus's? What if I cried? I couldn't cry at Gus's. That would be humiliating.

I loved him. I really did. I ached for him. I loved him as much as I loved Brian. My stomach lurched when I thought of him with someone else. I thought I might actually barf. I wasn't sure going to Gus's was a good idea at all. What if I made a fool out of myself in front of everyone? What if I did barf? Or worse, what if I burst into tears at the sight of him? I knew I had to go today. If I didn't go today, I'd cede Gus's over to Derek forever. Derek would definitely be there today; he didn't have practice. And I wasn't going to let him think he'd gotten to me. I couldn't let him or anyone else think I was hiding from him. It was my damn place first anyway. Not his.

I quickly sucked down the entire halfsie. I exhaled hard through my lips, pulled my Mason Pearson out of my book bag, brushed my hair, then pulled out my little mirror and put on some Bonnie Bell Dr-Pepper-flavored lip gloss. Just the smell alone was soothing—some weird chemical concoction that somehow smelled exactly like a freshly opened soda, even if it tasted totally gross. Whatever. I wasn't kissing anyone anyway. I tucked all my stuff back in my bag and headed on down the hill. I'd figure it out later. Everything will be fine. *I'll just keep moving forward.*

I'd gotten about halfway to town when I was met up with by David Fischer. David was a nice enough guy. Not quite one of our regular crowd but a frequent enough visitor and obviously eager to join. I'm sure he saw my newly single status as an opportunity. Just like I saw him as a way not to have to walk into Gus's alone. I was his entrée into the cool kids' inner circle. Social-climbing strategizing was something I could relate to. We didn't know each other very well, but I knew why he happened to run into me. We could help each other out. And he was definitely a left-field choice.

He fell into step with me. His wavy brown hair just grazed his shoulders. *He really isn't horrible-looking,* I thought. *Maybe with some cooler clothes and— Oh god, who was I kidding?* Anyway, he'd do for the moment. David was literally moving forward.

David was number one in the series of Nice Jewish Boys I would go out with for very short periods of time whenever Derek and I broke up. He was harmless, not bad-looking. Not tall or short. Nondescript would be the best description for most of them, and David certainly fit that bill. They were all nice enough guys, but not really all that interesting. If I had to say why I bothered dating them at all, I guess it was my way of checking in to see if maybe my mother had it right. Maybe she did know better than I did about the kind of guys that I should be dating. But nope.

David's family owned the largest flooring distributor on the East Coast. He was what my mother deemed "a catch." As it turns out, my mother was wrong. She never did know who was better for me than I did. I once heard someone say that you become a grown-up when you can admit your mother was right about some things growing up. Fine, so I guess I'm not there yet.

"Hey, Kat. Wait up. Are you headed down to Gus's?" David asked. His voice cracked, belying his attempt to sound nonchalant. His flushed-red face, the sweat beading up on his broken-out forehead, also seemed a dead giveaway. *Seriously,* I thought, *it's after classes and I'm walking in that direction. Where else would I be going?*

"Yeah, you?" I asked, truly casually. He'd really have to step it up a little if he wanted to step up to going out with me and hanging out with our crowd. I knew I was cute and all, but my being popular counted at least as much to him as my looks did. He'd never shown any interest in me before. I wasn't going to waste this opportunity by choosing poorly. Demonstrating that I could bring someone worthy into our group would be a coup. But bringing in a loser would make me look bad.

"Yeah. I'm ready for some 'za. Got a butt? I'm all out."

"Sure," I said and dug my Marlboro Lights out of my bag. "Here." I flicked the pack so one popped up. I looked at him and ticked off his attributes in my head. At least he was a good bit taller than I was, even in my boots. David had wavy brown hair, nice green eyes, so-so skin, and more metal in his mouth than I had ever seen before. Who knows what they were doing in there, but it sure required a lot of wires. He was on the varsity hockey team, although not on the first line. Still, respectable enough, for a sophomore.

His hand shook as he tried to light the cigarette. No lighting-a-match-off-his-fingernail bad boy, this one. He inhaled too deeply, and then coughed the cough of a novice smoker. I almost felt sorry for him. He was trying so hard.

"So, um … youwannagowithme?" It all came out in one very fast word.

"Um, OK," I answered and took off my glove to snuggle my small hand into his sweaty palm. Hell, it was better than walking in alone.

Gus's

Walking into Gus's with my hand firmly stuck into David's was a lot more fun than I thought it would be. I got a charge out of watching all the heads swivel and the chatter begin to reverberate around the room. I scanned the place quickly; there was no sign of Derek. "OK then." My booth was empty. I slid into the booth, pushing my book bag in ahead of me. I took the side with my back to the door so I would have time to compose myself when Derek showed up. I knew the sudden hush of the crowd would be my cue.

"Do you want a slice?" David asked.

"No thanks. Just a small Dr Pepper for me if you're buying." I smiled up at him through my bangs and wondered how you could kiss someone with that kind of major braces on their teeth. It had to hurt. How had I managed to get this far in my life and not kissed someone with braces? Just lucky, I guess.

David ordered his slice then came back to the table with my Dr Pepper. We held hands across the table, like all new couples do, while we waited for them to call his slice up. No way Chris was bringing his slice to the table. It didn't look like David knew the tip jar existed.

The door chimes rang out and just as I expected, I knew it was Derek by the way the noise level dropped in the room. All movement stopped. It seemed like even the jukebox stopped playing. I willed myself not to move my head a centimeter. I was holding my breath and biting the insides of my cheeks, unwilling to even flick a stray strand of hair out of my eyes. I did pull my hand away from David's to grab my soda, though.

I knew Derek was looking our way. I could feel his eyes on the back of my neck. I could feel the little hairs standing up like little antennae. *I was not going to look. I was not going to look. I was not going to turn around and look.* That resolve lasted about as long as the words did in my head. Of course I looked. And of course, he was looking right at me when I turned. He cocked his head to the side, threw me that grin, gave a short back-and-forth wave, and winked. *Freak! He winked! God, he was infuriating. I hate that wink*!

I felt my knees go to Jell-O even though I was sitting down. My stomach was continuing to do flip-flops. I yearned for him. My body craved him, like nicotine. I felt just like I did on the weekends when my mom wouldn't leave and I couldn't go anywhere to sneak a butt. I remember thinking, *I could get him to take me back. I could just curl up into him and whisper a "sorry, baby" and he'd be mine again. No! No way. No fucking way. He's the one who has to apologize to me. He has to try and get me to take him back. There is no way that I'm crawling back to him like I did something wrong. He's the one who is wrong.*

Rob and Robbie stood menacingly behind him. They looked at us like they'd like to physically remove us from "their" booth. I saw them, laughed, and waved back. There was no way I was going to fold. He could fucking fold first.

They sat elsewhere.

"Pepperoni slice up!" came the call from the front counter. As soon as David got up to get it, Derek came over to talk to me.

He put both hands on the table and leaned over me. "David Fischer? You can't be serious. He's not exactly what I think of as your type, Kat.

He's not one of us. You're making me look bad here. Seriously." He spoke in his usual low, quiet voice, sounding somewhere between comatose and amused. His pupils were so dilated they almost swallowed up the dark blue of his eyes. It was hard to imagine how he managed to walk around without his sunglasses on, even indoors.

At least he is here with the guys instead of coming in with another girl. Maybe he really did want me back. He was so close I could almost just lean up and kiss him. I wouldn't of course, but I wanted to. I tilted my head up so that my lips faced his—just inches away. He had to give in first. There was no way I was about to hand him the upper hand. In my head, I was Pat Benatar singing "Hit Me With Your Best Shot." I was Chrissie Hynde, just being Chrissie Hynde. I was a cool girl standing my ground. Rob and Robbie looked on from their lesser table in the center of the room. This booth was mine before Derek even got to Mansfield. They only got to sit here because of me. I wasn't backing down one inch.

"Hope you guys enjoy your 'za" was my response, and with a wave of my hand, I casually turned my lips back to my Dr Pepper. I was determined to show him I wasn't at all thrown off by his presence. I put my hand around the cool plastic cup so I had something to hold on to. Derek pushed off the table like he was doing one of his three-fingered push-ups and left to go sit with Rob and Robbie.

I knew he was right about David, but I wasn't about to show it. David was an OK enough human. But he really wasn't my type. He was nice and all, but there was no spark there. Did Derek think I was an idiot? This was timing, not true love. But "The Greeks Don't Want No Freaks" by the Eagles floated through my head every time I looked at David. Derek called it, he wasn't worthy. He'd definitely be the guy barfing on his girlfriend's shoes.

I guess David and I had an OK enough time sitting in Gus's and talking, but by the time Dots got there at 4:45, it was clearly over. We were toast. I think we may hold the record for the shortest relationship in Mansfield history. Under an hour. We never even kissed. Honestly, we were over the minute David left the table and let Derek talk to me. We could never safely be left alone, Derek and I, not even in a crowded room.

I let David walk me back up to campus but gave him my cheek when he tried to kiss me goodbye. I really didn't feel like investigating what it would be like to kiss someone with that much metal in his mouth. I got the same feeling as when you accidentally touch the metal rim of a pencil to one of your metal fillings. The shiver that went up the back of my spine was not of pleasure.

My mom came to pick me up right on time that night in her giant land yacht; I wished I could be swallowed up whole by the cushy red velour interior. I asked her to crank up the tuneage on BCN and leave me alone. I told her I needed the music to help me to study for a French test so she wouldn't ask me about my day. French was always one of the toughest subjects for me, so she left me alone with my nose in my notes. French and math were the two subjects I had to work on to keep up decent grades.

Some days when we were in the car together, she looked like she had something she wanted to tell me, some words of wisdom to impart. This wasn't one of those days. And I wouldn't have listened if it was.

Too bad my brain was on Derek, because I really did need to study for that test. I'd gotten a seventy-five on the practice that morning. It was so completely ungood to be me today. She would never let me out of the house if I didn't pull off at least a B in French II. None of my grades had ever been under that threshold. Not even math. My social life would be seriously compromised if I got grounded.

Tuesday Morning

December 9, 1980

I'm not exaggerating at all when I say I returned to a completely different campus the next day. People were wandering about in a daze. Teachers were openly crying. Classes were canceled, and services were to be held in the Mansfield Chapel for the first time I'd ever seen. The white-steepled classic New England church building had always been there, but no one ever went in it. It was part of the look of the campus but up till now had always been empty. Not on this day though. At 11 p.m. last night John Lennon had been shot in front of the Dakota apartment building in New York City.

Derek came up to me as soon as I got out of the car. He grabbed me by the hands, not even waiting for my mom to pull away to pull me close. My mom gave him the evil eye but had to get to her Jazzercise class, so she didn't have time to stop the car to yell at me about my taste in boys and my reputation.

I could tell Derek had been waiting at the day-student drop-off spot for me to show up. He looked like he'd been out in the cold for a while. He always got red patches on his cheeks when it was cold. His eyes were red. He had obviously been crying. He was also obviously massively wasted. I wasn't sure on what, but he was totaled. He wasn't drunk. He wasn't at all agitated or mad. I guessed maybe he'd taken some downers—we called them Roscoe's Happy Pills because most of the supply came from Willie Roscoe stealing them from his mom and selling them on campus—because Derek was super calm and slow.

"Oh my god, Kat-Kat. I'm so glad you're finally here. I need you. We can't fight. We can't be broken up. I love you. I need you to be with me, not that idiot David Fischer. I can't live with the idea of you with someone else. If I die, I want you by my side." He held me tight and spoke into my hair.

Yes, my druggie boyfriend was melodramatically comparing himself to the latest musician to join the Dead Rock Star Hall of Fame. And OK, technically that was slightly crazy, but I didn't care. He wanted me back. He said it first. Life was good again. I mean, I was horribly saddened by the senseless death of John Lennon and all, but it was still a much better day for me than the day before had been. I would go on to spend the whole day looking sad and sitting in groups of students and teachers singing "Imagine" and "Strawberry Fields Forever," but inside I was on cloud nine.

Derek stepped back, put both of his hands behind my head, and stared directly into my eyes. "I was an idiot, baby. Please take me back. Please go out with me again. I know you wouldn't cheat on me. I was stupid to be jealous of those guys looking at you. You're so pretty. You can't help it if guys stare at you. I know you're not like her. Please give me another chance." And we were back together. Nearly three days of abject pain, and I was thrilled to fall back into our adolescent madness again.

I wasn't sure if by "her" he meant Anita Pallenberg, whose cheating led to Brian's death, or his mother. Derek would rarely talk about his mother, but when he did, he'd hint that his parents had been arguing the day of her death, intimate that it was probably about her infidelity, and suggest that maybe her car accident wasn't an accident. Maybe it was a suicide, or maybe it was something worse. He definitely blamed his father for his mother's death, but he'd never come right out and say he thought his father had a hand in it. Instead, he'd talk darkly about how enough money and power made it possible to take care of any problem.

I suppose I should have worried about how much Derek compared himself to Brian. It's not like he was truly delusional, he didn't actually believe he was a long-dead British rock star. But it was almost as if he felt he was Brian's reincarnation. Even though Derek had already been born when Brian died. Honestly, even if you accepted the idea of dead-rock-star reincarnation, pre-death reincarnation was a bit of a stretch. That's part of why the idea that Derek could have been one of the kids, one of Brian's by-blows shipped off for adoption in America, made so much sense to us. It was possible he was adopted and his parents just kept it secret. Logical even, especially when compared to him being a pre-death-reincarnation incarnation. It's a wonder we weren't all locked away in the loony bin.

* * *

I think the teachers had a worse time of it that day than we did. While we loved to think of ourselves as baby hippies, none of us actually remembered the sixties. We were too young. But many of our teachers had been part of it. Albeit most of them from a safe trust-fund-baby prep school vantage point. Our teachers almost all grew up in our world, left for part of the sixties and seventies, and came right back to its comfort and safety in the eighties. John Lennon was one of their great heroes, and they couldn't believe that such a great talent and a great force for peace could be snuffed out so violently. They were truly shaken. It took until we came back from Christmas break for the school to run normally again.

Derek and I must have broken up twenty-five times during sophomore year alone. As did lots of our friends in relationships. It was part of the drama of dating. Drama was what relationships were all about. How else could you tell how someone felt?

We were rarely broken up for more than a day or two. Derek acted stupidly sometimes, but he never crossed the line with me. He never hit me. He never threatened me. He rarely drank at all in front of me. He'd wait for me to go home before he started drinking. He never hurt me, but we knew he could, and that scared me. I think it scared him too.

Whatever he was up to over the weekends when I couldn't be there, most of the time I could just ignore. I didn't see any of it happen, so it didn't exist. Often, he'd break up with me because I wouldn't have sex with him. He'd get angry and put it off as being a show of my lack of commitment to him. I'd counter that if he really loved me, he would wait until I was ready.

It wasn't like we weren't doing a lot of fooling around, but it was all fully clothed. Feeling the way his body responded when I brushed up against it through layers of clothing was as far as I was willing to go. The Monica Lewinsky era was not even close. So Derek would cause a dramatic breakup fight with me and go have sex with someone else. That way he wasn't cheating on me, since it happened while we were broken up. Then he'd come crawling back to me professing his undying love.

I'm sure there were at least a couple of times when he went off and found some stupid girl without even bothering to break up with me. If they weren't smart enough to demand he not have a girlfriend to do it, he didn't always see the need to go through all the bother. In those cases, it wasn't cheating on me if he was too drunk to remember it. It was always some clueless freshman. Those girls were easy. Some dumb frosh would come running up to me and brag about being Derek's new girlfriend. I'd just laugh and tell her I didn't believe her, and Derek would deny it ever happened. Even though I knew, somewhere in my head, that she was probably telling the truth. I could bury that knowledge. Because I also knew, no matter what she did with him, the truth was, she wasn't taking Derek away from me. I was his girlfriend.

And plenty of times, he'd be right there. He'd walk up to us talking in the halls, nod hello to the girl as if he knew her from somewhere, and walk away with me, hand in my back pocket, like everything was just the same as always. I knew it was wrong. And I knew that it was wrong that I was gloating a little bit that he wanted to be with me anyway, even if he had to go elsewhere for sex. It wasn't his fault the idiot freshman girls kept throwing themselves at him and insisted upon believing that fucking someone meant you were a couple.

It never changed. Freshman girls would always assume that if they slept with someone, they were automatically boyfriend and girlfriend. Silly rabbits. Maybe that's a thing I should mention to Bree, but exactly how do I start that conversation?

"By the way, darling, don't have sex with boys because you think that will automatically make you their girlfriend." Then what? Would she ask me then why she *should* have sex with boys? Or when? Then what could I say? "Never"? That's not right. "Not yet"? This is all just too much for me. It's better not to bring the subject up at all. She knows all the basics. She doesn't want to hear this from me anyway. I left a box of condoms in her bathroom once and said, "I want you to make sure you are safe, okay?" That's about all I've ever said to her about sex. I don't think her fingerprints are even on the box. I think she put it in the dresser drawer using tongs.

I would gladly have disintegrated into the seats of the car if my mother had started talking to me about sex. I am ever so grateful she never said a word. I'm pretty confident that Bree feels the same way. After all, she didn't want to continue our sex conversation past "OK, Mom," either.

Summer Follows Spring

Winter and spring went on. Breakups, makeups. The usual assortment of classes, games, and homework designed to keep us from spending too much time sucking face and smoking dope. At the end of sophomore year, Derek and I broke up for the summer because it was stupid to pretend we weren't going to go out with other people for three whole months. And I wouldn't feel comfortable dating someone else if I had a boyfriend back home. My guess is it probably wouldn't have bothered Derek quite as much, but he agreed.

He was going off on an Outward Bound program in Montana for the whole summer — Outward Bound being the early-eighties code word for rehab. He said his dad didn't want him home and getting into trouble. I was being sent, against my will, to a Jewish girls' camp in Upstate New York for eight weeks. It was conveniently located right near a Jewish boys' camp, so we could make new Jewish opposite-sex friends all summer long. Every weekend's Friday night Shabbat dinner and Saturday night dance was coed and held at alternating camps. We also had special sports and theater events together in case we missed an opportunity to mingle. I dated the only non-Jewish counselor at the boys' camp that summer. Just let them try and make me do something. I'd find a way around.

Mostly, I missed Derek. I wrote long, longing letters from my bunk. I never sent them. Letters were stupid, and Derek told me he didn't have any privacy at home, that his dad read all his mail. I called a couple of times near the end of August, hoping he was back and would pick up, but I hung up every time an unfamiliar voice answered. The days before email, cell phones, and caller ID were a mixed blessing. I was terrified of having to speak to his dad, even to say hello politely and ask if I could speak to Derek. I was so panicked I might have even hung up on Derek, thinking he was Jack. Long-distance calls sounded so tinny, it was hard to recognize even voices you knew well.

I've spent probably hundreds of hours on shrink couches trying to figure out why I kept getting back together with Derek. I still don't have any answers. I was young and in love. There was such an intense physical connection between us. No one else ever made me feel that way. My body felt the way being "in love" is described in books—heart palpitations, weak knees, sweaty palms, dampened underpants. And even besides the physical sensations, when I was with Derek, I was part of an epic romance—something bigger than our little lives. We were like Romeo and Juliet, like Brian and Anita. When I was with Derek, I was my fantasy self. And sure, even at that tender age, his family's wealth was part of it. It's really fun to be able to have anything you want just by making a call. And Derek could.

One Friday night junior year, Derek told me to meet him in front of the main school building at noon on Saturday. He wouldn't tell me why. I told my mom I was meeting Dots in the library and told Dots I was using her as an excuse and not to call my house. I had my mom drop me off at eleven thirty in front of the library so there was no chance of overlap. I wore jeans, a white alligator shirt, my denim jacket, and of course my high-heeled clogs. I looked cute, but not cute enough for my mom to get suspicious. I spent twenty minutes putting on makeup in the library's girls' bathroom then headed across the quad to wait. Derek pulled up five minutes later in his red Alpha and leaned over to push the passenger door open for me. I threw my book bag and my Coach purse onto the floor of the passenger side. It wasn't exactly warm out, but it was warm enough to have the top down.

"Hop in. I've got a surprise for you. You'll like it. I promise."

No matter how much I wheedled, he wouldn't tell me what the surprise was. A few minutes of cow path roads and we were on the highway and headed into Cambridge. He parked in the wicked expensive Harvard Square garage. My friends and I usually parked out at Alewife and took the Red Line in. He grabbed my hand as we left the garage and came out into the cool sunshine and said, "Come on! Let's motor. You really don't want to miss this." He was so happy he was almost bouncing on his feet.

I was dying to know. As an exciting mystery trip, driving into Cambridge on a Saturday afternoon alone was already pretty good. I didn't have a clue what could possibly come next. Derek led me right out of the garage past the Coop and to the door of an old office building on Mass Ave. This was my surprise? An office building? He held the door open with a flourish and bowed deeply. "My darling Kat-Kat, your wish is my command. I live to please you."

I had no idea what the heck was going on, until we walked into a room that was set up for a movie screening.

"No way!" I think I might have screamed a little, afraid I was wrong.

"Way," he answered with the most smug, self-satisfied look on his face, and folded his arms across his chest.

"Shut up!"

"You are not gonna want me to shut up, lover girl. Because I am presenting you, Miss Kat, the opportunity to watch the one and only bootlegged copy of *Rock and Roll Circus* that currently exists on the Eastern Seaboard of the entirety of the USA. Pick a seat, young lady. Your movie will start in three minutes. I'm getting you a Dr Pepper and some super-buttered popcorn. Just the way you like it. Because I am the best boyfriend ever."

"Oh my god! I can't believe this is real! How did you get this? Thank you, thank you, thank you! You are the best boyfriend ever!" I covered his face with kisses.

"My dad knows a movie guy. George Harrison is his kid's godfather. My dad said something to him about his kid wanting to see it. So he sent a copy here for me. I think the office building is one of my dad's or someone's. I dunno. His secretary, Fran, set it all up. Fran takes care of all our details."

We watched the film curled up together in a ratty old armchair with me on his lap the whole time. No one came in. No one bothered us at all. It was as if invisible elves took care of everything. There was popcorn and soda, but I didn't know from where. It wasn't really a movie theater, just a room. I was so enthralled by being one of the very few allowed to see *Rock and Roll Circus* that I barely noticed how terrible the movie was. And how wasted they all looked. I didn't even pretend to object when Derek moved his hands from on top of to under my clothes as we cuddled. We were moving ever closer to being an "everything but" couple in our sex life anyway, and it made him so happy.

I'm not sure I can think of another day that was so full of pure teen joy. I actually got to watch the most coveted bootleg in the entire Stones canon. Because Derek could even make *Rock and Roll Circus* appear.

Just because it was something I wanted. Dots was going to explode when I told her! He really was the best boyfriend ever.

In my fantasy future life, I could totally see myself growing up and marrying Derek. We'd live that kind of California existence that is so enticing to Massachusetts girls, hot tubs, hiking, going to Colorado for some winter weather. It was my teenage girl's idea of what grown-up life would be like. All pleasure and no responsibility. Setting it in the exotic land of California made it even more so. The idea of being married, of being allowed into the adult world, was so fascinating. It's the Beach Boys tune "Wouldn't It Be Nice."

And I thought Kat Wilkeson looked awesome as a signature. Sophisticated as we were at Mansfield, we were not immune to the time-honored practice of girls practicing signing their names combined with the last names of their beaus, just to see the flow, to play with the sound of it. It has probably been happening since last names were invented. College, and for some of us even grad school, came first, but marriage was our ultimate destination. How else was the next generation of preppies going to get there? It was an unwritten part of our responsibility.

Even in those name-doodling days, I knew that Derek and I didn't really have a future. But to be honest, neither did any of the other couples we knew. We were teenagers. And really, in the early eighties, who did have a future? We were probably all going to die soon in some US/USSR final showdown. The world's economy was in the toilet. This was the time of punk nihilism. How realistic my idea of fantasy grown-up life was didn't matter much under those conditions.

I did recognize that Derek was different though. He was following Brian down too dangerous a path. I hung on for as long as I could. Probably for longer than I should have, but I always had my snap. I could pop out of the drug culture at any time. And I did love him. I had no doubts about that. He had my heart. And I had his.

Being in love with Derek was part of who I was. And I know Derek loved me, in his own damaged way. He was just a broken boy. He tried to prove his love for me so many times, with stuff, with words, with grand romantic gestures, but the one thing he wasn't ever able to do for me was the thing I needed from him most. I needed him to not throw away his whole life on drugs.

For all the time I spent trying to figure out what kept me with him, I was equally confused about what kept him with me. Roof rule be damned, we were so different. I tried on different personas, but I was a good girl who would eventually move on in life to be a productive adult. He was a lost boy with no thoughts of what would come next, because he didn't think he had a next. His mother was dead. He had no other family. No close friends left behind in California. And his father had essentially abandoned him to a string of well-paid caregivers.

I think part of why he kept coming back to me was that I was the only one around who cared enough about him to say no to him. In our last little bit of time together, I thought that maybe I could save him just by telling him no. And I think maybe, maybe that's what he thought too. Because he did treat me differently than he treated everyone else. I was special. I was on a pedestal, all by myself. And that pedestal was so high that I was allowed to tell him no. I could get him to stop and to be in control of himself. He'd go away furious sometimes, but he'd never physically hurt me.

No one else ever said no to him. Not Rob and Robbie. Not the other girls. Certainly not the school, which was making a bundle in fines for every infraction he got caught at, major and minor. To give Mansfield the benefit of the doubt, I don't think the administration knew how bad it was. He never got caught at anything they would have had to throw him out for. And there was certainly no shortage of examples for them to look to; tons of kids got into youthful trouble at school, but they pulled it together once they got out into the real world. Derek got into plenty of trouble; it was the pulling it together that he never figured out.

The absolute worst of all for Derek though was that his dad never said no to him. Saying no would have required paying attention to him. His dad obviously found it easier to say yes, throw some more money at him, and think he was done with parenting. Derek responded by caring even less about his own well-being than his dad did. In 1981, Derek was getting five hundred dollars a week for spending money in a town with four stores. Honestly! Where did his dad think all that money was going? Would it even be possible to legally spend that much? How much pizza did he think a kid could eat?

Watching the way his dad dealt with Derek was when I figured out that all the money in the world can't fix the problems caused by having all the money in the world.

That was when I decided what my life was going to be like when I was a grown-up. My family would have enough money to not have to worry about it but not so much that I had to worry about other stuff. First-class plane tickets are truly awesome. Having a private plane brings a whole other level of complication into child-rearing. I know it isn't entirely fair, because I knew plenty of kids at Mansfield whose families had lots of money and they were just normal, upstanding citizens. And I know that poor kids can also be a mess. But it did seem to me that the richer the family, the more screwed up the kids.

So what does it say about my best-laid plans for my life that I married into one of the richest Mansfield families anyway? I don't know. Maybe that I'm really not so great at laying plans? I didn't marry him because of his money. I know that. I married him in part probably because he never gave up asking me. He never gave up on me. He always loved me, no matter what persona I was trying on. He loved the real me, even when the rest of the world didn't. He was my rock, my champion, on my side no matter what. I was everything he ever wanted. We'll have to see what it's like now that it's going to be just the two of us for the first time in, really, almost ever.

Together we have consciously strived to make sure Bree avoided most of the pitfalls of a wealthy childhood. We both saw some of the same things at school. We don't lead an extravagant life. We have a nice house and cars and a club membership, and we take some very nice vacations, just like everyone else in town, but nothing extraordinary. We don't stand out. We live just like all our neighbors live. We don't overextend. We don't live like we already have his parents' money.

Bree isn't completely clueless though; she is old enough to know that the Grammy and Grampy money is there, and it is considerable. We are all very careful, very committed to wanting to keep her grounded, but she is one of only five grandchildren who will inherit quite a pile when the day comes. I have always tried to make sure Bree could experience the world as a regular person first. A rich regular person, but still, a regular person.

Junior Year

September

The Outward Bound summer did change Derek, but not for the better. Maybe it just accelerated things for him, but to me, it was the perfect example of super-rich kid problems. His summer away with lots of other kids with similar issues gave Derek the opportunity to learn from them. They were all already experts at getting and hiding their drugs of choice. The higher-degree-of-difficulty summer taught them all the tricks. Derek came back to Mansfield drinking more, even in front of me. He was still careful not to get out of control when I was around, but he was also enjoying a much greater variety of drugs, very little of it pot. He was spending tons of cash on mushrooms, acid, coke, and heroin.

Heroin was where I bailed. Or where I told myself I was bailing, anyway. I knew he had been doing it for a while, but then he started talking about it all the time. He said it would make me feel like nothing else. I'd never have any worries about scoring, he had a guy, and he'd always take care of me. He wasn't shooting or anything like that, that kind of thing was for junkies. He just smoked it. He said everyone knew it really wasn't addictive if you smoked it. It was just an amazing nice blissful mellow that made the world feel so good.

I didn't believe a word of it. It made him boring. He didn't want to do anything. It made his pupils little pinpricks and his eyelids look too heavy to lift. It was boring. So unfun. So un-me.

And my sense of self-preservation wouldn't let me go there. Not even with him. I just couldn't. Heroin was scary. Coke just made you not want to eat, so I was OK with that. I could be more bubbly, more talkative, more fun, and skinnier? Sign me up! Coke was my drug of choice for a little while. Mostly as long as someone else, mostly Derek, was buying. I didn't have that kind of cash to spend regularly. And really, girls didn't have to. Boys almost always bought our drugs. After a few months of doing coke kind of regularly though, it started to make me weird. Coke started to make me someone I didn't like. Someone I was scared I could turn into if I wasn't careful.

We were at a party at one of the houses in town. Not sure I even know whose house it was. Some girl. A friend of a friend, someone knew her. She wasn't someone who went to school with us, but she wasn't a townie-type townie either. I sort of remember that maybe she had gotten thrown out of one of the other prep schools and had to come home for the rest of the year? Maybe she was hoping to go to Mansfield next year? Something like that. She was throwing an epic parents-are-out-of-town house party. Kids were there from all over. My parents didn't have to pick me up because I was getting a ride home with Will Austin, a senior day student who lived not far from me. He was my usual ride back from these things my junior year, so I didn't have to deal with my parents, and I was his usual ticket in.

Dots and I had decided to splurge before this party, and we bought ourselves a heavy quarter ounce of coke. Neither of us was dating anyone special at the time. We did lines in her room at Holden while we got ready. She had a super-cool polished agate stone that we'd dedicated for this purpose. It had rings of oranges and browns in concentric circles going out. It was about the size of a forty-five record but without the hole in the middle. So much cooler than a mirror. Because we couldn't risk any teachers finding evidence, while Dots licked the stone clean, I shoved the folded-up foil with a tiny little bump, maybe a bump and a half, left in it into my jeans coin pocket. It may have been the only thing that could have possibly fit in there. My Calvins were so tight I could barely breathe.

Later, at the party Dots asked me if we had any left and I flat out lied. I looked right into my best friend's beautiful brown eyes and lied my face off without blinking "Nah. Maybe check Willie Zeets. That's who I scored from today. His cousin brought some weight this week. They're running cars up from the school in Connecticut."

Then I locked myself in the bathroom alone to do the little bit I had left. That moment is pinned in my brain. I can feel the tiny square of foil. I remember the glee at having a line to myself. I remember how smart and thin I felt. I can see myself, looking in the mirror and pushing my hair off my face over and over. It felt like there was a tiny strand of hair too small to see that was stuck in an eyelash or somewhere and I couldn't make it go away. I can see my teeth clenched, my tight jaw muscles hard lumps below the hollows of my cheeks. I can see the blood caked around my right forefinger's cuticle, from where I'd been chewing on it all night. I can taste it too, the blood on my lip mixed in with the tiniest metallic hints of coke, after running that finger over the inside of the foil again and again and rubbing it on my upper gum just above my front teeth.

BAM. BAM. A fist hit the door, hard. "You gonna be in there all night?" I had no idea whose voice it was or how long I'd been in the bathroom. I jumped about five feet. I came out of the bathroom, smiled at the senior hockey player waiting not so patiently, and avoided Dots for the rest of the night. She caught my eye before I left for home, and I knew she knew. And even in my hyper-exhilarated state, I was ashamed of myself. Will Austin and I made it home before midnight, so my mom couldn't yell at me. I told her I was exhausted from dancing at the party. God only knows what she thought our parties were like—tea and dance cards maybe—and tried to sleep. I ended up just writing in my journal until four.

I called Dots the next day in abject misery and fear of what I had become. "I am so sorry, Dots. Will you please forgive me? I will never do anything that horrible ever again. I swear. I am the worst friend, and you are the best."

"What'd ya do? Kill my cat? Replace my shampoo with Nair?"

"Seriously, Dots, cut it out. I know you know."

"So say it. You wanna apologize, mean it. Spell it out for me."

"I was holding last night when you asked. And I lied to you. I am a terrible person who is not worthy of the friendship and trust and love you give me. I am so sorry. I will never lie to you again. I feel like an ass. Coke makes me weird. I'm over it. Totally dunzo. Are we OK?"

"Kit-Kat, of course we're OK. There are no drugs big enough to come between us. We're the Glimmer Twins. The Dynamic Duo. Not even death could harm our friendship. Don't do it again, K?"

"I swear, Dots. I swear on Brian I won't. I'm done with coke forever. Completely. That girl is not me. That coke girl scares the fuck outta me."

I liked being high as much as the next girl, but it was the social part that I really loved, being with friends, happy, giggling, feeling good. Hiding in the loo licking tinfoil after lying to your best bud was not the kind of drug experience I enjoyed. Or one I ever wanted to have again. I hated the idea that something could have that much of a hold on me.

I never did another line. Not even during those elementary-school-parent social years, when everyone was back at it again with a vengeance. I was lucky enough to get a glimpse of what kind of a monster I could become. I knew how easily I could become just another addict, lying to the people I loved and doing whatever I had to for more. I would never take the chance of letting that happen to me.

Heroin really did make Derek boring. He didn't want to do anything, even make out. It didn't seem to matter what I wore. He didn't even notice my boobs anymore. He didn't want to go hang out at the Gazebo, or go to the Cave, or go cow tipping, or do anything fun. He just wanted to hang out in his room alone, snort, or step outside for a minute to smoke and listen to music with his headphones on. He didn't even want to bring his boom box out onto the quad so we could all listen to music together. He wasn't exactly the best advertisement for a fun drug experience. I was bored.

We might not have stayed together for more than the first couple of weeks of junior year if it hadn't been for Ashley Dix—bane of my existence, demon spawn, source of all evil in the universe. Human I hate most on the planet. I'm not exaggerating even one tiny little bit. I still hate her with every fiber of my being.

Ashley Dix

My first encounter with Ashley Dix set the tone for our entire relationship. Yes, I do mean to this very day. And yes, I do understand that it is ridiculous that two grown women would be continuing to fight their prep school rivalry all the way into their forties, and yes, we damn well are, and damn well probably will be until we are dead. And I will always win. So there.

Ashley was a freshman my junior year. It was only the second day of classes, and Dots and I were gossiping about who hadn't returned and why, and of course about what my plans were for dealing with Derek. When Ashley first bopped up to us, we were in the rotunda, just after morning assembly. It was one of those warm first couple of days of school when everyone mills about, schedules not fully settled, unable to remember where they were supposed to go next, still more in summer mode.

Ashley stood in front of me with a huge smile on her face. She spoke in a sweet, breathy, childlike voice and in upspeak, ending each sentence as if she was asking a question. She took ridiculously long pauses between sentences, like her lungs had to work hard to keep up. Which was just as well, because you often needed a moment to figure out exactly what the words that had come out of her mouth actually meant.

It was confusing because her evil words never matched her tone or her sunny California-girl exterior. She looked like a surfer girl just off the beach, with long, perfectly legitimately beach-blond streaked hair, slim hips, flat chest, and the shiniest, straightest, longest, most perfect teeth I had ever seen. All of that and a sweet little button nose. She was, in one word, adorable.

Ashley was always running her tongue over her upper front teeth. Probably because she was afraid her true nature would burst out unbidden and serrated fangs might suddenly appear. Mostly she kept those hidden. It astonishes me to think that she was only fourteen and yet a fully-fledged demon. Who knew that the devil himself had a child from Mill Valley?

Dots and I watched her approach, and we separated a half step each, allowing her to come into our sphere. We stopped our conversation and met her gaze when she came near. We were polite upperclassmen. We would grant her an audience. I was expecting to hear some sort of hero-worship questions from her, a new girl barely hiding her reverence for the older, more knowledgeable girls by asking us about frosh nonsense. Rarely ever in my life have I been so wrong.

"Hi?' She simpered, it was my first taste of her horrendous upspeak.

"Hi," I replied, trying to be patient with a freshman who needed an excuse to talk to the cool girls.

"Are you Kat …? Kat Tarkoff?"

"Uh-huh."

"Hi. So I'm Ashley? … And I just got here? … And I just wanted to let you know? … I just met this super gnarly hot guy? … Derek, Derek Wilkeson? I asked around and everyone said that you were his girlfriend?" Giggle. "So I wanted to come over and see the competition? … But now I see you, it's kinda hard to believe? You don't look like any competition at all? So, fair warning, I'm totally going to take him away from you?" Giggle. "I just wanted to get a good look at you and let you know, ya know? This is gonna be easy-peasy." She made a giggle noise again and turned away and then right back toward us. "Oh, and I don't know if you know it or not, but you have a huge zit right on the end of your nose? Bummer, for you. I'm sure?" Giggle. And then she bopped down the hall, listening to what I can only imagine was organ music from hell playing inside her little demon head.

I blinked a few times, and I think my jaw might have literally been hanging open. *Did she just say what I think she said?*

"Did she just say what I think she said?" I asked Dots, still unable to process what the hell had just happened. Still blinking rapidly.

"Oh yeah, she did."

"That insane bitch! That total little baby frosh bitch! Who does she think she is? Is she out of her freaking mind? Why would anyone behave like that? Who talks like that? What the hell is wrong with her?"

"Um, yeah. That was weird! But, um, hey, Kit-Kat, you know, maybe use this. You know, with the whole Derek sitch and all. Maybe just let her take him off your hands? Not your problem anymore?" Dots and I spent hours on the phone those first couple of days of junior year trying to decide whether I should stick it out with Derek in the hope that this was a summer phase he would come out of now that he was back with us, or give up, acknowledge this was who he was, and break up with him for real.

"Are you out of your damn mind, Dorothea? I am sure as hell not going to break up with him and let that stupid little baby frosh bitch think she stole my boyfriend. Stupid little nonsense rabbit. She has no idea who she's dealing with. See what we can find out about her. What dorm is she in? She's not in Holden, is she in Colby? Who else hates her already? Anything anyone's got on her? Hey, do you have any Clearasil in your bag? Is that a new bag? I like that cream monogram on the dark-brown-cord background. It's super elegant. I can't believe I have a fucking zit coming up."

OK, so, maybe the reason I didn't break up with Derek the beginning of junior year even though he was no fun and doing dangerous drugs, was mostly just to make sure that Ashley Dix knew she wasn't capable of even being my competition. Of course, the little devil child became super popular; she was super cute, and fun to be around, if you didn't mind the invisible horns and the sulfur smell. And of course, everyone said Derek had sex with her that first weekend. It was like people lined up to tell me that one. I waved them all off. That was one of those stories I was never going to admit I believed. Even if I had walked in on the two of them actually having sex, I wouldn't have admitted I believed it. As far as I was concerned, Ashley was a freshman whose very existence was beneath needing noticing.

I walked right up to her in the dining hall at lunch on the Monday, after everyone said they were fucking all weekend, with Derek's arm around me and his hand firmly squeezing my butt cheek while in my back pocket. And I introduced myself to her with a smile. I looked right into those demon eyes and said, "Hi? I'm Kat. Kat Tarkoff. You must be new?" Ashley could spend the whole weekend on her knees if she fucking wanted to. That boy was mine until I said different.

She has spent the rest of her days hating my guts. I hate hers more. Not a bit has changed between us since those days. I know it's unbecoming, and even silly, for a fully grown adult married woman to think that way, and I don't fucking care. I hate her ugly, demonic guts. She is the devil.

Honestly, I have truly never met a nastier human. She hides it well from some people, but there is true evil just under that shiny exterior. And I will happily confess that any graffiti still extant at Mansfield about her, her name, the sucking of, etc. … maybe could be my doing. Since the day we met, she has always had the ability to bring out the worst in me.

I practically growl at the sight of her even to this day. Just hearing her name makes me hiss. And I am fine with the knowledge that she feels exactly the same way about me. I'd be concerned if she liked me—she is that terrible.

Since shortly after she graduated, Ashley has been the alum editor of the school newsletter and at the beginning of her tenure, she managed to "lose" every single one of the emails I sent in for Class Notes. I had to call the alumni office to express concern and to make sure the news of my wedding was included. Fortunately, I was marrying an important fellow alum and I could rub Ashley's nose in that too. I win, every time.

My greatest vindication is that even though she listed all three of her weddings, with pictures of each of her elaborate and tacky dresses, she's now back to "Ashley Dix—happily single" in all the alumni publications. Meanwhile, I get to send in perky greetings for the newsletter every year along with our Christmas card featuring my beautiful girl, my rich husband, and my perfectly groomed dogs. Just thinking about her reaction when she opens my card is one of my greatest joys of the holiday season. She probably lights it afire with a fingertip.

Our interactions are the lowlight of any reunion weekend. Except for those first few minutes when convention demands the kind of catching-up conversation that involves getting to contrast my life with hers. Then there is just that little mini modicum of schadenfreude on my part. Just a tiny skoosh. Little bit. Wee, really.

Every time we are forced together, we have to pretend to be adults. Our mouths always smiling while our eyes get to glare the daggers we would prefer to be throwing. Knowing that she has to listen to me talk about my perfect life and keep a smile plastered on her face makes it worthwhile. I'm sure the ridiculous amount of Botox she's using these days helps. Her whole head is frozen. She couldn't form a frown on her face if her life depended on it. Injectables must be such a great help to her in keeping her ugly inside from showing on her outside.

I am so happy that Ashley doesn't have any kids going to school with Bree. We'd have sent Bree anyway, not like that satanic slag could keep my daughter away from our school, but it would have taken a lot more than a convertible to convince me it was OK to let Bree go if I knew she was going to have to deal with the spawn of demon spawn. I would have had to buy a house up there to protect her. Maybe start a garlic-and-holy-water farm or something.

Buying a house near campus isn't a terrible idea. Lots of people buy weekend places in the nearby countryside while their kids are attending Mansfield. We could do that. It could be a good investment. Real estate is cheap in farm country, and it would be so relaxing to be able to get away. Maybe I'll look into that when I get home.

Fortunately for the universe, Ashley hasn't yet reproduced. I know I can't control everything that Bree will encounter, but at least she is safe from the ultimate expression of evil, Ashley edition.

Spoon River Anthology

The fall play my junior year at Mansfield was *Spoon River Anthology* by Edgar Lee Masters. *Spoon River Anthology* is exactly the play you'd do if you were an English teacher bored out of your mind with, and unwilling to put on, *Our Town* again. And if you hated audiences. And actors. It is a dreadfully dull series of monologues. I auditioned and got a bunch of good roles. Since actors weren't exactly clamoring to be in it, everyone who was cast got to play multiple characters. It was horrid, but at least I felt like a star.

The staging was as scintillating as the play. We sat on various-height risers and boxes in period costume and rose, spotlit, to do our monologues. I got to showcase my talent for accents and was even allowed minor costume changes, as I was playing characters of many different ages and classes and I'd demonstrated the ability to keep small bits of costumes hidden behind a box riser. Mr. Summers said I had real talent and potential and I should keep the drama department in mind when I started looking at colleges.

My career path was chosen. I was bound for college in New York—no way my mom would let me go as far as California—and from there, I'd get discovered. Maybe Broadway, maybe TV too, or even movies. I was sure I'd regularly be on the cover of *People*. I'd be celebrated for my fashion sense as well as my acting talent. I'd go to clubs every night and date actors, and every girl in America would want to be me. I'd get my own line of clothes and an Oscar.

Suburban mom is kind of close, right?

Derek didn't have any use for the theater, so I was on my own most of the time. He'd come see me in the show and bring flowers, but he wasn't about to hang around rehearsals or help me run lines or anything. "Those aren't the kind of lines I'm into," he'd say with a laugh.

I had my theater friends for that kind of theater thing anyway. Mansfield is small, so the techies and set people and actors all hung out together. There were lots of fun people in the cast and on the crew. Seniors mostly. Guys mostly. Mansfield was seventy-five percent boys back then, and it's always been easier for me to surround myself with more guy friends anyway. It's so much better than having to deal with insane girl-world drama, and you never have to carry anything heavy. The Twillies, short for the Triple Willies, were our main techie and house guys. Willie Hooks ran the lighting, Willie Zeets was in charge of sound, and Willie Glimmerglass, a fellow junior, was the stage manager. They were super-fun guys.

The Twillies were always together. They always had pot. They were nice. They were smart, fun to hang out with, and always willing to help me out. Willie Hooks was the nicest of them. And the silliest. He would often get down on his knees and swear dramatically and with great gesticulation in an exaggerated Errol Flynn-Robin Hood accent that he'd never let anyone put a green gel on me, no matter how stuck-up I got from being a star. He always had such a flair for the dramatic. Maybe he should have been an actor. Of course, only a career in finance was in the cards for him. His parents might seem cool, but they weren't that cool. The green gel is a classic techie trick—they use the unflattering color slide when they are fed up with a particular cast member's antics. Will was so over-the-top back then. I had great times with all the Twillies. We were such tight buds that year. And of course, Will and I always had a thing between us. He always watched over me.

On the whole, though, junior year was just a stone-cold drag. Throughout the early part of the school year, Derek and I would hang out after class at Gus's and wherever, but I didn't really want to spend a lot of time at the Cave. It got really cold really early that year. And besides, by the beginning of November, I was swamped. We were all swamped, but in addition to all the schoolwork, I also had to study my lines. I couldn't be a waste product all the time. Derek stopped even asking me to do anything more than get high and take the occasional Roscoe Happy Pill. We had less and less time to spend together as the year moved on. We were too busy. Well, I was too busy. He was too wasted.

Mansfield was not at all subtle in their cranking up the pressure on juniors to be studious and responsible so we would be seen in the best possible light on our college applications. Everyone and everything around us was about getting ready to send us on to good colleges. After all, where we went to college reflected directly on them. They needed to make sure our acceptances looked good to the alums, as well as the parents, because that's what brought in donations. Well, that and our continued success at hockey.

Fall was devoted to building up our extracurriculars and getting us prepared to take our first serious try at the SATs in the spring. Prep schools normally have the kids take the PSAT both freshman and sophomore years to take any surprise out of the testing situation. Then they get you the specific help you need based on those tests.

Since I placed high enough on the PSAT to be a National Merit Scholar, I wasn't really all that worried about how I would do on the SAT, but I had plenty of friends who were already studying for a test that was months away. I didn't need any extra tutoring, even in math, but there was not much else to do except join all my friends in quizzing each other and taking practice tests.

I think I probably had most of the questions from every old test in the history of the SAT memorized by the time I took the damn test. And as every one of those tests predicted, I did just enough above average in math to be fine and got an almost perfect score in English. I missed one question. I thought about taking it again but decided not to try for perfect. I had done well enough to be in the top one percent. I didn't really think my scores were that big a deal, but my mom carried the paper with my results around in her purse for years and would accidentally drop them whenever she met someone she had to brag to. It was completely embarrassing.

Everything we did junior year was more urgent, under more pressure, and under way more scrutiny. Everything was about how it would look to a college admissions committee. Sports were really important, chorus was really important, grades were really, really important, having fun was going to have to take a back seat until after our college applications were in, senior year. This year belonged to Mansfield. We could have fun again once we got done what had to be done.

Mansfield's crackdown on us was so hard that my party-barometer sense was on high alert throughout the entirety of junior year. Derek wasn't as cautious, but still didn't want to get thrown out and have to deal with his dad. He spent more and more time alone in his room. I knew he was going deeper and deeper into a drug fugue, but I didn't know what I could do to get him out of it. Or even if I should try to. It was his life. His decisions. I had enough to worry about trying to take care of myself.

He sure didn't want anyone's help. He probably would have been happier had I decided to keep him company in his addiction than if I tried to help him out of it. He might have even given me a purposeful little push toward wider experimentation without letting me know.

During one of our longer breakups that fall, Derek gave me a couple of joints one afternoon. I thought it was just a peace offering, but it turned out that the pot was undoubtedly dusted. I can't say for sure that he knew the pot was tainted. But I can't say that he didn't either. He definitely could have been wasted enough to have given me the dusted joints by accident. Whatever way it came to happen, by the time Dots and I were walking back from our first trip to the Cave in two weeks, we could tell we hadn't been smoking just pot. We were way fucked up, and there was some kind of hallucinogen involved.

That day was gray and nasty, New England mid-autumn drear, that kind of damp cold that seeps into your bones, no matter how many layers you put on. After we scored a couple joints from Derek—which wasn't at all weird; he was always good to loan me a joint or two, even if we weren't a thing at the moment—Dots and I decided that the best way to ignore the weather was to take a short sojourn to the Cave and see who was there. Then it was back to the salt mines for us both. We had a ton of work to do.

When we got to the Cave, it was obvious that no one else was of the same mind, so there was no bonfire started and no other friends around. Bummer. We sparked up quickly, each took a few hits, and started to head out from the clearing. It was too cold to be outside without gloves and threatening to rain on us any minute. So we just smoked one little joint between us, in my pretty Pegasus roach stone, and after I put everything back in my wallet, we began to walk back up the road toward campus.

Almost right away, instead of feeling good like usual, I was feeling a little weirdly paranoid. I heard a jingling sound behind me, like a thick dog chain. I turned and well behind us through the mist, there was this weird-looking old man, someone shabby, with a long, scraggly white beard, no one I'd ever seen near town before, walking a gigantic black dog and carrying a huge red Coleman lantern. He was swinging the lantern in what seemed to me to be a threatening way. He made me think of the Headless Horseman from Sleepy Hollow. The jingling noises of the dog chain stopped as soon as I turned back to face forward. I turned around again, and the guy and the dog and the lantern were gone. Vanished. There were no houses around. No other streets to turn on to. Where could they have gone? I wasn't about to wait to find out.

"Run!" I screamed at Dots. And we both took off as fast as we possibly could in hiking boots. We ran full speed as the rain started, the whole quarter mile until we got to Main Street. We stopped under the streetlamp to catch our breath. The light from the streetlamp made the drizzle that had just started all sparkly and multicolored.

"Did you see that?" I asked her, bent over at the waist and breathing hard from all the effort. *Ooooh, my shoelaces are really pretty—like little red licorice strips.*

"Why'd ya yell like that? You scared the crap outta me. Wait, did you see something in the woods?" Dots said at almost the same time. She was equally breathless. We really needed to quit smoking.

"Back on the road"—at least my breath was coming back—"didn't you see that weird guy ... with the dog, the lantern? Did you hear the dog chain rattling?" I let my voice trail off. Dots was looking at me like I was nuts.

"I didn't see anything. I thought I heard music though. Somebody was playing 'Magic Bus' full volume. But I couldn't figure out where it could be coming from since we were the only ones there."

We looked at each other in alarm. I could tell we were thinking the same thing.

Dots spoke first. "Do ya think … maybe we're trippin'?"

"Are we trippin'? Shit, I think we're trippin'."

"We must be trippin'. Did Derek say anything when he gave you the pot?"

"Nah, he just said 'enjoy' and smiled. I mean, he winked, but he always winks at me, the weirdo. Freak. Asswipe. I hate him. He dosed me. I can't believe he fucking dosed me. I have things I have to get done this afternoon. I don't have time for this!"

"Yeah, and me too. Quelle douchebag your ex is, Kat. All right, be calm. We're good. OK, if we are trippin', we better go someplace safe. OK. Where can we go? Um, OK, let's go down to Doc and chill. We can get a soda, watch TV, and try to stay calm until we come down. OK? We just won't talk to anyone else until it wears off, OK? We're gonna be OK. OK? Don't worry. We didn't smoke that much. It won't be that long." Dots hugged me as she rambled on, sounding like she was trying to reassure herself. Even tripping, Dots took charge and organized things. Better her than me. I was an anxious mess with whatever this was.

Our brand-new student center building was near the football field and replaced the TV lounge by the locker rooms that year. Willie Hooks's dad and his classmates were the main donors, and they named it for their beloved history teacher, Dr. Sherman. Doc Sherman was an institution of the institution; he taught there for fifty years and had just passed away two years before. His namesake, the building we called Doc, was opened with great fanfare. We had an actual ribbon-cutting ceremony and a whole school assembly outside the building, complete with the singing of the school song, at the beginning of the school year. It was an incredible student space, a two-level building, just for us. Practically no grown-ups allowed. It had three giant TVs, a pool table, a foosball table, a dance floor, and a snack bar. We wouldn't have to have dances in the student lounge in Blackstone anymore. There was an outdoor terrace for the nice weather with chairs, a chess and checkers game station, and a smoking area. It was designed to be run and staffed entirely by students, as a real-world econ lesson, so we knew we'd be left alone. It was totally bitchen. It was a giant playhouse, with heat and everything.

Dots seemed to be holding it together a little better than I was, so she held my hand and led me to one of the big squishy chairs in front of the biggest TV over the fireplace. We watched cartoons and drank Dr Peppers until my mom came to get me at six thirty. I told my mom I thought I might be coming down with the flu or something and closed myself off in my room. I should have known better than to trust Derek after that little stunt, but he was so cute and contrite, and I forgot to stay mad, once again, and before long we were back together again.

Two Days before Thanksgiving Break

Westford House, 6:45 a.m.

Right before Thanksgiving break, Derek and I were in a really good place together. We hadn't fought or broken up in weeks. Going into first semester exams, my grades looked like they would be very good, even in French. The Math outlook wasn't quite that rosy, but still, life was good.

As was fitting, Derek had what was widely acknowledged to be the best boys' room in the whole school, right next to the back parlor in Westford. Off the back parlor was a small back porch. Behind Westford was a thickly wooded area where you could quickly be far enough in so as to be completely hidden from prying eyes. It was a short jump off the back porch into the woods. Because of the angle of the trees to the sun, the back porch didn't get much light, so it often had icy patches even when the weather meant you wouldn't expect ice. The dark glossy paint didn't help in identifying the slippery parts. The wipeout danger was part of the charm of the place.

I knew I couldn't go into Westford this early in the morning, not even inside the front door, and definitely not into the front parlor, even with the doors all open. It wasn't parlor visiting hours. Being caught in an opposite-sex dorm outside of visiting hours was a very serious offense. Especially for the girls. The boys got in trouble, they were given a good talking-to, had to do massive weeks of kitchen duty, and there was even a suspension or two. But girls got booted immediately if they were caught in a boy's room. Girls were still a relatively new addition to Mansfield in the early eighties, and nothing scared the school more than the idea of student pregnancies.

That year already we had one poor girl who got bounced because they found her boyfriend in her room. Even though he was the one in an opposite-sex dorm. He was naked and hiding in her closet, so the school had a pretty good case for both of them being in really big trouble. No one knew who narked, but someone had to have, because they had to look pretty hard to find him behind all her clothes. He got suspended for the rest of the semester. She got the boot. The girls all protested how unfair it was to have different rules for boys and girls, but it did us no good. Boys couldn't get pregnant. She was out. He got to come back.

I wasn't about to push the envelope on rules they took that seriously. Outside the dorm was a different story. We could be outside on the porches all we wanted. And even if I couldn't go into Derek's dorm, it was possible to sit on the outside of the porch rail, lean way off the side with your legs hooked around the railing, and knock on his window. It was a great core exercise. The porch didn't extend all the way across the back to his room. Instead, there was a small space in between with a good drop under it where the ground sloped down steeply. The part of the basement under his room was mostly aboveground.

Or I could stand under his back window and yell from the ground below. That morning I took the safer option. "C'mon. We're gonna be late for breakfast. Exams start right after assembly. Wake up, lazy boy!"

Our trimester system meant exams were right before Thanksgiving break, right before Miniterm, and right before graduation.

"Keep your shirt on, I'm coming." He leaned his head out the window and grinned down at me. "On second thought …"

"Never mind that, I'm hungry!" I grinned right back. I really did love him. *It's time. Maybe right before Christmas vacation?* I was three-and-a-half weeks away from being sixteen.

Derek came out the door to the back porch and tied the laces on his boots while he sat on the small wooden bench that some nice Westford family had donated for exactly that reason. They probably imagined us getting a lot more healthy exercise than just walking to the Cave and back. I hopped up onto the porch ledge, climbed over the rail, and joined him. He was wearing a beige ribbed turtleneck with a plaid chamois shirt over it and a red down vest. *The boy is starting to look pretty darn preppy himself. And he is pretty smokin' for a preppy boy.*

He reached into his chamois shirt pocket and pulled out a small red leather box with gold tooling all around. This was most definitely a jewelry box! His voice was extra casual when he started speaking. "Hey, I got you a birthday present, since I won't be there for your birthday. My dad is coming to take me for a ski weekend in Vermont. I didn't have any wrapping paper. I know it's early and stuff. But it came last night, and I wanted to give it to you right away. I hope you like it. It looks like you—I mean, it looks like you to me, I guess." This may have been the most words I had ever heard out of him at one time. He stumbled a bit over the words. The more he talked, the more I could tell he wasn't quite the cocky, winking, easy boy I was used to hearing. He actually sounded kind of nervous.

I opened the box, and inside it sat a beautiful gold heart necklace from Shreve, Crump & Low in Boston. Hearts were my favorite! It had tiny diamond chips all around one side of the heart. It was gorgeous. It was perfect. It was me! "Oh Derek, I love it! It's beautiful! Put it on me, OK?" I sat on his lap and turned so he could hook the necklace behind my neck. Breakfast could wait a few minutes longer while we kissed in the freezing November morning air. I didn't care.

His voice was soft near my ear and a little tremulous. "I was thinking, maybe, if you can, maybe for vacation you could come home with me, for Christmas. I mean, you could stay at our house. My dad will be there and all. You could have a California Christmas with a Christmas tree and everything. Do you think your parents would let you? I mean my dad will pay for the tickets, and he'll be responsible and stuff. I can get him to call to talk to them and let them know it's on the up and up and all. If you want. Like if you don't have plans already or anything."

Derek knew that a Christmas tree was one of my fondest desires. One of my top grievances against my parents was their stubborn refusal to get a Christmas tree, or a Chanukah bush, as lots of their friends called it once they caved to their Jewish children's wishes. It was completely ridiculous, and it was so unfair. I just didn't understand what their problem was. Everyone else in the universe had one.

"I don't care what they call it!" my dad would say loudly and embarrassingly within earshot of other people. "It's a Christmas tree and it's a shondeh"—Yiddish for a shame. "No Jew should have a Christmas tree, no matter what they call it. A shondeh, I tell you!" Christmas trees came up in conversation and all of a sudden my father turned into Tevye.

I would always try to rush him out of the hearing range of normal people as quickly as possible before renewing my begging for a tree. "Everyone else has one, please, Daddy, please …" I wanted a Christmas tree more than anything in the world. I wanted the smell in my house, carols, presents under the tree, Rudolph, Santa, the whole megillah. It never happened. I always got almost everything I wanted from my dad, especially when I turned on the charm, but he wouldn't budge on the Christmas tree. It was so unfair.

And I knew how much of a huge deal it was for Derek to ask me to come home with him. He never wanted anyone to meet his dad. He never introduced Jack to anyone on visiting days. He never wanted me to have dinner with them when Christian was out East on business. Mostly he liked to pretend Jack didn't exist, except for cashing his allowance checks. He rarely wanted to talk about him, except when he wanted to almost sort of blame him for his mom's death.

There were other weird stories about Jack. Once Derek briefly mentioned something about some older girl, like eighteen, nineteen, who he had dated a few times. He said she started going out with his father after Derek came East. I guess it made sense, then, why he didn't want me to meet him. But ew, who would even do that? Date someone and then their father? That's just beyond creepy. Anyway, it sounded like she and Jack had since broken up. But shit, like Derek needed any more reasons to hate his dad? For him to be willing to bring me home, and for him to ask his dad to call to reassure my parents, was huge. It showed how much I really meant to him, how much he trusted me. Maybe everything really would work out? Derek would get better, and we'd be in love forever.

Inviting me home for Christmas break meant Derek wanted to get better. I just knew it. He'd stop doing so many drugs and clean up, and we'd be happy forever after. I was ready to show him just how much his love and trust meant to me. I was going to have sex with Derek, and it was going to be magical—transformative for both of us. We'd have this perfect love and this perfect life. We'd get right all the things that Brian and Anita got wrong.

I fiddled with the necklace so it balanced perfectly on the edge of my turtleneck. The chain peeked over the edge of the turtleneck, the heart bounced, and the diamond chips caught the light with my every step. We walked over to breakfast as entwined as we'd ever been. My life was perfect. Not fake-perfect. Perfect. Actually, truly perfect.

That Same Day

Just Later

I showed back up at Westford after my last exam that afternoon as happy as I had ever been in my whole entire life. The air was crisp and clear, the campus was beautiful, even the squirrels were cute. I felt almost about to burst into song. Even my algebra exam wasn't killer. I was pretty sure I aced it. I was going to figure out some way to get my parents to let me go to California for Christmas break. I knew I couldn't show them the necklace. There was no way my mother would let me keep it if she saw it. It wasn't an appropriate present for a young boy to give a young girl. Jewelry was the province of the older, the more experienced, and getting good jewelry from a boy could only mean one thing: He wanted something in return. She'd never say sex, *thank God*, but I knew that's what she meant. I didn't care, I was going to sleep with him anyway, not because of the necklace, but because of the faith he showed in us.

That afternoon I felt perfectly willing to risk my neck hanging off the side of the porch rail. I was in the best mood of my life. Getting ready to knock on his window, I wasn't even worried about slipping and cracking my head on the ground below. Nothing could bring me down. I was sneaking a peek into my beautiful boyfriend's room, expecting to catch a glimpse of him, imagining maybe even seeing him napping on his bed. Happy as anyone could possibly be.

But that isn't what I saw. In fact, I didn't see Derek in the room at all. Instead, I saw Ashley and her best friend Beanie sitting on his bed, wasted, red-eyed, and bleary-looking. They weren't undressed, but both looked suspiciously disheveled and puffy-lipped, as if there had been a lot of kissing going around. Then I saw Derek. He was in the far corner with his camera. He was taking pictures of them on his bed! Seriously? *Was he insane? The school would have evidence if he developed those pictures. What the fuck was going on? Did he really think he had a shot at both of them? Oh my god. We were in rural New Hampshire, not California. That sort of thing didn't happen here!* I could see all kinds of drug paraphernalia all over the room too. And there was a funky smell leaking out of his window. The three of them were in violation of pretty much all of the most serious rules we had, all at the same time. Whatever the hell else they were doing, they were not just smoking pot. I let out an involuntary noise, giving away my position, then a "What the fuck?"

What the fuck? It felt like my brain just hit a brick wall at two hundred miles an hour. Was he trying to get booted before break? Two girls in his room would get him booted. Or at least get them booted. Smoking anything in his room would most definitely get him booted. What the fuck had I just seen? What the fuck just happened to my life? It was just a few short hours ago this morning when everything was perfect. Now everything had gone to total shit. *What the fucking fuckity fuck?*

I should have run right to the dean's office and gotten the Hulk. I should have reported Derek, under the honor code. I should have reported those horrible girls, gotten the whole lot of them busted, gotten all of them all fucking thrown out and sent home. Those lousy, rotten, horrible fucking tramps. Oh my god, I hated them. Hated!

But of course, I didn't do that. There was no way I was going to run tattling to the Hulk. I may have just had my heart ripped out of my chest and tap-danced on, but I wasn't a nark. Why would he do this to me? Why would he do this to us? Why, when everything was so good? *What the fuck? Why?*

Ashley waved and smiled as she saw me outside. I was so close I could see her running her tongue over her teeth. Then she and Beanie hightailed it out of the room, giggling as they ran out the back door and right past me as I dismounted the porch. Someday I was just going to up and strangle that horrible little bitch. I could hear her and Beanie still laughing as they ran through the woods. This story would be all over campus by the time last bells sounded. Great. I would be fucking humiliated in front of the whole school, as well as devastated.

This was the absolute end. *Actually seeing him with another girl— oh my god, girls? How is that even possible? After this morning? After he said he wanted me to come home with him? After I decided I was going to sleep with him the minute I turned sixteen? Oh my god, I'm so glad we haven't yet—who knows what I could have caught, care of that tramp Ashley Dix! Gross!*

Derek came running out on the porch without any shoes on his feet. His camera was still around his neck. He was a mess. His eyes were so bloodshot that no amount of Visine could possibly be enough. He had on his turtleneck and blue paisley boxers that poked out over the top of the jeans he was still zipping up as he ran. He hit a patch of ice and slipped, falling down hard on one of his knees. *Good. I hope it hurt.*

I ripped the necklace off my neck and threw it at him. The bite of the chain on my fingers felt good. It was good to feel anything other than the aching pain that was wrenching my body. I didn't let him say a word to me. What was there to say? I wasn't about to listen to anything that came out of that lying mouth. Through the tears that fell despite my ordering them not to, I screamed at him that it was over. I yelled so loudly that my throat hurt. I told him that it was forever this time.

"Don't call me. Don't talk to me. Don't even look at me. I'm gone." I was crying and screaming, and it was probably as close as I've ever been to being actually hysterical. I had gone from perfect joy to abject misery in the span of a few minutes. I ran to the closest girls' bathroom, downstairs by the lockers in the school building, and didn't come out until my mom came to get me. I couldn't wait to have my own car so I didn't have to put up with being carted around like this. I didn't even try to hide that I had been crying. I told her exams were good and my boyfriend and I broke up and my life was miserable. And I didn't want to talk about it.

I was so embarrassed that I fell for his crap. That I believed for one minute that we could have had a happily ever after. What an idiot I was. I didn't even try to find Dots to tell her. I knew she had the late exam that day. Of course, she heard the whole thing from Ashley's hell minions five minutes after the exam was over, but she was too loyal to ask me what really happened. We never talked about it. I swore that no one else would ever break my heart like that again. I wish I had sworn instead that Derek would never break my heart again. But I didn't, and he somehow managed to find a grandfathered-in loophole to the vow I made.

I guess it just goes to show how stupid I was, because we did get back together again. I must have been some kind of addict too. Derek was addicted to drugs. I was addicted to Derek. Together we hit all the highs and lows a human could experience. It was physical, emotional, chemical, magical, whatever. We were special.

I refused to talk to him for weeks, but after we got back from Christmas break, he came up with some ridiculous story of being in the shower and coming back to his room to find Ashley and Beanie there making out on his bed. He said they were messing around and it was their idea, and they wanted him to document it. He was just an innocent bystander. They brought all this drama to him. And I bought it. I didn't fully believe it—all evidence to the contrary, I was not an idiot—but I bought it. I wanted to be Derek's girlfriend. I wanted to be back together, I wanted us to be us. His story was just plausible enough to allow me to tell myself I believed it.

I knew he was lying. I knew I was being stupid. I knew I needed to break away from him. I knew that this wasn't OK or right or good for me. But I didn't know what it would take to make me finally break our bond.

He got the chain fixed and tried to give me the necklace back, but I didn't take it. I told him my mom wouldn't let me accept expensive presents from boys. Truth was, I never wanted to see that stupid fucking thing again. That necklace had mocked me with its false promises of perfection. I hated it. It was poisoned.

In the Car

One Week Ago

I'm almost in tears, just thinking about that day, so when I hear "No Woman, No Cry" coming out of the bottom of my purse again, I'm a little confused for a moment. *Fucking hell,* I think, and an angry "What could he possibly want now?" escapes before I have the chance to modulate. I must have said it loud enough for Bree to take her headphones out.

Even with my eyes on the road, I can feel Bree's questioning look. "Wow. Too much coffee this morning, Mom? Do you want me to get it?"

Deep breath. "No, sweetie, I'm sure Daddy has just remembered something he needs me to pick up before I go home. It's easier if we just let it go to voicemail. I'll listen to it when we make our next pit stop. Didn't mean to go *grrrrr* at the phone. All this driving is a little tiring. Sorry if I startled you. What were you listening to while I've got the oldies going?"

"Nothing. You wouldn't know them, Mom." The headphones go back in, and I am dismissed back to the crises of my youth with a toss of her hair and closed baby blue eyes.

I have got to pull myself together. She cannot see me like this.

Winter into Spring

There are times when this all seems as if it happened just a moment ago and other times when it's so far off that I wonder if all this stuff really happened at all. We can't really have spent most of our time junior year, when we weren't up to our ears in work, obsessing about virginity, ours and everyone else's. Ad nauseam.

Surprisingly, I did manage to hold on to my virginity through my junior year. After Christmas break, even though Derek and I spent more time broken up than together, if an alien had landed at the front gate and asked anyone in that school who my boyfriend was, every single person—fine, except maybe Ashley Dix, the stupid bitch—would say Derek. All the other guys I went out with were placeholders until Derek and I would get back together again. It was the same for him. We'd date other people, but we'd always come back to each other. Hard as Ashley might try to change his mind.

Of course it was stupid of me to keep going back to him. I know that now. I probably even knew it then. But every time he said he was sorry, I believed him. Every time he said he would change, I believed him. Every ridiculous excuse was just good enough for me to suspend disbelief because I wanted to, so very badly. Every damn time.

All the breakups and makeups just added to our mystique, proving that Derek and I were part of something bigger. We weren't just an ordinary teen couple. We were epic star-crossed lovers. We were more like Romeo and Juliet, more like Brian and Anita, than regular mere mortals. Derek would break my heart again and again, but after a few days, or a couple of weeks, with some average boy, I'd want that feeling of being part of something special back. And he must have too. Because he kept asking. I have to say this for the boy, he was certainly creative in his transgressions and his excuses. He never broke my heart the same way twice.

So, in his own fashion, he lived up to his promise to change.

Derek and I were both planning to go to Switzerland for junior year Miniterm. The weather is so dreadful in New England in February that many of the private schools in the area add a two-week extra term just before our two-week spring break. The idea gained currency in the late 1960s to give the kids an alternative intellectual experience, something outside of the classroom. It quickly became part of our culture.

Miniterm gives everyone something to live for. Costa Rica is one of the most popular trips. You get to travel into the rainforest, practice Spanish in a village in the morning, and play on a beach every afternoon. It's warm and sunny, and no one pays a lot of attention to the drinking age. But I didn't take Spanish, so my parents never let me go on that one.

The trips are billed as cultural immersion, so parents don't feel that they are just paying for the kids to go on expensive vacations. Of course, they pretty much are just paying for the kids to go on expensive vacations. The students have to write a paper, keep a travel log, or record a photo journal or something, but that's really just cover, and everyone knows it.

There were on-campus artsy things you could do if your parents didn't want to pay for you to get away, but most kids tried to go somewhere for their last three years of Miniterm. Freshmen were strongly encouraged to stay on campus their first Miniterm. As a frosh, I took a mixed-media class and made papier-mâché puppets for our productions. Sophomore year, Dots and I went to England to study art and architecture and learn how to drink rum and Cokes. Junior year I was all set to go to Switzerland with Derek, to ski and practice my French. I couldn't think of a more romantic place to surrender to love than in the Alps! I pictured us, a roaring fire in the fireplace, champagne, me in a fancy nightie I'd somehow smuggled into my bag. I could almost hear Rod Stewart singing "Tonight's the Night."

Once again, we were in a good patch, and I had decided it was time. We were an everything-but-actual-sex committed couple, and the virginity thing was just getting cumbersome. Still, I was looking for a more romantic setting than the Cave. Besides, it was too cold to do it outside, and anyway, I sure wasn't going to risk being caught in his room. I rarely went too close to Westford after the Ashley/Beanie incident anyway. The sight of the porch still made me a little sick to my stomach.

This time fate intervened instead of heartbreak. A week and a half before Miniterm, I fell off the stage during mock sword-fighting class—my drama elective—and I broke my left leg. The doctors all said that I was really lucky that it was my only break. Yeah, right, lucky! I was going to be on crutches for five or six weeks. At least *Spoon River Anthology* was over. It wouldn't really be a problem for me to be on crutches to audition for the spring musical. I'd be off of them before showtime.

Everyone at Mansfield was really super great and really super helpful the whole time I was on the stupid crutches. The Twillies helped me paint them baby blue and glue on rhinestones and fake pearls. If the crutches were going to be my constant companion for that long, at least they could be an accessory I could work with.

In the hospital, I figured I looked so pathetic that my parents would have to let me go on the trip anyway. Even if I couldn't ski, I could still practice French, and that was a huge part of the trip. Most of it, really. But they were having none of it. They just flat out refused to listen to reason.

My mother said "absolutely not" even though I explained that skiing was only a small part of the cultural experience I would have in Switzerland. Speaking French was most of it, and I really needed the French practice. How would having a broken leg stop me from that? I could still talk. It was so unfair. *How could she not trust me?* I think she probably knew exactly why she couldn't trust me, broken leg or no. My mother wasn't about to just hand me my bag and let me go on off on a romantic—school chaperones notwithstanding—European trip with my gorgeous Hitler Youth Brigade boyfriend. I may have thought of her as clueless, but she wasn't stupid.

My revenge has been long enduring. For the rest of my academic career, I blamed my lousy French grades on her refusal to let me go to Switzerland that Miniterm. Even though I went to Quebec senior year. My inability to conjugate is her fault.

Derek went on the trip anyway. As did Ashley. I stayed home and did a leather-tooling crafts Miniterm. I was able to sit at the crafts table with my bad leg extended on a shorter footstool underneath. Boy that was some fun, especially compared to the romantic days I imagined Ashley having with my boyfriend. Good thing she was so far away when I had sharp tools at hand.

I still have one of the belts I made that Miniterm. Or at least I did until I let Bree pack it to take to Mansfield with her. The belt doesn't really fit me anymore and looks super cute on her anyway.

The day after Ashley got back from Switzerland, she cornered me and my stupid crutches in front of the downstairs girls' room in the main school building and said, "If my boyfriend treated me like that? ... I'd dump him? ... Of course, no one would ever treat me like that?" When I just looked through her like she wasn't there, she said it again, louder. In a moment of enormous self-restraint, I did not whack her with a crutch. It's one of my greatest regrets. I should have broken both of them over her head.

As spring started to work its way through the New England gloom, I sort of gave up on the idea of ever having sex with Derek. On some unconscious level, I must have decided that not sleeping with him was the last great hold I had over him. I was still the girl who told him no. The girl he couldn't get. Just barely out of reach, even for the great Derek Wilkeson. The other boys at school were fun enough to make out with and whatever, but no one else ever made me think about what it would be like to rip their clothes off. I didn't get that same charge out of feeling them swell when they ground into me. I didn't get a tingle in my pants just thinking about doing it with them.

Besides, if I had sex with any other boy at Mansfield, it would be all over school by the next day, and the next time Derek and I got back together I wouldn't have any plausible reason to turn him down. *I'm waiting for the right time* was understandable. *I slept with another guy but won't sleep with you because I love you too much and I'm afraid you will dump me once we finally do it and I no longer have that hold over you* sounded batshit even to me, and I was the one who was thinking it. It was safer for me to stay the Virgin Queen.

Summer

The summer between junior and senior year I got a job working for a family from our temple. Steve and Laurie needed someone to come along and play with their kids during their ten-day late-June-into-July vacation in Maine. They were happy to have an extra pair of hands along but didn't want to be free of their kids for the entire vacation, so it wasn't like I was constantly on call. I would be off duty every night after nine, and I was free to go out after that, as long as Steve and Laurie were home from dinner, to join the teenage festivities along the central strip of the little town and on the beach.

The three girls were adorable, a six-year-old and three-year-old twins. I got paid $150, which was a huge sum, and was responsible for taking care of the kids and generally keeping them out of their parents' hair during the day so Laurie and Steve could have some couple time on vacation. After being out in the sun and cold salt water all day and given dinner, ice cream, and a warm bath, the kids were in la-la land by eight. Even on the nights when Steve and Laurie went out instead of making dinner at the cottage and watching TV while sitting on the couch holding hands after, they were home by nine fifteen on the weekends. It was incomprehensible to me, but I was so very grateful for it. That was still early enough so I could go out for an hour or so to get an ice cream at Durland's Candy Shoppe or see who was hanging out on the beach or at the arcade. I technically had a curfew of midnight, but they didn't stay up to enforce it.

My parents were happy. They knew the family from our synagogue and thought I couldn't get into too much trouble under their roof. I was happy. I didn't have to be a camp counselor at the Jewish girls' camp all summer. Laurie and Steve were happy. They wouldn't give me any problems about going out as long as I did a good job when I was looking after the girls. Laurie and Steve were in their mid-thirties and pretty realistic about their expectations for taking a sixteen-year-old on vacation with them. They just wanted a little alone time. Which still gave me plenty of time for fun.

We got to the cottage late on Friday afternoon. The traffic on 95 was a total nightmare. Before E-ZPass, the Hampton toll used to back up for miles. The kids bolted out of the car, cranky from being stuck for so long and eager to move around. From the outside, the cottage was super cute. It had weathered gray shingles and robin's-egg blue trim. Best of all, it was just a couple of houses away from the beach.

The girls and I escaped the car and went inside to get drinks of water, use the bathrooms, and explore while Steve and Laurie unpacked the car. The windows were all open and a light breeze made the white curtains dance about. The interior of the cottage smelled of salt spray and marsh grass, with just enough of an underlying hint of that industrial-strength-cleaner scent to make you feel comfortable with the fastidiousness of housekeeping.

We raced up the open-backed wooden stairs to find our rooms. The twins showed no fear at the rickety, uneven treads—they were just happy to be let loose. Upstairs was a former attic space divided up into two rooms separated by a little hallway with a shared bath at the back of the house. The rooms had warm wood paneling, with each room's trim painted a single pastel color, it's wooden door painted to match, and floral bedding in the same colors. There were little signs on the doors saying Beach Rose and Hydrangea. I thought it was a really cool touch and wondered if my parents would let me paint my door a funky color. The girls' room was larger and had a full-size bed with a twin bunk over it. The twins would sleep together below in the full. Big sister Emily got the upper bunk. From my small room, I could almost see the water, if I leaned out the window. I could hear it, anyway. The crashing waves would lull me to sleep every night.

Laurie and Steve had the downstairs master bedroom and bath. Three big rooms completed the house: a large eat-in kitchen; an open living room with a couch and chairs, the TV, and a game cabinet; and a huge screened porch across the front. The porch had green wicker rockers on one side and a white wooden picnic table on the other. The backyard play area was full of that itchy scrub grass that grows in sand, the kind that hurts when it catches between your toes. It hurts, but it feels like summertime, so it's also kind of good. The cottage wasn't very big, but it had everything you could want from a beach house.

I was on vacation! It would be easy enough to play with the kids on the beach all day and the teenagers on the beach at night. I took this job also thinking it was going to be the perfect time for me to rid myself of my virginity. I'd be away from home and my all-seeing-mother's eye, so I wouldn't have to worry about getting caught. Virginity had become this annoying appendage that kept me apart from the wider adult world, and I was sick of it. I wanted to get it over with before school started in the fall, or I'd be stuck until next summer, or even until I got to college. Ick, who wanted to go to college a virgin?

I didn't need to be in love with the boy. Heck, I didn't even want to be in love. I wasn't going to fall in love in a few days with some random guy I met in Maine. I'd already had my coup de foudre, and you only get one of those. And even if I was still in love with Derek, he wasn't the right guy for this job.

I hoped to meet the right candidate and jump to the other side of the experience chasm. But it couldn't be just anyone. It wasn't like I was going to go out and have sex with some townie or anything. Maybe I'd meet someone from Canada or Chicago or some other far-off place? Above all else, it couldn't be someone who could in any way possibly be a source of rumors getting back to Mansfield. I had to be in control of this story. I'd be the one to decide if I was going to tell it at school. Even as a child, pragmatism was of my strengths.

Beach Day

Our days at the beach were all pretty much the same. I dragged the kids down the hill and across the road to the beach. I put Lily and Rose, the towels, and some snacks into a wagon and had Emily walk next to me. They were all slathered up with sunscreen and hidden under brightly colored hats. The beach was crowded with local renters and Saturday day-trippers. The hats made it easier to keep my eye on the kids at all times.

The frigid water kept most people on the sand, but a few hearty souls were in the sea, jumping waves and bodysurfing. We didn't go swimming right away. Instead, the girls and I built dribble castles and played in the warm pools left on the beach by the receding tide. By the time late morning came around we were hot enough to jump into the water. At first my feet hurt so much. It was like tiny needles stabbing into my anklebones, at least until the numbness set in. As I became accustomed to the frigid water, I ventured farther in, still not too far. With the little ones in tow, I didn't go in much past my knees. The girls giggled and splashed; their plump little bodies seemed to be impervious to the cold.

I was having so much fun. I couldn't believe I was getting paid for this. I even made a new friend, that first day, named Allie. She set up her towel and charges just next to where we were. Allie was tall and had masses of long, dark curly hair and had already been there for more than a week taking care of two boys. The family she was working for was staying for the whole summer. That seemed like a long time and made me glad I was going home after ten days. It was great to be away from the 'rents for a little while, but I didn't want to work with kids all summer. After this gig was up, I was going to work in the mall for a few weeks. I could use my discount there to buy new clothes before I went back to school.

Allie's family had the house behind us, one up the hill, away from the beach. Our backyards were attached, which was a great bonus. The kids got along well and were happy to play together. She was also off duty after nine, so we decided to meet up to check out the arcade and T-shirt shops in town that night. At noon we took the kids home to get them out of the sun for a couple of hours. Lunch and nap time would take until two. We'd staked out our section of beach, but in case we didn't run into each other again for the kids' afternoon beach session, we made a plan to meet up in front of our cottage on Shore Road just after nine. We were instant besties.

The girls and I took refuge in the cool interior of the cottage. Everything looked so dark in those first few minutes inside after being out in the bright sun all morning. Poor Lily cried that the dark scared her. I cuddled her until she calmed down. My eyes soon adjusted, and I made us some lunch, which we ate on paper towels at the picnic table on the screened porch. That way I wouldn't have to wash dishes. The girls wolfed down more Fluffernutter sandwiches than I thought possible. It was like they were starving. They washed the sandwiches down with big plastic cups of red Kool-Aid. I cleaned up their sticky hands and faces, but there was nothing I could do about that bug juice staining their mouths. That was just going to have to get worn off in the ocean.

After lunch we went inside for some quiet time. Emily watched TV with me in the downstairs living room while the twins napped in their bed. She was curled up on my lap, thumb in her mouth. Emily dozed off for a bit too but would never admit to needing a nap like her baby sisters. At some point while they were all snoozing, I eased Emily off of me, onto the couch, and snuck outside. I hid around the shaded side of the house and sucked down a quick smoke to quell my nic fit. I knew without asking that smoking in front of the girls was most definitely OOQ—out of the question.

I was able to smoke a lot less over summers and vacations than when I was at school, so it didn't turn into a hard-core addiction for me until I left for college. It was my true-love vice from college on, until I found out about Bree. I quit immediately and never took another puff. I know I'm a nicotine addict. I'm not one of those people who can pick it up and put it down. I'll never be able to have even one cigarette ever again without going right back to a pack-and-a-half-a-day habit. I keep saying I'm taking up smoking again the day I turn seventy. It's been over fifteen years, but I still miss it sometimes, especially when I'm stressed.

I wanted to make sure I didn't scorch the kids in the sun on my first day, so we played in the house for a while after nap time. Then I slathered them up again and off we went. This time I added a radio to the pile we were hauling to the beach so I could listen to music while we played. Their mom didn't want wet suits in the house, so they changed into play clothes when we came in for lunch. That meant new suits for the afternoon trip. I rinsed out their morning suits and hung them out on the line. I was happy to do it, it was great cover for another quick smoke.

I kept on my mint-green string bikini from the morning since I didn't go in far enough to get it wet and because it was my current favorite suit. Over it, I wriggled into a pair of white terry shorts with chocolate-and-mint piping. Unlike the little girls, I was old enough to tan and was working strenuously on it. I planned to be golden-skinned by the end of the ten days. Bain de Soleil and a sparkly pink Lip Saver were my constant companions. Once we reestablished our spot on the beach, I could see the afternoon beach scene was much the same as the morning, and we played accordingly. Allie and her kids must have found something else to do, because they didn't return for the afternoon session.

After the beach I got the kids home, bathed all three at once in the tub—that was easy—and fed them hot dogs, cut up grapes, and mac and cheese for dinner. Laurie and Steve came home from their day off somewhere and dinner out relaxed and happy. By seven, the kids were conked out. By nine, I was free. I think Steve and Laurie wanted me out of their love nest as badly as I wanted to be gone.

Once we were off duty, Allie and I walked around town, trading life stories. We both wore cut-off jeans, black polo shirts, and zip-up hooded sweatshirts—mine from Mansfield, hers a Maine one. The nights in Maine are cool, even in the middle of summer, and you almost always need a cute little hoodie. We looked in all the little shops in the little honky-tonk town. We ate coffee ice cream, giggling "That's my favorite flavor too!" We tried on earrings, laughed at T-shirts with rude sayings, and finally ended up where the boys were, at the arcade.

It's funny to think how quickly you can make a deep emotional connection with someone. Allie and I were best friends for those ten days. After that, we wrote for a couple of months, and then never saw or heard from each other again. I sometimes wonder whatever happened to her. I wonder what she remembers from that summer. I remember her talking about her boyfriend back home—they had done everything but— and her speaking with great longing about giving herself to him when the summer was over. She was clearly way into him. I privately thought that letting him know was giving him way too much power over her.

That's one of the pieces of advice I have said to Bree. "It's important to make sure that any boy you date is just the tiniest bit more into you than you are into him. They need to want you more than you want them. Otherwise, they take advantage."

I confessed my plans to Allie to find the right boy. She didn't say anything about my plan either, but I think her private thoughts were that I was giving some new boy way too much power over me.

Jack Was the One

Before I even knew his name, I knew he was the one. I chose Jack as the one to help divest me of my virginity even before he turned around to notice me. He was completely engrossed in a game of Tetris, so I had a chance to study him. He had nearly chin-length blond hair; he was thin with long, wiry arms. I liked the way his arm muscles popped as he pushed buttons on the game. He had a very intense look about him when he played. Brows furrowed, eyes locked on the screen. Total focus. Later that week I came to rue that focus and his desire to have his name in the top slot in every game in Durland's Arcade. I wanted to be outside in the sun and fresh air. He wanted me to stand there and watch him play. So unfun. I could pretend to be Supportive Girl for a couple of hours, but I made excuses to meet Allie whenever I could.

Before all that though, all that mattered to me was that he was really, really cute. He looked like he could have been the preppy younger brother of the guys in Lynyrd Skynyrd. He must have won his game, because he looked quite pleased when he straightened up from his video game crouch. I was happy to see he was very tall. I've always been a fan of tall guys. He was wearing a battered white popped-collar alligator shirt, a pair of equally battered Nantucket Reds, and docksiders. His preppy signifiers called out to me, as mine must have to him, with our matching sailor bracelets and casual airs. He hooked his thumbs into his belt loops. I noticed a Deerfield key ring attached to one loop.

"Szup?" he said in Allie's and my direction. We locked eyes. He smiled. Nice teeth.

"Nada," I replied. "We were just watching you play. You look like you know what you're doing at ... what's that game called? It looks cool." This said winningly despite the fact that the top of the stupid machine said TETRIS, and as a pinball girl, I despised video games. As I spoke, I engaged in not only the required combination hair-flip/giggle gambit, but also my very own signature move of staring straight at him for a moment, breaking gaze to look demurely at the floor, and then sweeping my eyes back up to his as if I was being pulled toward him. Turns boys to mush every time.

Jack responded as I hoped he would, asking if he could join us for a walk down on the beach. We chattered away, and I soon found out he was about to be a senior at Deerfield. Perfect—a well-respected school, not in our division so our teams would never play each other in sports. He had everything I was looking for. He didn't know anyone else at Mansfield. I didn't know anyone else at Deerfield. My instincts were right on. Jack was exactly the boy I needed to meet on this trip.

July 3rd

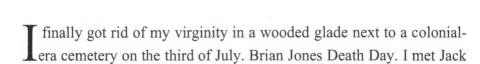

I finally got rid of my virginity in a wooded glade next to a colonial-era cemetery on the third of July. Brian Jones Death Day. I met Jack on the beach that night wearing all white to set off my tan. We both knew why we were there.

We'd tried to have sex the night before, but Jack wasn't prepared with condoms, and by the time we'd figured that out, all the convenience stores were closed. He said he thought I might have them with me. I suppose that should have been a big clue that he wasn't as experienced at this as I thought he was. He tried, although not very hard, to convince me we should do it anyway, but there was no way. That was well past my threshold for risk. I wanted it over with, but I wasn't going looking for that kind of trouble.

So, on the night of Brian Jones Death Day, we were both fully aware of where this was heading, even though we both pretended to be a bit surprised that our clothing was actually coming off. My original idea was that the Fourth of July would have been perfect. Fireworks literally bursting overhead for my first time seemed kind of cool to me. But the timing didn't work out that way. Jack had a family event he wouldn't be able to get excused from and was going home on the fifth. Tonight was our chance. I thought about Brian the whole time I was waiting for it to be over.

Now, of course, I know that Jack didn't know what he was doing any more than I did. At the time, he seemed like a very sophisticated older man, even if he was utterly befuddled when confronted by a front-clasp bra. He was already seventeen and certainly at least implied that this wasn't his first rodeo. Even then though, in my state of innocence, it didn't seem like he knew quite what to do or how to do it. We were both obviously really nervous; the joint we smoked kept getting stuck on my lip it was so dry, and his hands were a little shaky when he passed it to me.

Jack and I walked arm in arm up the path from the beach, held hands to cut through the cemetery, made it to the glade, spread out our beach blanket, and smoked a big fat doobie. Even though this was what I wanted, I was still jittery as all hell. *What if it hurts? What if my mom knows? What if she can tell when I get home?*

Jack pulled a small bottle of Southern Comfort out of his jeans pocket and offered me that as well, but I declined. Barfing would definitely ruin the mood. I remember his unsteady hand as he smoothed out the blanket and leaned over to start kissing me. His breath smelled like Southern Comfort and cigarettes, a sweetly smoky combination I really liked. Soon we were lying on the blanket and his lips were going down my neck while his hands went up my shirt. When I got dressed that night, I thought the front-clasp bra would make things easier, make it so I wouldn't have to take my shirt off and expose my whole back to the voracious Maine mosquitoes. But since Jack didn't seem to know what to do when he didn't find the clasp where he thought it would be, I had to untangle myself from his arms and sit up to unhook it myself. Once my boobs were free, his hands were all over them, twisting nipples right and left and generally acting like they were knobs on a TV set. It seemed sort of rude to yelp, but a couple might have escaped me. I was kind of relieved when his hands went down to unzip my jeans.

The zipper noise sounded super loud and startled me a bit. I looked around to make sure no one was anywhere near our hideaway. No one appeared. Jack's fingers poked around inside the front of my underwear for a couple of minutes before he decided I was good and ready and our pants should come off. He pulled mine off first. His followed pretty quickly. I was so glad it was dark, with only a little bit of moonlight shining through the trees. I didn't want to touch his thing, and I really didn't want to look at it. Or him. I was so glad that keeping my eyes closed seemed appropriate to the situation. But there I was. Too late to back out now. He took my hand and guided it to his penis. I wasn't sure what I was supposed to do with it. Fortunately, I only had to keep my hand on there a second or two while he opened up the Trojan wrapper. He rolled the condom on, rolled on top of me, and stuck it in. *Ouch, that did hurt.* Two or maybe three thrusts later, it was all over. Then we were pulling our jeans back on and getting ready to walk back home in time for curfew. I didn't feel like I wanted to look him in the eye. I was afraid he'd see I was disappointed and feel bad. We held hands on the way back to my cottage, and he kissed me goodbye with a little too much tongue. I kept trying to think about Brian and dedicating this to him on our day.

Laurie met me at the door. It seemed to me that she eyed me suspiciously, but she didn't say anything. I was careful to stash my bloodstained underwear in the back of my drawer so I could save it to put it in the wash next time I got my period. I did the same thing with it when I got home, so my mom would never notice anything strange about the laundry. My only journal entry for that night was "Is that what everyone has been raving about all these years?" Turns out no, he just wasn't doing it very well.

But if it wasn't good, at least it was over. Now I didn't have to worry about showing up at college as a virgin. The best I can say for my first experience is that at least it was over quickly. That, and no one would ever have to know until I wanted them to know.

I called Dots the next day. She was thrilled for me and also a little jealous, even though I told her it wasn't all that great. Didn't matter, she slept with her boyfriend that night. She couldn't let me get too far ahead.

Jack had a family thing on the Fourth and he was headed home the following day, so we didn't get the chance to see each other for long before he went home. That was fine with me; I was looking forward to him leaving. It seemed almost embarrassing to be near him somehow, now. He kept telling me he'd call me as soon as he got home. I knew he would. As a matter of fact, he wouldn't stop calling. He was like a puppy with a new squeaky toy. He called me nearly every night for the first semester of senior year. It was somewhere between flattering and stalkerish.

Jack and I went out once more over Christmas vacation the next December. He picked me up at home in his dad's car, wearing a button-down and a tie. My parents were quite impressed, even if my mom did still call him part of the Hitler Youth Brigade. At least he was polite. We went to the Victoria Station steak house at the mall. Then we went back to his car, and he tried to take off my clothes. Turns out he just wanted to have sex with me again. Going out to a restaurant held no appeal for him. For me it was just the opposite. I told him I'd rather not. Disappointed, he drove me home, and that was the last time I saw or heard from him.

I never did tell anyone at Mansfield except Dots. And of course, the news never leaked. Dots would cut off her Belgian loafer-shod feet rather than betray me. Even though by our senior year there were more than just a few girls who weren't virgins, I still didn't want to be lumped in with them. It was enough that I knew. I was ready to move on to the next phase of my life. I didn't need to take Mansfield with me.

Senior Year

September 14, 1982

We were just a few days into senior year when Derek and I got into a huge fight. It was a Tuesday evening after classes and sports, but September, so still daylight. We were at the Gazebo. I was a little stoned, but Derek was massively way drunk and almost incoherent.

I remember telling him I thought that maybe he shouldn't drink any more that night. I remember saying it wasn't safe to have a bottle out here in the open like that. The Hulk could materialize out of anywhere. I don't remember it clearly, but I think I may have even tried to take the bottle away from him to hide it. I wasn't going to drink it. I just wanted to make sure he didn't get into trouble. My memory is a little fuzzy, but then I can hear him calling me a cunt, telling me to "Let go!" and then his hand flying up and him hitting me. Derek really hit me. He didn't threaten to hit me or pretend to slap me. It was a hard backhanded smack across my face. He hit me. His hand was bigger than my whole face and he hit me.

I had never been hit before. I don't think my parents ever even spanked me. It hurt! My cheekbone felt cold, then my whole face felt hot, then I was cold all over and wanted to throw up. My cheek stung, and I could taste blood in my mouth. I think I was in shock. I think Derek was too. I started crying, and then he was crying, and I think we both knew that it really was the end. There was no excuse that he could come up with for this. It was over. Finally, Derek + Kat was really, truly over.

I remember him sobbing and telling me he was sorry, saying he never meant to hurt me. He would go run to the nurse and get an ice pack. He would make it up to me. Nothing like that would ever happen again. He didn't mean it. It was a reflex, an accident. I can still hear him—he didn't know what made him do it. It would never happen again. He was so sorry.

But there was no taking that back. It wasn't a punch. He never beat me or anything like that. He didn't keep hitting. He only hit me once. But once was enough. We were done. I was done. We finally found out what it would take for me to break up with Derek Wilkeson. I covered the bruise on my cheek with makeup until it faded. I think my heart stayed cracked forever after.

After that night, senior year just sort of happened to me. Like the reverse of *The Wizard of Oz*, all the bright colors were gone out of my world. I went through the motions. Like I said to Bree, it was just school. We did our homework, we played sports. College applications took up the first half of the year. Waiting, the middle part. Parties were all we had time for once the acceptances came in.

Derek and I still saw each other around. Mansfield is a small school and with only three hundred kids, we couldn't help it. We moved on to hang out with slightly different crowds, his ever druggier and darker. The heroin kids. I spent more time with the theater and music kids. We were still wasted most of the time, but benignly, mostly on pot, occasionally some shrooms, but nothing crazy.

Once or twice, Derek and I accidentally caught each other's eyes and forgot for a moment how we were with each other now and smiled. Then

I'd remember and pull down my mental gates. I never sat next to him in a class or got closer than arm's length away. I didn't trust him. Also, mostly I didn't trust me. I knew I had excused almost anything Derek did before, and I was afraid I would again if I let myself get close to him.

I wasn't about to let my life follow that ugly path. I controlled what I could control, and so if I couldn't control my own feelings when I saw him, then I just wouldn't let myself be near enough for him to realize what I was feeling and let him pounce on my weakness for him. I could control what he could see about me. I was an actress. A good one. I could act like I was over him. I kept one of my friends by my side if I was anywhere outside of class where he was likely to be. I knew that I could never, ever again let myself be caught alone anywhere where Derek was. I knew he'd try to talk to me. I knew I couldn't be trusted if he did.

Instead, I acted like everything in my life was perfect and exactly the way I wanted it. As I have done ever since. There are some life lessons I don't ever seem to learn.

The New Girlfriend

Turns out maybe I didn't have to worry so much about us being alone together ever again. Amy Avalon started at Mansfield the week after Derek and I broke up. I remember the day she got there with perfect clarity, because I swear, she showed up and I physically felt the connection between Derek and me snap. Derek saw Amy and resonated with the kind of energy that had been previously reserved only for me. Like Derek, Amy was a transfer, a boarder, and a barely functioning alcoholic. Unlike Derek, she was a work-study (read: charity-case) student. Amy had cascading copper curls, pretty blue eyes, and a spectacular tennis game, which is what got her into Mansfield. Amy did everything Derek told her to. Amy was everything that I was not. Tall, athletic, docile. They made a big show all over campus of falling in love, and soon every time I saw them, my heart was ripped out of my chest anew.

I was a walking Phil Collins song, "Take a Look at Me Now," barely able to hold it together when they were around, arms entwined, or hanging out in the hallways, Derek's hand in her back pocket. Just like we had been. Every time I saw him lift her hair to kiss her neck, it was like a screwdriver being plunged into my heart and rotated. It was stupid that I thought that he would only ever do that to me. But ye gods did that hurt. It was almost more than I could take.

In some ways it made it easier. At least once Amy got there it didn't matter if I would have taken him back. Now he didn't want me. I can't say I took much comfort in that. Or in the other boys I dated senior year. Mostly I just couldn't wait to leave Mansfield and get on with my life.

Unlike Ashley, Amy was never mean to me. Amy was never mean to anyone. Amy was very sweet and very amenable to everyone, never raised her voice or argued. Mostly, Amy was just absent. Or more accurately, there but not there—a pretty, silent, wispy ghost. She was like air. I couldn't even hate her. Beautiful girl, totally wrecked all the time, but our tennis team needed her.

Who knows how they discovered she was a natural? The school legend said that she was playing on some local small-town Pennsylvania court one day, with a racket she got at Goodwill, and was spotted by some sort of scout. From there she won, and then lost, a scholarship to one of the finest New England prep schools. She ended up being recruited to Mansfield after being asked to leave the other school her first week, for violating the honor code. I heard she was caught with a water bottle filled with booze in her dorm room. I guess we really needed to shore up our girls' tennis program more than we worried about having yet another waste product on campus.

Amy seemed to love vodka and Derek in equal measure. She was so thin you could almost see her bones. I think most of her calories came from booze. I don't think I ever saw her eat a single bite of food, and I would spy on her whenever I thought I could without giving myself away. I'd pretend to be spacing out, looking out a window or at something just beyond her, underneath my bangs, but really, I was studying her every move. I was trying to figure out what she had that I was missing. I was trying to figure out how she broke Derek away from me. Even though I was the one who broke up with him, and even though

I certainly didn't want him back, I still wanted him to feel attached to me. He was like a phantom limb now.

Other Mansfield kids had different reasons for trying to ferret out the great mystery that was Amy Avalon. One of the epic questions of senior year was how Amy, without any money, never ran dry in the great New Hampshire booze desert. No one knew how she did it, but she kept the supply lines open. There were rumors about a coach, but I find that hard to believe. The school might have looked away, but they wouldn't have helped an obviously troubled student get booze. As far as I know, no one ever figured out how she did it.

I think of Amy as a wraith, she was just about translucent in her pain and her need. She and Derek deserved each other, complemented each other, and encouraged each other. I look back now and thank all the high school gods and goddesses that Amy came along when she did. Who knows what I might have done otherwise. For all the pain he and Amy being together caused me, I was better off. I have always been lucky like that.

I consoled myself by thinking that maybe that was the real reason Derek clung to Amy. Maybe it was so there was no way he could hurt me again. Maybe in his way, he was protecting me. Maybe it was his way of keeping me safe. I tell myself it's the only thing that makes any sense, on those rare occasions that I ever think about him at all.

Connecticut/Massachusetts Border

One Week Ago

Bree and I get to the border. Bree is bouncing up and down in her seat, doing her happy car dance. We point to the giant turkey on the sign and intone "Massachusetts Welcomes You" in voices filled with glee. I can see a great big grin spread across her face and hear her say, with the kind of delight she used to be able to muster up regularly, "Hey Mom. I gotta pee. You know who has really nice bathrooms?"

We have been doing this same shtick since she was old enough to talk, so I'm thrilled to play along. "No, baby. Who?"

"Why, I believe Aunt Lillie's Pie Plate is just off the next exit here. And some say Aunt Lillie has the cleanest restrooms in all of Massachusetts."

"Wow, really? Well, I don't know that I've ever heard that before. Maybe we should just stop there and see for ourselves. I know I could use a little break. Stretch my legs a bit."

"Maybe. Hmm …" She brings her hand up to her chin in mock thought. "And you know, while we're there, I hear Aunt Lillie's apple crumb is marvelous."

Bree draws out the word *marvelous* like a bad Katherine Hepburn imitator, and I'm biting the inside of my cheek so I don't crack up and lose this moment with her. When I regain control, I say, "Really? Well, I must admit that I'm rather partial to her strawberry-rhubarb myself." By now, the car is halfway down the off-ramp, and we're both looking for the first glimpse of the Aunt Lillie's sign above the scrubby pines off the highway. Her bright pink glowing beacon to the weary traveler. As soon as we near the parking lot, Bree opens the window to try and get a whiff of fresh pies baking. She looks like our old golden retriever Mojo with her head halfway out the window. My heart is full to near bursting at how adorable she is.

We pull into a parking spot and sit down at a table by the window. I try to not think about what my encroaching wrinkles look like under the unforgiving fluorescent lights of Aunt Lillie's. Or what a slice of pie will do to my calorie count for today, especially after sitting in a car all day. Aunt Lillie is clearly not my buddy. Bree slides across the hard plastic bench with gusto—so thrilled to be here she nearly falls into the open space between the booth and the window. I can't help but see my happy little girl again and I laugh.

"Let's get a sampler! C'mon, Mom, you barely ate any lunch. Share it with me, Mom. Please, please, please, Mummy. Mummy, please!" Begging always works, even though I tell her it doesn't.

At least I don't have to worry about her eating. We're not one of those horrible skinny-mother/fat-daughter pairs that are so common in our milieu. It breaks my heart to see those chubby girls looking at their lineless, hyper-toned, hyper-blond mothers with a mixture of fear and longing. I always want to say "Have a burger for Chrissakes" to those moms. "Your job is to take care of her and let her feel good about herself.

So eat something, and then send the poor kid to fat camp. It isn't a competition between you two. She gets to be pretty too."

In the fog of sugar aftermath—I had a bite or two of each of the three small slices—Bree keeps at me with questions I seriously consider answering, at least semi-truthfully. If only I can figure out how. She sticks her fork into the apple crumb and asks, "OK, so when you were at Mansfield, was there any boy who broke your heart? Any boy whose heart you broke? Tell me anything, Mom. C'mon, I know you dated in school. Can you pick any three guys you went out with and tell me anything you remember?"

I feel like she's got me cornered. If I don't answer her questions correctly, in a way that sates her curiosity, she'll continue to dig. I feel like digging could prove to be disastrous, so I need to choose these stories well to placate her.

It's a little like when she was young and became convinced by a particularly evil-looking letter opener of mine that I was secretly a trained assassin/secret agent who had given all that up to be a mom in the suburbs. She invented all sorts of stories about my past, and I'd go along but pretend she had it all wrong. Of course, I pretended she was wrong in a way that convinced her she was right. It's one of my best acting games, and we had many hours of fun with it.

I suppose she invented glamorous stories about me because it was fun to imagine this tiny little housewife dealing in danger. But also because she didn't really know me, any more than I knew my mother. We never really know anyone else. We just see the little bits they are willing to let on to us.

The stories she was asking for now were more important. Not a bit of silly, fun spy story, but a comprehensive and believable narrative that would keep her from following any further along the fault lines of my prep school life. I was going to need to summon up all my semi-atrophied acting talent to weave a story that was complete enough to satisfy her yet also completely innocuous.

I don't trust myself to even say Derek's name to her. I'm afraid my voice will give something away. But I can tell her about Zeke, really Xerxes, the Persian boy I dated to drive my mother out of her mind. He was absolutely drop-dead gorgeous, with thick black hair and dark almond-shaped eyes, but the driving-my-mother-crazy part was a terrific bonus.

Zeke gave me a gold necklace that had a large disk pendant with Arabic writing on it. My mother threw about the biggest fit I ever saw her have when I came home with that one. She made me give it back. He and I didn't go out for long. He was super cute, but I think his mother was as unhappy about him dating a nice Jewish girl as mine was with me dating a Muslim boy. His mother had a bit more influence. Bree loves to hear about how bad I was and what all I put my mom through. The Zeke story is a great one, with only a little kissing and virtually no drugs. There's no heartbreak there. We had a little bit of fun together, but that was it.

Then I decide I will tell Bree something about Skeet, the boy whose heart I broke. I haven't thought about what I did to Skeet in a long time. It takes me a few minutes to organize my thoughts and figure out which parts I can tell. I think about Skeet while I talk about Zeke. Skeet was the last boy I dated at Mansfield. I lost track of him after he left school. He didn't graduate with us, and he never sends anything in for Class Notes. I really hope that he is OK now.

Senior Year

Late October

After Derek and I broke up for good, and after I scandalized my family by dating a Muslim, I scandalized the entire school by dating a junior. I was tired of trying out Nice Jewish Boys, plus I think I might have actually run out of them by then. It was time for something new. Because of my late birth date and the propensity even then for parents to hold back their boys, I was younger than at least half of the boys in the junior class. So it wasn't like I was dating someone younger than me or anything.

Scoggins Kuntz Mackenzie was never called anything but Skeet by anyone because, well, at least in part, because his parents had named him Scoggins Kuntz. Even the elderly wildcatting relatives for whom he was named weren't thrilled to be memorialized in that way. His grandparents didn't understand why his loco parents insisted on using their family names as Skeet's Christian name. Fortunately, the boy found his calling — and nickname — at a young age as a clay pigeon shooting marksman. He was Skeet thereafter.

Skeet was six months older than I was, even though he was a year behind in school. He was the scion of not one but two Oklahoma oil families. Hence the names, making his lineage unmistakable, I'm told, to the sort of people who knew about those things. Even before we started dating, we were super good friends and hung out together all the time. He was sweet and funny, and absolutely beautiful. He had sheepdog-shaggy blond hair and these dark-brown "take me home" pound-puppy-dog eyes. He had the longest, most sweeping, dark eyelashes I had ever seen. They curled up at the ends like his eyes were smiling. He stood just a bit under six feet tall and was the lead guitarist in one of Mansfield's premier new wave bands, The Sandinistas. Within a week of my breakup with Zeke, Skeet and I were spending all our time together. By the first time we kissed, at seven fifteen, before morning assembly, in the little smoking area by the headmaster's house, our relationship seemed inevitable.

Despite all of his coolness and the easily verifiable fact by when his birthday was that he was older than me, Ashley gave me all kinds of crap for "cradle robbing." She was the prime instigator pushing the story of my pathetic behavior out into the wider community. Even after Derek and I were through, Ashley's hatred of me didn't abate.

Ashley's opinion, stated loudly and with great enthusiasm in the girls' locker room, was that obviously I couldn't get any of the senior boys to go out with me, so I had to move down the food chain. Everyone knew that she was just mad because Derek didn't go running into her open arms and always-open legs after we broke up. My opinion, stated equally loudly and with equal vigor, was "At least he had been willing to be seen with me in public."

I think it's possible that the other girls might have had to physically separate us that time. Normally, I'm not one to go after someone with my tiny little fists, but there are times when it's the only option. I might have been a lot smaller than Ashley, but I could kick her ass given the right motivation. And her very existence was enough to be the right motivation. I remember being lifted off the floor from behind, I think by Stupid Jennifer, while I was trying to take a swing at Ashley. Cooler heads kept us more than arm's length apart, and we left the locker room out of two different doors, swearing at each other but without any outward scars. I should have broken free and knocked out some of those weirdly perfect teeth.

Sweet and kind as Skeet was, his family life was complicated, even by our ship-the-kids-off-to-boarding-school eighties standards. There was one girl at Mansfield who had four stepmoms and five stepdads and half siblings all over the place. Zibby's family tree project went on for five pages, and that only covered her closest relatives, but even she conceded Skeet's family made hers look like amateurs.

The way he told it, his mom was the perfect oil heiress, at least until she turned twenty-four or so. She had the requisite embarrassment of beauty queen crowns lining her bedroom wall. Each one of them was a step, beginning with her coronation as Miss Something-or-other-county-in-the-middle-of-nowhere and leading all the way up to her highest triumph as Miss Oklahoma. Sadly, she was robbed of the Miss America crown by some bimbo from Alabama. After that disappointment, she promptly retired from the circuit in order to marry the oil baronet next door; Skeet's dad had been her intended since they were infants. Their union brought about a merger of their parents' companies and Skeet as their only child.

When Skeet was almost three, his mom went completely crazy by Oklahoma standards, dumped her husband, left her perfect home and her perfect life, and moved out to San Francisco to smoke dope and live in a commune. She got a court in California to award her full custody. At the same time, Skeet's dad got a court in Oklahoma to award him full custody. As a very young child, Skeet was kidnapped by each of his parents. More than once. Eventually, Skeet's dad was onto another former-beauty-queen wife and brood, and allowed his ex-wife to have primary custody. His dad meant well. He was involved in Skeet's life. He paid for Skeet's schooling, shooting, and travel, and he saw Skeet every summer and on alternating long school holidays, but he no longer seemed to feel the need to hire men to shove Skeet into a waiting black Town Car to be whisked off to an airport and returned to the Promised Land.

Among the further complications of Skeet's story is that his maternal grandparents agreed that his mom was an unfit parent, simply for preferring the California hippie life to living on a nearby ranch. They sided with his dad and cut his mom off without a penny, thinking this would bring her to her senses and, therefore, home. Didn't work. She didn't want their filthy, capitalist pig, oily cash anyway. At least not until the mid-seventies, when she launched what went on to become the first of the very successful hippie-luxe clothing lines. By then, the whole situation was far less contentious, and she accepted a loan from her parents, which she was able to return with interest when the company took off. Until then, though, Skeet's childhood was spent in great comfort and riches whenever he saw his dad or either set of grandparents, but at home, he lived in not-quite-genteel poverty. He had his choice of horses to ride at his dad's houses. At home with his mom, they ate government cheese.

It didn't matter whether he was living in comfort or need though, both of his parents tried to make him feel guilty for enjoying being with the other. By the time he got to Mansfield, he was kind of a mess. Skeet was yet one more psychologically fragile boy I was drawn to.

Skeet and I dated for almost the whole rest of senior year. He was such a good human and was the only other person at Mansfield besides

Dots I came close to confessing my summer secret to. But I still didn't want to deal with those complications. Although I really liked him and had a great time kissing him for hours on end, I didn't want to have sex with him. I didn't feel anything resembling lust. I'm not sure I've ever felt great lust for anyone but Derek. The hubby and I have fun, of course; our sex life is great, but having a baby does kind of put a bit of a spanner in the works. Everyone knows that. When we were first married, I was too overwhelmed over Bree to have time for lust.

Telling Skeet, though, was too complicated for me to want to deal with. While it was possible for a boy to understand the idea of a girl holding on to her virginity, they were completely flummoxed by the idea that a girl might have once had sex, then decided not to for a while, especially when this time the girl was being presented with the opportunity to have sex with them. It was easier to let him think I was still dragging around the ball and chain of virginity than to explain my feelings. I never lied to him, I just let him believe I was a virgin much the same way I let Bree believe I was a trained assassin—by denying it in such a way that implied it was true.

I know Skeet found it so easy to believe I was still a virgin because he thought I was holding out for Derek and me to eventually get back together and that I was still waiting to finally lose it to him. That would be dumb, it was never going to happen. Derek and Amy were rock-solid. But I know that's what Skeet thought. Like I was secretly waiting for Derek to ride in, sweep me off my feet, and ravish me. That wasn't it at all. I only had a little bit of senior year left, and then I'd be able to reinvent myself in any way I wanted. Why would I let these people define who I was for my last bit of time here?

People's perceptions are often so much more important than reality. The secret to getting what you want is to act like you already have it.

Want to be popular? Behave as if you already are. Want everyone to think you're rich or smart? Use a few small signifiers. Show the world you already are whatever it is you want to be. Act as if you know they believe it, and soon enough everyone will. Confidence comes from acting confident. "Fake it till you make it" works.

I wouldn't have done it if I had known what the consequences would be, but I crushed Skeet. We were together from right after Zeke and I broke up until a couple of weeks before the prom, long enough to have a six-month anniversary. But for the record, Skeet broke up with me.

And he did it right before prom. Which we weren't going to go to anyway, because only geeks went to school-sanctioned and chaperoned proms. We were going to go to the alterna-prom at Willie Glimmerglass's barn in town that night, but still, I needed a date. It was humiliating to be a senior girl all alone at such an important event.

Skeet said he was breaking up with me because he knew I was still mooning over Derek. He was sick of being a stand-in love. He was sick of waiting for me to realize he was the better man. Even as love-wronged teenage boys go, Skeet was being a bit of a fucking drama queen about the whole thing.

I could not believe he was breaking up with me right before prom! I didn't care what he was sick of. He was supposed to be my boyfriend, and I was supposed to have a date for the party. So now I was going to have to either find a date fast or go to the alterna-prom alone? How could that possibly be? How could he do that to me?

I think he thought that by starting all that drama, he could get me to tell him he was wrong. But that backfired. Because I was too pissed off about having to find another date super pronto to care about what he thought. The only thing that was worse than thinking I might have to go alone and deal with the gossip and whispers and pitying looks was knowing that Derek and Amy would definitely be there. I could just see how happy my humiliation would make Ashley. I knew she was going with David Fischer, who had finally gotten his braces off. He must have needed to get laid really badly to be willing to take Ashley somewhere in public. Gross.

I was seething mad at Skeet for leaving me in the lurch, and I wanted revenge.

This coincided with me being in a mean-girl phase. Mean isn't one of my natural attributes. I wanted to change that. I wanted to be ruthless, feared, and admired. I wanted to be more Alexis than Krystle. I wanted to be able to be as awful as Ashley.

Since Dots was always happy to be Rosencrantz to my Guildenstern, we conspired to stage a dramatic fight right in front of Skeet's math class. We waited for the bells to stop, then hit the hallway stage. Dots started with her lines.

"Oh my god, I can't believe you! You are such a tramp. No wonder he dumped you! I can't even be friends with you anymore. I can't believe you were still seeing him the whole time you guys were together! He's a good guy. He doesn't deserve that. You are such a toxic bitch!"

Dots even managed to look at Skeet as if she was surprised that he was there when he came out of class. Maybe she should have been the actress and I should have gone to law school. With any luck, this little scene might also make Amy give Derek the hairy eyeball and push a little wedge between them as well. There was no uncertainty as to who was involved; even the teachers were able to name the unnamed players in this production.

I remember seeing Skeet rush off, looking as though he'd been punched in the stomach. I tried really hard not to feel any sympathy for him. I was a mean girl, with a hard shell, and I had no room for feelings.

"Good," I said to Dots. "Serves him right for breaking up with me and messing up my life."

I was so wrong.

That weekend, Skeet's roommate walked in on Skeet about to hang himself in their room. I heard the Hulk ran in and saved him. I never saw or spoke to him again. I never found out what happened to him next. I tried to ask a couple of times, but no one would ever tell me anything. It was like once he was gone, we weren't allowed to mention him again. I still feel bad. I feel like I should find him and apologize. Sometimes I start to look him up to do exactly that, but I'm so embarrassed by my behavior, I wouldn't even know how to start apologizing.

I know if I really wanted to, I could find him through the alumni office. I think about it sometimes, but then something else always comes up, and I get too busy, and I forget. And what if something bad happened to him after Mansfield? I know I should finally really try to get in touch, but it's complicated.

Of course, I know that it wasn't just my stunt that made Skeet try to kill himself. He had lots of other problems. But I sure didn't make his life any better. That performance was the end of my very short career as a mean girl, out to hurt people just because I could.

* * *

I can tell Bree about Skeet as a tale of unintended consequences, to demonstrate what can happen when you go against your basic nature. Her basic nature is so very lovely. Before she is off without me, maybe I should tell her that reinvention is all well and good, but you shouldn't try to go against your essential self. That never goes well.

Bree and I get into the car, all full of pie and happy for the beautiful day. After starting the car and turning down the radio, we sit in the parking lot while I tell Bree nearly the whole story of Skeet, leaving out the virginity part and anything but a quick mention of Derek—no name, just "some other guy I kind of dated." Bree seems so astonished that I am confiding in her that she is rendered momentarily speechless, and I get a momentary break. I stomp on the brake and look behind me to make sure no one is walking past or backing up, before I put the car into reverse.

But before I can even back the car out of the parking spot, Bree starts asking some even worse questions, and I have to throw it into park again.

"Mom, stop tap dancing around things. I know you're hiding something from me, you put that blank nothing-to-see-here look on your face, you purse your lips together hard, and you start doing that twirly "I don't want to deal with this" thing with your fingers whenever Daddy calls. Is something happening with you guys?"

I can't escape, my throat tightens, my fear is real, I can feel the shallow breathing start, and I will myself to yoga-breathe. I can't believe she knows. I have been so careful. I feel like I must be bright red and sweaty. What the fuck do I say now?

"Nothing is happening, sweetie. Grown-ups sometimes have grown-up issues, baby girl. Everything will be fine."

"Bullshit, Mom, everything isn't fine. Is that why you're sending me away?"

"I'm not sending you away, Daddy is," I snap at her. *Shit, that didn't come out right.*

I take a deep breath and try to start again, more calmly. "Don't be silly, darling. We aren't sending you away. It has always been the plan that you would go to Mansfield, just like everyone else in the family. We've talked about this about a million times. You said you wanted to go. If you don't want to, fine, I'll turn the car around, and I will be happy to take you right back home. Mansfield can keep the fees as this year's donation. Daddy and I have had our disagreements about this. I would be thrilled to have you stay at home with us a little longer. Daddy is a little more keen than I on you following the family path right this minute, so you will be a four-year senior. But if you don't want to go or don't want to go yet, that is completely fine. You can be home another year and then we can reassess."

"And sit at home watching you two molder? I do have eyes, Mom. I know you think I'm just a baby, but I'm not. I know you guys hate each other. I'd rather be stuck in the wilderness than be home with you two pretending."

"We most certainly do not hate each other, young lady."

"You do a damn good impression of it then."

"Language, Bree! Look, Daddy and I have our own things to talk about, but we both love you."

"Oh great, here comes the 'we'll always be a family and always love and take care of you no matter what happens between us' speech. Spare me, Mother. I know how it goes. All my friends have heard it and warned me about it. Then Daddy marries a twenty-five-year-old and I get to babysit the new batch of brats."

"This isn't about you!" I scream at her. *What the hell is the matter with me?* I'm shocked at myself. Or my lack of self. This isn't like me. I am the one who always makes sure everything is about her. She seems shaken by my words.

I take a breath and try to salvage this conversation. "I am very sorry I overreacted and yelled at you, Bree. Daddy and I will be fine. We'll be up together to visit you for Parents' Weekend." I vow to kill him with my own two bare hands if he doesn't make it for Parents' Weekend. "You will be fine at Mansfield. You'll love it. They already love you. I am being selfish about you leaving home because I will miss you so much. Now can we please stop all this miserable nonsense? Isn't there anything pleasant you want to talk about? Anything happy?"

"Sure, you want to tell me now what you were really like in school? I bet you weren't nearly as good as you pretend to be."

I'm trying as best as I can to hold it together, but I can't help but glare at her while I say as evenly as I can, "You cannot possibly still be on about that, young lady." I blow my bangs out of my face by exhaling hard over my upper lip. Then I stomp hard on the brake, throw the car into reverse, and head back to the road. This road trip is starting to seem endless. Why did I think this would be fun? Why did I think telling her anything about my past was a good idea?

May, Senior Year

The weeks between the Glimmerglass alterna-prom and graduation run together. The weather was gorgeous, the days were long and warm. We had all gotten into college. Sure, some of us were happier about where we'd be in the fall than others. But the raison d'être for prep school is to get kids into college, and we were all in somewhere. Even with the pressures of exams, they weren't really all that tough on the seniors. We were mentally done with school, even if we weren't actually. And there was so much fun stuff to do before we left. We had Senior Skip Day, another party at the Glimmerglass barn—those parents were saints—and then Thoreau Day, when the whole school got on buses to go to Walden Pond and the kids all got high in the woods while we were supposed to be communing with nature. Which we were actually doing, just while very, very, very stoned.

Even while enjoying all the festivities Mansfield had to offer, I was already in New York City in my head. I had gotten into NYU School of the Arts to study drama. I'd stuck to my plan for my future, no matter what my mother said, and was going to concentrate on acting rather than getting a history degree and going straight to law school, which I'm sure she assumed would be filled with a good selection of Nice Jewish Boys for me to settle down with. I could always go to law school in a few years if the acting thing didn't pan out. At least it comforted my mother no end to think that I'd be in a whole city filled with Nice Jewish Boys.

Exams were easy. Graduation week was nothing but graduation run-throughs and parties. Run-throughs were really tough, because somehow I got stuck walking down the long carpeted aisle last and I was paired with Derek. Don't tell me the universe doesn't have a sick sense of humor. It was made worse by Derek trying to make small talk with me. "Hey, Kat-Kat, you think Chrome Dome is going to powder his head for graduation? Otherwise, the glare might kill us." "Kat-Kat, how about those Sox? This might be the year." I refused to even look at him. I was not about to get tripped up by that smile when I was almost out of here and far away from these people for good. I kept my eyes firmly on the bright blue carpet. The Mansfield logo embossed throughout made for a hideous rug but a great distraction. I concentrated on walking slowly — heel, toe, stop, heel, toe, stop — finding my seat, and not looking into those blue eyes that I feared could still knock all the sense right out of my head. Derek was some sort of reverse Medusa, making me melt instead of turning me to stone.

I don't know why he kept trying to talk to me. He was happy with Amy. I was happy to be getting the hell out of here and heading off for the bright lights of New York City. What more could he want from me? Would he win some kind of prize if I admitted I still loved him? The only thought that kept running through my head was staring right back at him and saying *Enjoy this, buddy, because this is as close as you'll ever come to walking down an aisle with me.* But I knew he would laugh, and he would know that I was thinking about walking down an aisle with him. So I kept my mouth shut and kept walking, heel, toe, stop, heel, toe, stop.

Honestly, was it really necessary for high school-level graduates to have to do that much rehearsing to walk from the rotunda down a long carpet to sit on some rent-a-chairs under a tent? It was a straight line! According to the music teacher and the guidance counselors, yes, it was imperative that we not mess this up. They kept telling us how important this ceremony was to our parents and that it was our responsibility to make sure it went perfectly. Our parents had paid a lot of money for our education, and this ceremony was their chance to celebrate. Or some such teacher blather. I tuned out that lecture too.

The parties were easier, as well as more fun. As long as I kept away from Derek and Amy, I was fine, even without a boyfriend. I was done with prep school boys. The couple of weeks since Skeet left were the longest I had ever gone at Mansfield without a boyfriend, but I was fine. It was fine. I was so cool I could go to parties alone. And there was no one worth dating here anyway. This place was fished out. I was ready to date men, not boys, anyway. Ashley's dad had accidentally proved that at the cast party for *West Side Story*.

In my defense, I had no idea that the creepy old guy who reeked of Aramis was Ashley's dad. And it certainly wasn't my fault that he was hitting on me at the cast party at the Glimmerglass's barn. I can't believe their parents let them have another party after the mess of the alterna-prom and the one for Senior Skip Day. At least the barn was pretty far from their house and had its own plumbing. Their hayloft was littered with clothing and half-empty cups of beer, and I don't think they ever got the deposit back on the keg the lacrosse players rolled down the hill at the alterna-prom. Willie Glimmerglass was stage manager for all the plays, and he somehow was able to convince his parents that it was all just high-spirited hijinks, and they were the best parents in the world for going along; besides, the theater crowd was different. We all thought they were the nicest/dumbest parents in the world for getting us another keg.

So I didn't know who this creepy man was or why he was there. He just introduced himself as Bob, not Bob Dix, father of demon spawn. Maybe he wore so much cologne to mask the sulfuric family scent. Who knows? And who lets their dad come to a cast party anyway? That was just too bizarre to think of. Creepy Bob kept trying to bring me drinks, even though I told him I didn't really want any, and he kept asking if I wanted any "grass." Gross. I told him I was allergic. When I walked to another part of the barn, he followed me. I could not get away from him. When trying to get me liquored up and stoned didn't work, he asked me about method acting, and what I thought about Brando and Stella Adler. Like, what? He was sitting on the edge of a couch, leaning forward with his legs splayed out, with one hand on the knee of his corduroys and one on his hip while his bad Mr. Brady toupee did a little dance on his head. It was hilariously nauseating.

My making fun of him in the line for the bathroom was totally warranted, no matter what Ashley said. I didn't even know who he was! And I don't know why she let him stay at the party anyway instead of shooing him away once he dropped her off, like any normal person would. Also, there was no way he was hitting on me because I had played Anita as so trampy that he just assumed I was older. Seriously, how would that even make any sense? I was a senior; how much older could I have been? Did he think I was a teacher? I don't think so! What kind of creep hangs out at their kid's cast party trying to give intoxicants to underage girls? Honestly, the whole family is deranged.

Anyway, Bob being Ashley's gross father notwithstanding, older men were clearly interested in me, so I no longer needed to bother dating children. Prep school boys were no longer worth my time. Neither were gross old men with demon children. But college guys would do just fine.

Graduation Day

Graduation Day was a spectacularly beautiful May day, exactly as is decreed. Sometime over the past couple hundred years, some wiseass headmaster issued a proclamation stating that Mansfield Academy's Graduation Day would always be beautiful. The fact that it always happens in late May—which means it's a pretty safe bet for nice weather—helps a lot. Maybe we get some divine intervention as well. Whatever the reason, it almost never rains on us.

My parents dropped me off early, so I could get ready with my friends. They understood that we all wanted to get dressed together in one of the dorms and cry and hug and take pictures and swear we'd write. And on that one day, my usually completely unreasonable and uncool parents were surprisingly cool about driving back and forth to school just so I could be part of the on-campus scene with all my friends.

The morning of graduation I got out of my mom's enormous car at the top of the hill quad drop-off spot for the last time. The background chattering that accompanies any major school event seemed even more pronounced than usual. When I got out of the car, the voices all seemed to stop for a beat. Then they started up again, louder and faster than before. It felt strange, like when you've missed something big that everyone else is already in on. Dots grabbed me by both hands as soon as I got out of the car and made me sit on the bench in front of the rotunda. Graduation wasn't for hours, so we weren't shooed away.

My mom waved as she drove off. "See you soon, Graduate!"

"Kat, did you hear yet? Something horrible has happened. For real." The look in her eyes let me know she was not pulling one of her lame jokes.

"Dots, what? Is it Derek?" I knew it was. It had to be. Nothing else would make her make that face.

"Sorta. It's Amy." Dots sucked in a deep breath. "She's in the hospital."

"What? Why? Did she have to go get her stomach pumped?"

"No. She and Derek got into a huge fight on the way back from the party last night. What I heard was that they both wanted the last bit of the bottle of vodka they brought with. It sounds really bad, Kat. Like her jaw is broken and maybe some other bones. Her face is messed up. Her eye. Maybe more. Rob and Robbie tried to pull him off, but he just kept pummeling her. I just … I … ugh. I wanted to be the one to tell you, Kat. I didn't want you to hear it from just anyone. Oh Kat, I am so sorry."

I tried to make sense of Dot's words, even as I started peppering her with questions. "Where is he? Is he in jail? Did they manage to get him on a plane home instead? Jesus, his dad is going to kill him for fucking this up so close to graduation. Oh my god, I didn't even get to say goodbye. I mean it wasn't good with us, but I thought I'd say bye today. Just bye. Just for old times." I could hear my heart beating in my ears.

"Oh sweetie, I'm so sorry, it gets so much worse." A giant exhale. "Derek is here. He's graduating. His dad was already here, he's staying at the Coach House Inn. I guess Derek told Rob and Robbie to call him last night. Mr. Wilkeson drove Amy to the hospital. No ambulance. No witnesses. They were jumped by townies on the way back, is the official story. Derek, Rob, and Robbie fought them off, but Amy was hurt. Mr. Wilkeson is covering all the hospital bills, and Amy's parents aren't pressing any charges. Since no one is willing to press charges, and no one saw anything, nothing can be proven against Derek. He's graduating. His dad was up with the headmaster and the Hulk all night. Buffy Johnston told me that her mom told her that the family gave some humongo, humongo, humongo donation to the school, and that's why Derek gets to graduate."

This part came out of Dots in one long string of words with almost no breaths in between. It was the verbal equivalent of pulling the Band-Aid off as quickly as she could.

She gave another giant exhale. "I'm so sorry, Kit-Kat. Are you OK? It's gonna be OK. You're going to be OK."

I sat there with my head in my hands thinking I actually might have to throw up. *That could have been me.* "Is she going to be all right?" I managed to say out loud. I was freezing cold, even though the bench was bathed in bright sunlight. I looked down and could see my hands shaking, but I couldn't feel them. I had no idea how I could even stand next to Derek that day. That poor girl. How could he have beaten her so badly that she needed to be hospitalized? Why? How could he do something like that?

I went back to Holden with Dots to put on makeup and try to pretend everything was OK. My shaking hands made eyeliner impossible. So I let Dots do my wings for me, badly, but whatever. I told everyone who asked that I knew nothing more than they did. I tried to make it really clear that I didn't want to know any more, so when they found out any more, they shouldn't come running back to tell me.

No, I didn't want to smoke a joint in the back garden, and no, I didn't want any of the champagne that was being passed around. I just wanted to get the fuck out. I wanted this to be over. That poor girl. At least I had waterproof mascara for today. I could totally justify crying my eyes out. Given that my mom was certain to cry, she'd think I was crying because she was crying.

There was no way my parents would be clued in enough to be part of the crowd gossiping about Derek and Amy. They weren't close enough with the other parents or any of the teachers. They would never hear anything about it. And they wouldn't ask me anyway, even if they did.

Amy never played tennis again. Her vision was permanently damaged. But she did finish Mansfield with a full scholarship and went off to a private college afterward. She's never been back for any school event since she graduated. I heard from someone that she works in finance.

Derek managed to corner me, just as the appointed commencement time finally came. We were all assembled at the back of the hallway leading to the rotunda. Dots had been torn from my side by the programming gods. She had been my protector all day, but once the proceedings started, she had no choice but to be in her place up near the front rather than at the end of the line with the two of us. The other eighty-something kids of our graduating class felt like a wall of people between me and Dots, allowing Derek to capture me.

I was standing near the board, and he put his arms on either side of me just below my shoulder height, trapping me like always, low enough to block my ducking out without bringing everyone's attention to us. He knew that a scene was the last thing I wanted. That's why he did it that way. He'd trapped me like this so many times before. He leaned in slightly, not menacingly, and spoke to me very softly.

"Kat-Kat. I swear to you. It's not what you think. It's not what you heard."

"For Chrissakes Derek, get help. I can't make you better. You can't make you better. That poor girl. Get help." Those were the last words I said to him before we went our separate ways. The music cue started, and he let his arms fall to his sides.

Dorm Hallway, NYU

October

Derek called me the first week in October of my freshman year of college. Pre-cell phones, Mansfield always published a list of everyone's college along with their dorm phone number so we could keep in touch. It's strange for me to think that's one of the things they don't do anymore. They don't have to. Everyone has the same mobile number practically from birth. I stood in my new hallway, smoking butt after butt, hanging on to that old gray pay phone handset, listening to him slur in my ear. It was good to hear his familiar voice. Even after all that went on last spring.

"My dad has something going in New York next month. I can fly in with him on the plane. So easy. It'll be fun. I'll take you to the '21' Club as an early birthday present. We'll show the old farts how to party, Mansfield style. Damn, I miss you Kat-Kat."

"Don't you have school?"

"Nah, I bailed. College just wasn't my bag. Maybe I might try one of the super-crunchy NoCal more fun ones next semester. There is one called Redlands? Redwoods? Something like that ... My dad's setting it up. Meantime, I could come visit. It'd be like the old days, but no dorm masters. It'll be fun. Come on … let me come visit you and take you out."

He went on and on, about how much he missed me and how good we could be together now that we were grown-ups. He could come to school in New York, maybe even NYU if I wanted him to. Later in the call he stopped talking about coming in November and switched to saying that if he could only get his shit together, he'd come back East and look me up. He could fly in anytime I wanted him to. I held on to the handle so tightly the plastic on the receiver got hot. It felt so good to hear him. I could almost see his face while he talked. I missed him so much it was a physical ache. But I held my ground and didn't tell him to come visit. I stuck to what I knew I had to do. I told him the only way he could come see me was if he was clean. I didn't mention Amy or any of our other stuff. I didn't need to. We both knew all our ghosts.

By the time we hung up, I knew it was never going to happen. He was never going to get clean. He was never going to be OK. I finished my cigarette and sat down in the hallway next to the phone, hearing Carole King's song "So Far Away" in my head. Once I had that hard cry out of my system, I went back to my room thinking I'd never hear from him again because I insisted he get his shit together. I shoved down the pain of that thought and went out that night to Heartbreak and the Mudd Club with my roommates. Done.

As it always was with Derek, we were only kind of done. Over the years at NYU and just after, I thought about calling him whenever things weren't going my way. And maybe he thought about me too. Strange things happened once in a while that made me think maybe he was keeping track of me.

I studied acting in London for my junior year abroad program, and one day when I got back to my dorm, I had a message at the front desk saying I had a visitor while I was out. Reception said he was a tall blond American man who said he was visiting England and would stop by again but who didn't want to leave a name. He didn't come back. I didn't need a name, I knew it was Derek.

After college, in various crappy apartments, I got magazines I hadn't ordered delivered to my door, fully paid subscriptions with no gift names. Random ones. *Country Living*? *People*? Why? But I always felt like it was him telling me he knew where I was.

When answering machines first came out, I'd get these weird messages on my machine. A few bars of songs, odd old ones, nothing that meant anything specific to us, no Stones or Dead, not Geils or "Stairway" or anything like that. Once it was "Baby Come Back" by Player. Once it was "Long, Long Time" by Linda Ronstadt. And the last time I got a message like that it was "You and Me" by Alice Cooper. Completely random. The messages weren't left on dates that were important, and it was before machines had caller ID, so I could never say for sure that it was Derek. But I knew. Maybe it would have been different if we had connected back then. Who knows?

NYU was a lot of fun. I had fun. I learned a lot. I dated well, graduated respectably, and then shamed my parents by working as a waitress and at other menial jobs while waiting for my big break. I was always good, but not quite good enough.

I didn't bother going to my five-year reunion at Mansfield. I had nothing to say to anyone. I was just a year out of NYU and didn't know what I was going to do with my life. I really didn't want to go to law school even though my parents wanted me to. I figured if nothing came up in acting, maybe I'd be able to get a job in fashion in some way, but I never really did anything about that—other than reading lots of magazines and being a fashionable girl about town. Getting a regular job would limit my ability to audition, so I temped and waitressed and took acting classes. I was following a well-trodden path. I had nothing going to talk about at reunion. So I stayed home, ate a pint of Frusen Glädjé coffee ice cream with a spoon, and wondered when my big break was going to show up already. When would I have a life good enough to show up at reunion for?

If I could have known that this is where I would be now, I wonder if I still would have climbed aboard the Big Ship Suburban Mom Lollipop that sailed to my rescue. Would the me that I was then consider the life I have now as good?

A few years later, nothing much had changed. I was still waitressing, temping, odd-jobbing, auditioning, and living in the world's smallest apartment, which my parents paid most of the rent on. I went to a New York City Mansfield alum party because I literally had nothing else to do that night and met up again with Will—no longer Willie—Hooks. The party was at his parents' place on Park Avenue, so if I had thought about it, I guess I would have thought that it was a good bet that he would be there. I went for the free food and drinks. He went because his mom made him.

We ran into each other by the bar and got to talking about old times and what we were doing now. It was super fun to see him all grown up. I heard all about what he was up to, and he told me that he always expected me to turn up on his TV someday, not in his living room. After several years out in the working world, Will was heading back to school again and staying with his folks while he looked for an apartment up by Columbia. He had gotten a job with Morgan Stanley right after college, but recently quit to start B-school, with an eye toward going back there, or maybe somewhere else, at a higher level when he got out.

After we reconnected at his party, we started hanging out a lot, and we just sort of naturally started dating some. Life was just like high school. Nothing ever changed. Will still wanted to be my knight in shining armor. And since I still didn't know what I wanted other than a paying acting gig, I let him while I waited for my big break.

On paper, Will had everything; he was good-looking, smart, sweet, and with the potential to make serious money once he was done with his MBA. And of course, he had major family dosh. We were happy and compatible, but I can't say sparks exactly flew between us. Will was comfortable. He was nice, attentive, great at knowing exactly what I wanted and needed. He always seemed so pleased just to have me on his arm. I never imagined that could change.

Six months went by, and without ever talking about it, we were dating exclusively. We each had a drawer in the other's apartment and key privileges, but I still wasn't ready to leave my ratty East Village studio for his slightly less ratty upper-Upper West Side abode. Besides we were both so busy. He was busy with school. I was busy with auditions. Everything between us was easy. Will was always there to comfort me when the callback didn't come. I helped him study. He was the perfect boyfriend. I was the perfect girlfriend. Other than still waiting for my big break, my life was perfect.

Will wanted us to move in together. What Will really wanted was to marry me, but it was too soon. And it has never been in Will's nature to push me to do anything. He just does things and sees if I will go along. I wasn't ready to get married. I needed to have a little more time to see if my big break was around the corner before I could make a lifelong commitment to anyone. We were still young. I needed to put my career first.

I knew he wanted to give me an engagement ring that Christmas. He would point out other girls' rings to try and get a sense of the kind of ring that I liked. I tried to put the right spin on the whole thing by saying things like "A girl would have to be crazy not to love getting a ring like that in a horse-drawn carriage in Central Park on a perfect spring day." I said it as if I had a vision of our engagement in my head, and that I knew just how I wanted it to happen and what I wanted it to look like. In all honesty, I was trying to buy some time. I sure didn't want to say no. But I wasn't yet ready to say yes.

Was it possible to say "not yet"? Will was such a great guy. I didn't want to lose him. He was so good to me. What the hell was wrong with me that I wasn't ready to commit to that kind of love and adoration? Who needed an acting career that didn't love me back?

Will heard me and held off on giving me a ring for Christmas, settling instead for an Elsa Peretti gold bracelet and a trip to Vail for a ski holiday. But after New Year's, he really stepped up the pressure for me to move in with him. My lease was up at the end of March, and it was ridiculous to hold on to two places. It made sense to move in when my lease expired. I knew we'd probably get engaged soon after. It would be this spring, and it would be in a horse-drawn carriage in Central Park.

I also knew that if Will was the perfect boyfriend, then it stood to reason that he would be the perfect husband too. I knew that I should be thrilled that he wanted to marry me. He was a catch and a half. I just couldn't shake the feeling that I was waiting for something to happen. Something that was going to point me in the direction I was supposed to go. Something finally did. Bree.

Family

Will and I got married at City Hall just a couple of weeks after we found out I was pregnant. The mayor presided. I guess Will's folks were friends of his. I wore a trim white suit and a forties-style cap with white netting. I didn't look any fatter yet, so the pictures show nothing but a happy couple eager to start their life together. Will's parents and brother and sister were there. My parents didn't show up. They were still mad about the whole him not being Jewish thing.

In the long run, it was just as well. The last thing I needed that day was my mother discovering I'd gotten myself knocked up by the goyim. It was hard enough to be throwing up every morning. Will's parents weren't the type to count wedding day to birthday on their fingers. They were just happy to see their baby so happy. And thrilled to have another grandchild on the way. If a City Hall elopement wasn't exactly the wedding they envisioned for their youngest son, they never let on.

Eventually my mom got over it, and she loves Will. I think she likes him a lot more than she likes me most of the time. He was so helpful when my dad died. He made sure all her finances were set and all the details were taken care of. And of course, when Bree came along, she helped to smooth things over between us. The common love of a child is a wonderful bond. Even between my mother and me.

Will and I quickly went from being a couple to being a trio. It was an easy transition. We were a family. I had Bree on my birthday, and she really is my best birthday present ever. I can't believe how quickly it has all gone by. I feel like I just got to hold my baby girl in my arms for the first time only moments ago and now she is already gone.

Will has had a big job for a number of years now. We throw a party for his team at our house every spring, and I pretend to be interested in what's going on. I'm very adept at nodding and pretending to pay attention. And I'm a stellar hostess. I'm great at knowing all the names and marital statuses and children of everyone who works for him, so I handle all of that part. I'm sure I could do a reasonably good cocktail-party-level impersonation of someone who works in his realm, from what I've gleaned over the years, but the money stuff just bores the hell out of me. Whatever he does, it keeps us well provided for. And of course, the real money will come along later.

Sometimes it feels as if once I made that decision all those years ago to be a good and caring wife, I became a character in my own life. I just go along and play my part.

But I know that it really goes back before that. The die was cast for the rest of my life by one mistake, and I've been doing penance ever since. I did this to myself. I put myself in this cell, and I threw the key out the window.

I didn't know it was possible to be forty-two and feel fifteen; right now I do. This must be what a midlife crisis feels like. I feel like I'm bouncing around in time.

Maybe a midlife crisis is when you figure out that this isn't a dress rehearsal, this is your life, and it's the only one you've got. It feels like a freight train is approaching and my foot is stuck on the tracks.

Lately, I find myself overwhelmed by the sheer number of people I have to be nice to on a daily basis. From the housekeeper to the grocery store clerk to my in-laws, the mailman, Bree's coaches, the lady who always takes the spot next to me in yoga … The list just goes on, and I have no choice in the matter. I have to be sunny and pleasant to everyone. All the time. Every damn day. I don't have a real job, so that is my job. I know being nice shouldn't feel like such a burden, but sometimes it's all just so exhausting. I know I sound like a terrible person. But I also know it feels awful to never be allowed to have a down day.

Because it's not the smiling and being nice that is so hard. It's the having to. It's constantly being on guard to keep up this perfect façade. I've been struggling to pretend everything about my life is perfect for so long, and I am so tired. And the number one most terrifying thought to me is that other people can see the cracks in my façade when I get tired.

So I smile and keep things organized and moving smoothly, and no one else ever sees any seams in our life. The cash is always on hand to pay the housekeeper. I always remember her kids' and the gardener's kids' birthdays properly. The refrigerator is always full of beer and milk and healthy snacks. My legs are always shaved, my nails and toes are always perfectly manicured. I can pull together a dinner party at our house on a moment's notice or I can get reservations for ten at the hottest new restaurant around. I exercise every day and only eat one meal a day. I drink one glass of white wine a night.

But as perfectly as I am holding things together, I still can't stop obsessing over what happens next. What will happen to me when I'm not happy, pretty Kat Hooks anymore but some wrinkly old lady? What will I do?

And who will I be next? I've reinvented myself plenty of times over the years, from nerdy Jewish girl to cool stoner kid, to girl about town, to wealthy suburban mom. I try to tell myself I'll be able to handle whatever comes next. *Fake it till you make it, you always come out on top.* But it is getting harder and harder for me to not hear the doubts screaming in my head. I know all of my previous reinventions were possible because of what I look like.

Maybe I should pick up photography again? I need a creative outlet. Besides, if I'm taking the picture, I don't have to be in the picture. I haven't kept a single picture taken of me in the last year. Not even the ones with Bree at her eighth-grade graduation. I've erased every one. All I would see is impending doom.

Driving Bree, I start to feel the panic rising again about what I'm going to do in that house without her. Will seems to think we're going to be kids ourselves again, with plenty of time for each other. He tells me he can't wait to not have to check if she's really asleep before we have our usual hushed, married, don't-wake-the-baby sex. He thinks it's going to be one big party, chez nous. But I'm sure between his workload and hockey schedule and my Junior League and yoga and tennis we are not going to have quite the time for the second honeymoon he says he envisions. He says he's going to spend every Saturday chasing me around the house. I know better. He'll be too busy for me.

Bree and I may have been going through some tough teen times for the past few months, but still I don't know who I'm supposed to be without her. And there is that talismanic quality about being able to walk around town as the mother of a beautiful girl. She proves you were once a babe, back before you were a mom. *Yeah, I may look like this now, but once upon a time, I tell you what, I used to look just like that.*

I don't have any idea what I'm going to do with myself when it's only Will and me. Maybe if we'd had other kids, but I had two very-early-stage miscarriages, after Bree, and I was just so sad. Will said he hated to see me like that, so he didn't think we should try for more. We were a perfect family just the three of us. And I was so busy taking care of Bree that I didn't really think about it. But now I'm lost. She is all I have. Sometimes I am so angry at Will and at myself for letting her go. Not when every instinct I have is telling me she isn't ready. Or do I just feel like that because I'm the one who isn't ready? I'm worried that I can't trust myself because I'm subconsciously trying to force my instincts to tell me what I have to hear in order to make the outcome I really want to happen.

Sometimes I think maybe we should try for another baby. I'm not too old. There are plenty of women my age in town with newborns. But then we might have to deal with the whole fertility thing. That wouldn't be surprising at all; I'm forty-two. And then what if it turns out the problem is Will, not me? Does that happen to men when they get older too? And what if the doctor said that—then where would we all be? No, we're much better off with having just our one perfect child. I nailed that can of worms shut years ago and shut it will damn well stay.

Anytime Will and I have sex lately, all I can see when I close my eyes is the B'way cosmetics corridor at the Bloomingdale's on Fifty-ninth. I don't even know why, I haven't been there in ages. I'm not even sure the floor is still there. But that's all I see in my mind, the black and white squares on the floor and the bright, colorful packages on the counters. Bizarro, right? Shouldn't I be thinking about Chris Pine, or Chris Hemsworth or Chris Evans or someone like that? What the hell is wrong with me? Bloomingdale's? Am I so broken that I can't even fantasize right?

I was doing a daytime temp gig at Bloomie's as a Clinique beauty adviser, when Will and I met up again. I loved that coat. It made me feel so official. Besides waitressing jobs at night and the occasional go-see, I was a perfume sprayer. Then I got a temp gig as a Clinique beauty adviser and got to wear one of those crisp white lab coats. I loved that coat. It made me feel so official. Even back then I didn't have the kind of exotic looks that would put you at the Lancaster or Sisley counters. I was the friendly all-American type of beauty.

Maybe with Bree gone, I should try to get a job. I could probably just go get a job at a Clinique counter again. It would be fun, playing with makeup all day long. I love makeup. But now I'd probably get hired as a mature-skin adviser, and I definitely don't need that reminder weighing me down, every day, thanks. Photography sounds like a much better plan.

Maybe I should finally join the community theater group in town too, now that I won't have to work around her schedule. I miss acting, and it would be fun to make some new friends. But the same problem crops up—could I really deal with the parts available to me these days? I'm well past the ingénue stage. If I got cast as someone like the elder Madame Bovary, I might just throw my own damn self under a train.

Drop-off at Colby House

One Week Ago

As we turn up the big hill onto campus, I see the iron gates that herald our arrival and I have a moment of sheer panic. *Why am I doing this? This is a bad idea. Why am I letting her go when I know it is a bad idea?* But I look over at my golden-haired beauty, my sweet baby, the one who has never given me any cause to worry, the one who tells me she really does want to be here, and I think, *Why do I want to hold her back?*

I drop her off at Colby House, a white wooden Victorian with lacy gingerbread trim and a set of welcoming all-weather wicker furniture out on the front porch. I can picture her doing her homework in the cozy porch swing or curled up on one of the comfy floral cushions on the chairs.

We drag her stuff out of the car, up the long set of stairs—*mental note: that carpet has seen better days and needs replacing; ask if we can donate*—down the hallway to the right. I laugh to myself at the Wi-Fi notice in the hallway. The whole campus is a hot spot now. They were still trying to teach us COBOL when I was here.

I'm happy to see her room. She's close to the bathroom, and she has a view of the main road through campus, so she can see what's happening on the quad and who is going into or coming out of the library. I'm even happier to see her room is one of the ones that is really hard to sneak out of. She'd have to climb out over the dorm mother's apartment, drop down, and scramble across the porch to get out after curfew. It's still possible, but the second floor is so much safer than the first.

And I am totally thrilled that we signed up for the concierge maid service. Her trunk is already unpacked and at the foot of her bed. Her things are in drawers and hung up in the closet. All Bree has to do is unpack her toiletries and suitcases from the car. The Ralph Lauren pink madras comforter and crisp white sheets with pink rickrack and her monogram in pink on the pillowcases I picked out are already on the bed. Her laundry will be picked up and done once a week, and there is one less thing for me to worry about. I reach out a hand to smooth out the already perfectly smooth bedding. I'm still trying to figure out how to say goodbye. Even though I know it is only for a few weeks. It just seems so final.

I give her a big squeeze, kiss her forehead, and pat her hair and hug her some more until she finally says, "Mom, it's time to go. I'll be OK. I'll call you tonight after I get back from dinner. It's time for you to go home, Mom." Bree shows me her standard confident tilt to her chin, but her eyes are starting to shine a bit with tears, and her bottom lip is dangerously close to quivering.

I know I can't let her cry in front of me, so I lean over for one more hug and kiss, and whisper in her ear, "Seriously, no matter what, do not eat the Turkey Tetrazzini. It's not safe for human consumption." The joke, part of our long-standing family schtick about the dining hall, has its desired effect, and she throws me out of her new life with a giggle.

The clarity I've been groping for the whole trip comes upon me in that one moment, and I realize that she really is a lot more like me than she is like anyone else. She'll be just fine. I'm hit over the head by the thought that if all goes well, I won't know what her prep school experience is like any more than she'll know about mine. I will only hear the stories she wants me to hear. And that's OK.

Hospital Parking Lot

Today at Dawn

I got the call at three this morning. I was in the car by three fifteen. Thank God her friends didn't just leave her there in the woods. Thank God they called in the Hulk—I'm so thankful he is still there—and he got her right to the hospital. I pull into the parking lot just as the first pink lights of dawn start to shred the sky.

The only thought in my head is recrimination: *You had one job!* And it's true, I had only one job, to keep her safe, that was it, that was all I had to do. And I couldn't even manage that. I let her go off to Mansfield, knowing what it would be like, and not knowing if she was able to handle it, because I made a dumb promise to Will when we got married. I have been so cowed, so beholden, that I gave over every other decision in my life to him. I allowed him to act as my common sense instead of listening to myself. Instead of doing what I knew was the right thing for Bree. I put her here. I put us all here.

And now my baby is lying in a hospital bed because I was too much of a coward to listen to my own instincts.

I throw the car into the first spot and run to the door. I don't even bother locking it. I don't care if it gets stolen. It would serve me right. I know I look like a crazy person, yoga pants, sweatshirt, no bra, hair a bed-head mess, and no makeup on. I don't care. I rush to the front desk, tell them who I am, and beg them to tell me where she is.

I tiptoe into her room, afraid of what I will see. She looks so impossibly small. So tiny, hooked up to all kinds of monitors and IVs and who knows what else. There is no tube down her throat. That must be a good sign, right? She is sleeping, so I just sit by her bedside, waiting for her to wake up, willing her to be OK. I sit there for an hour and a half before she stirs.

She blinks her eyes five or six times. It seems like she's trying to figure out where she is. "Mummy, I'm so sorry."

"Shush, baby, it's OK. I'm here. You're gonna be OK. It's OK."

"We were playing a game. It was drink or say what you'd done with boys, and I didn't want them to know I hadn't done anything with boys. I didn't want to look like a loser. So I just kept drinking. I don't know what happened after that. I don't remember."

"It's OK, sweetie. Your brave and wonderful friends knew that you were sick and risked getting into trouble to get you to the hospital. I've already talked to Dean Heinemann. None of them will get into any trouble for being smart enough to go for help. You could have died. They saved you. They did exactly the right thing. They won't get in any trouble, baby. I promise. You aren't in any trouble. No one is in any trouble. It's all going to be OK."

Bree starts sobbing and whispering "I'm so sorry." Over and over again.

I sit on the edge of her bed and hold her, careful not to crimp anything that might be important. "It's OK, baby. I'm here. I should have been honest with you. I should have told you all the trouble I got up to, so you knew what could happen. Everyone makes mistakes." And I sit by her bed and tell her almost every story I can remember. I tell her about drugs and drinking and throwing up and being lucky at not getting caught. I tell her nearly everything. I tell her everything but the truths I can't bear to.

February 28

Nearly Sixteen Years Ago

One freezing-cold, blustery Monday in late February, Derek called me. Totally out of nowhere. I had the passing thought that it was Brian's birthday. I hadn't seen Derek or spoken to him in nearly ten years. He said he found my number in the Mansfield directory and was in New York, so he decided to give me a call. Luckily, I was home, hiding under my covers, eating ice cream, after yet another rejection. This one from a soap opera. Evidently five feet tall was just too small to be seen on the small screen. I was "too tiny for TV." Casting directors always said things like that, as if you could do anything about it. Trust me, if I had any ability to make myself taller, I would have done so ages ago.

I was too depressed to go waitress with a big smile on my face, so I called in sick. I was perilously close to facing the fact that my big break wasn't going to happen. In fact, I was now nearer to thirty than twenty-five, and I was so sick of hearing how pretty and how talented I was, but still hearing no. All I wanted was a crappy paying acting gig. All the gods were offering me was a good husband. I was going to need way more ice cream and maybe some hot fudge sauce and mini marshmallows.

When I answered the phone, I almost didn't believe it was really him. It was so random. But it was. His voice was the same. That voice still sounded so good in my ear. I think my body recognized it before my brain knew who the hell I was talking to. My heartbeat quickened and my body softened, and I was suddenly back to being a schoolgirl, and I didn't give a shit about casting directors or acting or anything else in my stupid life. It was that soft, slow voice, that mellow Marin County drawl that always did me in.

Derek wanted to know if I could meet him for a beer at the Ukrainian bar on Second Avenue. I kept my voice light and casual as I answered "Sure," but my hands were shaking and my stomach was churning. The bar was only a couple of blocks from my apartment. And I deserved some cheering up after the rotten day I had. Will was at his apartment working on a huge paper he had due on Monday, so I knew he wouldn't come down here tonight. What could be the harm in having one drink with an old friend? I didn't spend one single moment thinking about all we'd put each other through. I just wanted to be near an old friend again for a little bit.

It all happened so fast it was like it was happening to someone else. One minute I was lying in bed with my head in a carton of ice cream, and the next I was leaping about searching for something cute to wear. I didn't even have time to properly freak out about seeing him again. If I had known, I would have gotten a hair appointment and done something about my roots—which were terrible.

This is madness. Why was I meeting him at a bar? For a moment I thought maybe I just shouldn't show up. But I said I would meet him. Blowing him off just seemed rude. So not done.

I went through my closet like a cartoon character, tossing clothes on the floor, trying very hard to find an outfit that screamed cooler-than-thou sophisticated New Yorker who is most definitely not trying too hard to impress the likes of you. I pulled on a black dress so short it barely grazed my thighs and added a pair of black leggings. *Definitely trying too hard.* I tried on several more combinations before I finally settled on black jeans, a black scoop neck Petit Bateau tee, and black cowboy boots. I was proud of being one of the few country music fans in New York City and besides, cowboy boots make me taller.

And I confess I did take some extra time picking out sexy underwear. Not like anything was going to happen or anything like that. It was just because nothing fills a girl up with confidence quite like a push-up bra and matching lace panties. Victoria's Secret isn't exactly a big secret.

I slicked on several coats of Lancôme's finest mascara and some pink shiny lip gloss. Then I wiped that all off and painted on brick red lipstick and smoky black eyeliner. I was a grown-up. I wondered if Derek would even recognize me.

I found him right where he said he'd be, on a barstool at our sometimes-trendy, always-trashy preppy slumming spot in the East Village. It had some unpronounceable Slavic name, but we all knew which one it was. It was one of Mansfield's unofficial NYC clubhouses. Raccoon Lodge on the Upper West Side was the one where Will and I hung out most. Dorian's was our preferred option on the East Side. You could almost always count on recognizing a rep tie or two. Usually it was pretty easy to spot because it was tied around someone's head.

When I got to the bar, Derek was spinning the stool around like a kid at a diner and drinking out of a longneck Bud bottle. He looked exactly as I remembered him. Blond bangs hanging into his eyes. It was like the years just melted away and we were back at our table in Gus's. He looked at me and winked. I almost giggled. Then I had to stop myself from welling up with tears. I was so overwhelmed to see the boy I'd left behind all those years ago. *Damn, why am I so emotional today? Totally PMS-ing.*

"Hey, Kat-Kat," he said. That voice. That California-boy look. He always looked so out of place in cold weather. Derek must not have gotten there much before I did. He still had those red patches on his cheeks when his face got cold. He had on a shearling-lined brown leather bomber jacket and a bright blue scarf hanging around the back of his neck. It looked homemade, and I wondered, with a small nibble of jealousy, if a girlfriend had made it for him. *Well, why shouldn't he have a girlfriend? I have a boyfriend. No big deal. Nothing untoward here. We are old friends, catching up. That's all.*

Derek got up from the barstool and enveloped me in a long hug, then he gave me a dry little peck on the lips, just a hello kiss between friends. It felt delicious to have the soft leather of his jacket against my face and feel the warmth coming off of his skin. I remember thinking his lips felt drier than I remembered and what an odd thought that was to have. I leaned my head into his chest and breathed in deeply, if furtively. He still smelled of Eau Sauvage, the cologne that seemed so sophisticated back then. *God, it's been a long time. Was he twenty-seven already? No, I was twenty-seven in December. He's twenty-eight. He'll be twenty-nine in June.* Looking at him more closely, I could see he wasn't exactly the same golden boy of years gone by. There were faint lines starting to form at the outer corners of his eyes. I prayed the same wasn't true for me. I couldn't believe it had been almost ten years since I'd seen him last. He was drinking beer instead of vodka, so I thought that was a pretty good sign. He definitely wasn't completely sober, but maybe he was clean? Maybe he'd finally figured out how to dabble, like the rest of us. Maybe he was better?

We talked and laughed for what seemed like hours about old friends and old stories. The only things neither of us brought up were Amy or Will. *He must know about Will and me.* We were having such a nice time, why ruin it? I heard all about who was doing what on the West Coast and filled him in on the goings-on of the New York Mansfield contingent. Mostly we drank. A lot. I can't drink beer, so his beer was swiftly joined by the bar's famous and cheap vodka shots. A dollar a shot, and they just kept filling up your glass until you told them to stop by turning the glass over or passed out on the bar.

Almost before I knew what was happening, Derek had his hand on the small of my back and was telling me how hot I looked. The bill was paid, and I was being steered out the door. We were leaving. My heart pounded furiously as we half-ran, giggling, stumbling, and kissing down Sixth Street, passing happy couples and sitar players showing through the windows of Indian restaurants. There we were at my building. Still kissing, we were inside, then upstairs, then at my door. At last.

The saddest thing is that I truly can't remember it. I remember getting to my place. I remember kissing. I sort of remember my clothes coming off, but my memory gets pretty fuzzy after that. I don't think I passed out, but I can't be sure. I mean, the next morning I could tell we'd had sex from the way my body felt and the way we woke up wrapped around each other. From the looks of things, it must have been pretty energetic too. My apartment looked like a dress rehearsal set from *9½ Weeks*. There were scarves tied to the bedposts, what furniture I had was askew, the ice cream carton was empty on the night table, and our clothes were in one heap next to the door. I can see that scene, but I can't conjure up in my mind the actual details of what it was like when I finally got to bonk Derek Wilkeson. All those years of wondering what it would be like, and all I've got is a hazy sense of fulfillment. Sometimes life is just unfair.

We woke up late the next day, hungover as all hell. I grabbed my jeans and shirt from the night before on the way to the bathroom. Good enough, I didn't have them on that long. Fresh underpants made the outfit clean. Glancing in the tiny bathroom mirror without turning on the light, I was so glad I woke up first. I could see last night's eyeliner smeared all around the top half of my face. Red lipstick traces wound faintly around the bottom half. And my mouth tasted like I'd slept with a small furry animal in it. I did the best I could with Cetaphil, witch hazel, and a toothbrush. Oh god, I was going to have to take another day off. I hadn't felt this bad in ages. I had to throw up again, and then brush my teeth again. Ugh, having to get out of bed to throw up in the middle of the night, that I remembered just fine. *Maybe I did pass out. Maybe nothing really happened. Maybe we just fell asleep together.* As long as I wasn't looking straight at the evidence in my apartment, I was pretty well on the way to being able to convince myself that nothing had happened. We were just friends.

Then Derek joined me in the bathroom. He splashed some water on his face, winked at me in the mirror, nonchalantly borrowed my toothbrush, and then magically looked good as new. At least I thought so. I smiled up at him, and my clothes came off all over again; his didn't have to, because he never bothered to put any on. This time there was no denying it. Something definitely happened. I remember passion and wonder and tracing my fingers across his chest, feeling his strong body surround me. I remember him picking me up and carrying me back to my unmade bed. A line of paralyzingly teasing kisses that started at my neck and this time went all the way to my feet and back up again. I remember knowing that what we were doing was really making love. We fit together so perfectly, as if we'd been doing this with each other all our lives. There were none of those awkward first-time moments. I was surprised by his tenderness; I'd expected him to be rougher. I was surprised by my desire. I'd never felt like that before. There was one moment, one moment when I could feel his heart beating through my chest, and we were one. I didn't think about Will, or the past, or anything, I just stayed in that breath for as long as I could. I remember it all.

We lay there entwined for a while, but eventually the need for food drove us out of each other's arms. Since my refrigerator held only three Diet Cokes and a very old container of deli salad, I thought a diner was in order. Odessa was only a couple blocks away on Avenue A.

Odessa

We walked in and grabbed one of the booths. I sat on the inside next to the window where I could watch people scurry past. The chill coming off the window made me feel a bit better. Derek slid in next to me. I knew the scary old lady waitress was going to have a cow when she saw his feet up on the seat across from us, but I wasn't going to tell him and ruin our peace. Let her do it. She came over, and we pleaded for "coffee, lots of coffee." When the waitress started to bitch him out for having his dirty boots on the seat, he didn't even turn to look at her, he just held up a fifty for her to go away. It was dismissive rich-guy rude. The waitresses here saw that sort of behavior all the time, from drunk people turned hungover slummers. They were used to it, and I'm sure they were happy for the easy money, but I found it totally gross. It made me think about who Derek really was as a man, and not in a way that made me happy to be sitting there with him. The waitress stuffed the bill into her bra and walked away with pursed lips. She'd hold the words in for fifty bucks, and he could put his feet wherever he liked. It wasn't her job to clean the seats anyway.

Derek ordered a huge omelet with bacon and cheese and all kinds of veggies. I was hungry, but the thought of food made me want to hurl again, so I stuck to the coffee alone. From the look the waitress gave Derek when he proffered the bill, I knew she was probably going to spit in our food anyway. I met her eyes and gave a sympathetic shrug as if to say, "Men, whaddya gonna do?" and hoped my coffee was safe. I pushed away any misgivings, and Derek and I talked easily for a while. I put my head on his shoulder while I let my stomach rumbles subside. The greasy spoon smell wasn't helping any.

I just wanted to have this little bubble of morning-after last for a little bit. The enormity of what we had finally done was beginning to seep in around the edges of my consciousness, but I willed it away. *Just let us have this moment. Please. Just let us have this.*

I can hear his voice in my ear as we sat with our sides pressed together on the crinkly vinyl seat. "C'mon, my Kat-Kat. Come out to California with me. I just bought this awesome place in Sausalito. They have a theater group in town. I'll donate a pile, and you can star in all the shows you want. Or we can start our own theater company. You don't want to stay here and be a waitress. Waitressing is such a drag. You don't need to let people order you around like that. I can take care of you. Let me. Come with me. The weather's wicked nice. No more cold rain. C'mon. You'll love it. You want to go to LA instead? Be a movie star? My dad's got people. If you have your heart set on LA, I'll make it happen for you there. My dad will set us up. We'll keep the Sausalito place for weekends."

"Derek, don't …" I groaned.

"Kat-Kat, I have to. This is my shot. You know it's always been you for me. Always. Even when I'm with somebody else, it's you I think about. All these years later. It's still you. And you can't tell me it's not the same for you. I know it is. The worst mistake I ever made in my life was letting you go. I never should have let that happen. I should have followed you to NYU. I should have said this to you a hundred times these last ten years. This is my shot, and I'm taking it. Kat, I want you to come to California with me. I want us to be together, forever. We can do this. We can be happy. We can get married. We can have babies. We can have whatever you want. I'll do whatever you want." He sounded like he had it all figured out and we could just go off and be some normal couple. Like we'd just broken it off in school because we were young. Like the drugs or the violence or Amy or the last ten years of our lives didn't happen, and it made all the sense in the world for us to just live happily ever after.

The impossibility of this relationship stabbed ever deeper, and I was having a harder and harder time pushing my thoughts away. My morning-after bubble was swiftly deflating.

"Derek, don't. I can't. I can't just pick up and move to California." I said it. It was hard to breathe. I desperately wanted his vision of our future to be true, so badly. I could almost touch an image of our happily ever after. I wanted that almost more than I wanted anything. But even more than I wanted his vision to be true, I wanted it to be right. And no matter what I wanted, I knew it wasn't right. What would happen if I did something he didn't like and he got mad, or he got bored? Then I'd be stuck in California with no job, no money, and no friends. I'd have no one but him to turn to, and he would use that to hurt me.

Holy shit, what have I done?

"Why the fuck not? You've got nothing here." Derek seemed surprised that I wasn't just going to fall into his arms and accept his generous offer. I knew he'd been practicing singsong-saying "Come on, come to Cali with me, Kat-Kat." He whispered it into my ear a few times before I answered him.

"Dude, I can't. I can't just pick up and leave. I've got a life here. I've got friends. I've got a boyfriend. It's not like you can just show up in New York after ten years and I'm going to turn my whole life upside down because you suddenly tell me I'm the one for you. Grown-up people don't do those things. We aren't children anymore, Derek. I don't need you to take care of me. I can take care of myself. I don't need you to buy me an acting career." Since I hadn't had more than a small role in anything since I left NYU, I didn't feel all that confident about that last bit.

"Oh yeah? How's that workin' out for you, Kat? You didn't seem to have anyone but me in your bed last night or this morning. I don't see any boyfriend keeping me away from you. If I was your boyfriend, no other guy would ever come near you." He leaned over and kissed me, then said in a meaner tone, "So when can I expect your movie to come out? Or maybe I missed your TV show?" I saw his jaw set the way it always did when he didn't get his way. Which made me think about Will again. *Will always makes me feel better about myself, not worse. Oh my god, how will he ever forgive me? He's always so good to me, and I am such a stupid messed-up fucking idiot. I am such a fuck-up.* I picked at the edge of the ketchup label to avoid having to meet Derek's eyes.

"I don't have a movie coming out. And I don't yet have a TV show. But even if I didn't have anything to keep me here, Derek, my deal hasn't changed. I'm never going to be with someone who isn't in control of his shit. Still. Ever. Never. And I'm sure as fucking hell not going to pick up and move across the country with you unless you're clean. I mean it. I haven't even smoked pot in ages." I held my breath for a moment before meeting his eyes to ask him the question I knew would truly doom us.

"So, are you holding?"

"Everything I have with me on this trip is by doctor's prescription only. Scout's honor." He answered, his eyes downcast, a small smile fighting to escape the corners of his mouth. *There was no way he was ever a fucking Boy Scout.* "But if there's something you want I'll get it for us. I can get you anything in the world, Kat-Kat. Say the word, it's yours. All I want is to make you happy."

I didn't need any more confirmation. I didn't need to hear anything else from him. It was enough that I could hear Neil Young singing "The Needle and the Damage Done" in my head. I needed to extricate myself from this mess. And so I did. I did what I had to do. I told Derek that even though he was absolutely right, that it was him for me and always would be, that wasn't enough. I told him that Will and I were a real thing, even if it wasn't the same as the thing we had. I told him we were going to be moving in together soon. I told him I really shouldn't have gone out with him last night and I would never do it again. I told him I wasn't at all sorry for what happened between us but that was all we would ever have of each other.

I was miserable and heartbroken, and one hundred percent, absolutely, completely, positively knew that I was doing the right thing.

I knew there was no way Derek would ever say anything to Will about what happened between us. Because if he did, he'd have to admit I picked Will over him even after that. It may have been ten years, but I knew him well enough to know that that was one thing he'd never cop to. We were at checkmate.

Derek stood up and pushed off the table. He could still do that three-finger push-up move that made me ache. I turned my head away. He didn't wait for his food to come out. At least he threw a twenty on the table, because I don't think I had more than a couple bucks on me, and I really didn't want to have to tell the waitress I had to go to the ATM and then pray there was enough money in my account to pay her with.

He walked out yelling at me that I should have a nice, boring life. He was done trying to get me to have some fun. He looped the blue scarf around his neck twice and disappeared onto the cold and crowded street.

No one at any of the other tables even looked up. I think the regulars were all pretty used to loud morning-after lovers' quarrels. Everyone kept to their own borscht.

I sent his food back for the staff and sat there for a long time drinking too many cups of their too-strong coffee, looking at the freezing rain pelting down outside the foggy window. At least the weather matched my mood. I moved to the middle of the bench once Derek left. I didn't need the cold to ground me anymore. I just needed some time before I could face my apartment again, with the scent of him still there. I just needed some time to think. I just needed some more time to figure things out. The waitress didn't seem to mind me taking up the space.

When I finally left the diner, I was determined to never speak to Derek again, never see him, never speak of him, never think of him. His existence would be totally erased from my life and my mind. I went home, cleaned up the mess in my apartment, lit all the scented candles I could find, cracked the window, and banished Derek's presence as I cleaned up the evidence of him ever having been at my place. My decision was made. After, I stood under the hot water of the shower until it ran cold and then got myself dressed and called Will.

I spoke to Will on the phone like it was just another regular day. Every fucking casting director in the world be damned, no one could say I wasn't the best actress on the whole fucking planet. I asked how the studying was going and how his day had been and if his paper was done yet. I asked him if I could come by tonight with Chinese food or if he wanted me to get something else for dinner or if he just needed another night alone to get his work done. I told him I missed him and would love to come up to his place if I wouldn't be in his way. I said all the things a good and caring girlfriend would say. Being a good and caring girlfriend wasn't a hard part to play. I was good at it. He made it easy. I could forget that I ever gave any thought to having any other kind of life.

I would forget it ever happened. I just made a mistake. There was no need to turn our whole lives completely upside down over one little mistake. So, I went a little way down the wrong path. At least I turned myself around quickly. I should be thankful for that. It wasn't like I chucked my entire life and followed Derek to California and then figured out I'd made a terrible mistake. I just drank too much and honestly, I can't even really remember much of anything. It happens to everyone. Everyone makes mistakes sometimes. This wasn't that big a deal. I didn't even remember it hardly at all. I just kept saying it until it became true.

What good would come of telling Will everything? Why unburden myself and cause him pain? Why ruin everything we have? Why, when it was so much easier to just say nothing and forget it ever happened?

Since Will said he'd love to see me for dinner, I let myself in and got his place all set up while he was at his study group. I took cash from his desk to buy Chinese food. I set the table with an actual tablecloth and real plates and chopsticks and took the food out of the containers so everything looked perfect. I wore the red cashmere sweater he'd given me as a Christmas present. He loves the way I look in red. Just a little bit of extra makeup to hide the greenish hangover cast, and I was right as rain. I even stopped and picked up a cheery bouquet of bodega flowers and set them in the middle of the table.

I surveyed the scene of domestic bliss and decided to like it. When he got home, I told him we were celebrating. I had told my landlord that day I wasn't renewing my lease. I explained to Will that I just needed to see what his place looked like with a bit of a girlie touch. If it was OK with him, with some flowers and a few throw pillows, I could work with his place and make it ours. During our conversation at dinner that night

I mentioned briefly that I'd run into Derek when I was out grabbing some food, and that was that.

I told Will it had been nice to bump into an old friend who happened to be in town. Derek and I had a quick drink, and I went home with that stomach bug from the weekend still bothering me a bit. No harm, no foul, nothing to tell. If he didn't believe me, he didn't show it.

Will didn't seem to want to spend any more time talking about Derek on our happy occasion anyway. He grabbed a bottle of champagne from the fridge and we took it with us into the bedroom to properly celebrate my moving in.

Sex with Will is nice. It's very loving. Even if it's not entirely the type of two-hearts-beating-as-one-passion thing, it is very comfortable. I was happy to be safely ensconced in his strong arms. He loved protecting me. I had dodged a bullet with Derek. I would never cheat on Will now that I was committed. I pushed all thoughts of Derek out of my mind. I got on with my real life. I hardly ever thought about him again, ever.

Sitting on the Bathroom Floor

My college friends and I refer to these post-college New York City days as "the vomit years." We didn't eat much, we drank a lot, so we threw up a lot. Most of my besties were fellow girls about New York, working whatever jobs paid enough to keep us in our apartments and didn't interfere too much with our social lives. All of us waiting for the right break. I was an actress/waitress/temp. Christie answered phones at Random House. Holly answered phones at Sotheby's. Sunni answered phones at ABT. All our boyfriends were in grad school, so we were on hold until they graduated and we got married.

My girls and I usually all went out together during the week; the weekends were for the boys. There was something happening almost every night—book parties and gallery openings. We supplemented our meager incomes by going to any event that had free food and an open bar, and if we ever had to choose between food and drink, we'd always pick the open bar.

Less than four weeks after I told Will I would move in, I found myself sitting on the bathroom floor, staring at a bright blue plus symbol on a stick. *This was not possible. I could not possibly be pregnant.* I was on the pill. Sort of. I mean, I was on the pill. I just didn't always remember to take it at the right time. And OK, Will and I had been to so many parties that month I might have missed a couple of days. And since I threw up every time I drank too much, those pills probably didn't count either. But nothing bad had ever happened before. I could not be pregnant right now. I could not be pregnant this month. This could not happen to me.

Shit. Shit. Shit. What am I going to do? I briefly considered not having the baby. But it was only briefly. I wasn't planning it, but I couldn't imagine not having it now that it was there. I was adopted and couldn't help but put myself in my birth mother's place. I could take care of a baby. I was old enough to be a good mom. I had a great boyfriend who wanted nothing more than to marry me. Maybe this was the sign I'd been waiting for. It certainly seemed like the universe was saying it was time to move on with my life.

I wasn't sure what I should do about Derek. I mean, it was technically, kind of, sort of, maybe, slightly possible that it was Derek's. Should I call him? Did I have to? Did I have to tell Will about Derek? Sitting on the cold bathroom floor holding the stick in my hand, I could hear the song "Torn Between Two Lovers" playing on the jukebox in my head. I started laughing, crying, and hiccupping at the same time. Mucus from my stuffy nose kept running down my face, and I swiped it away with the back of my hand. *I'm having a major fucking crisis and I've got crappy seventies soft rock stuck in my head? Like things aren't bad enough right now?*

I sat on the floor like that for a while, but once I got up, I knew that the best thing I could do was to forget that it was even possible that anyone else could biologically be the father. I didn't tell Derek anything, because if he was my baby's father I did not want to know. And I did not want him to know. Under no circumstances would my child be co-parented by a drug addict. I would tell Will I was pregnant, but I didn't see any reason to mention that there was a teeny-tiny, minute possibility that it could be not biologically his. I loved him and I didn't want to see him hurt.

Should I have told him the truth then? Probably. I mean, of course. I do know that. But my highest concern was taking care of my baby. So even if it meant not being such a perfectly good person, it was worth it. Since the moment I found out about her, Bree has been my number one priority. Will meant stability and love, and that's what babies need most. Derek was chaos and drugs and instability—no way my baby would grow up surrounded by that.

So if I settled, I settled for all the right reasons. I washed my face, fixed my makeup, and put on a big smile. Everything was going to be OK. Better than OK, everything was going to be perfect.

I never told a soul about that night with Derek. Not even Dots. It might be the one thing about me she doesn't know. That truth belongs to just Derek and me. Because once that kind of secret is spoken aloud, it's out there. And I cannot allow that to happen.

The first thing Will did when I told him was to get down on one knee and propose. It was the sweetest, most romantic gesture ever. He hadn't bought a ring for me yet, but he dug out his Mansfield ring for me to wear until we could go to Tiffany's over the weekend. Then *that* was the sweetest, most romantic gesture ever. I burst into tears when I said "Yes!" but I swear I said it with honest-to-god, real enthusiasm. I was determined to do everything in my power to make our lives together perfect.

And I have. I've done my absolute best to make Will happy all these years. To make us the perfect family. Everything I do is for him and Bree. Even if sometimes it seems like he doesn't notice anymore. Even if in spending all my time and energy doing all that for them, I somehow managed to forget to be me.

It wasn't like our engagement and elopement came as a surprise to anyone or anything. After all, we'd known each other forever and we were living together. Why wait for him to graduate? Will had been telling all our friends for ages that I was the girl he decided he was going to marry when he was sixteen years old. He told everyone that once I said yes, he thought it best to whisk me off to City Hall before I could change my mind.

I quit waitressing for sitting at home proofreading Will's papers and gestating. There was no need for me to make any money, and Will thought that being on my feet was too much stress on the baby. And even though I kept at it half-heartedly for a couple more months, I eventually quit trying for acting gigs that never came.

I didn't call Derek to tell him that Will and I were getting married. I was afraid if I called him, he'd try to talk me out of it. He'd tell me that I'd be bored as a house cow. He'd say I needed more adventure than Will could give me. More than that even, I was afraid if I spoke to him, he'd somehow know I was pregnant. And the math there was pretty simple. I couldn't allow him the chance to ask those questions or demand those answers. I might always carry him around in my heart, but he would not be part of our lives. He could not be my child's father. He was not allowed to mess up my baby's life.

Looking at Bree as objectively as I possibly can, she could be related to either of them. They have the same basic coloring; they are about the same height. Besides, Bree looks just like me, not like either of them, other than the blond hair, and half the time I forget that I'm not really blond. There's really no way to tell. I mean, short of a DNA test. Bree has my blood type, which is dominant, and none of us have any genetic health issues, except if you count the possibility of addiction being genetic.

This problem at Mansfield is no reason to think that she might have a genetic propensity toward drugs or alcoholism. She's just a kid. She just made a mistake. There is no reason for her life to be turned upside down for a mistake.

If Will has ever suspected Bree might not be his, if he's ever wondered what happened between Derek and me that night, he's never let on. He adores her. She's his baby girl.

After Dropping Her Off

One Week Ago

After I leave her at Colby, I am determined to get right back on the road. I want to get home before it gets too late. There is the other truth I can't tell Bree, even though she knows something is wrong. Will is having an affair. It started six months ago. When he hired a new assistant, Kayleigh, who looks exactly like I did at twenty-eight. I mean, honestly, how unimaginative can one man get? Shortly after hiring her, suddenly he started having late-night meetings, weekend conferences, and more tournaments than you could shake a hockey stick at. Did he think I was an idiot? His team only plays in the Fairchester League. Will started running again and doing sit-ups, for god's sake. Seriously? Sit-ups? Did he think me a complete fool?

The absolute worst part was that when I first figured it out, I told myself I didn't care. I chewed on the insides of my cheeks and told myself I only cared in an "I can't fucking believe he's making me look bad" way. I told myself I didn't care in that punch-to-the-viscera, "Oh my god, he's fucking someone else, I'm going to die" way I felt when I saw Derek with Amy. *As long as my life stays the same, if he wants to sleep with someone else, fine, that's just one less thing for me to do around here. Fine. I don't care.*

How pathetic is that? How pathetic am I? I was as disgusted by myself as I was at him. Could I not even be honest in my own head? Of course I cared. Of course it's a terrible betrayal. He broke our marriage vows. I mean, I may have done some less-than-perfect things, but I never did that. Not once we were married. Not once we were engaged. Not once I agreed to marry him. Once I committed to Will, I committed completely.

Thinking about the mess of my life is all just too much for me to continue driving. I have to pull the car off at the first rest stop on the highway and collect myself before it is safe enough for me to continue home. I put my head back on the leather headrest and let the memories take over. I feel the tears leaking out from behind my closed eyes, I don't bother to try holding them back. I cry for Derek, for Will, and for myself.

When I think of you now, I think of you doing those three-fingered push-ups over and over. As many as we both could stand. I'd walk down the hall, look into the weight room, and there you'd be, looking back at me in the mirror. You were this sixteen-year-old-bronze-and-golden-boy statue. I was fourteen, terrified that I couldn't catch my breath after you caught me looking at you.

I think of you every time I hear "Stairway to Heaven." I feel your hands at the small of my back, my hands around your neck, us swaying together, bodies pressed as tightly as can be.

I see you coming off the lacrosse field, throwing that grin at me over your shoulder. I see those aviator sunglasses, the tip of a Visine bottle sticking out of your pocket, smoking a butt at the Gazebo. I see you lying in the sun, on the hill going down to the Pond, eyes closed, singing Dead tunes softly to yourself. I see you freezing your ass off that first winter—this too-cool California boy trying to stay warm while getting high in the New England woods.

I never see you dead.

I have now been to two high school reunions without Derek. We're coming up on the third. The first one, our tenth, was bad enough. But he was newly dead, and I was so stung by the shock of it. Our twentieth was tough, because by then it had really set in that I'd never see him again. I was just so damn mad at him for dying. This next one, I'm not sure how I'll get through. Our twenty-fifth? Twenty-five years since we graduated? How is that possible?

* * *

It was one week before my tenth Mansfield reunion. Will and I were newlyweds. I was just starting to show a little baby bump. I was carrying small, so I wasn't really worried that anyone would be counting on their fingers at reunion. It wasn't a thing that was done. At least not in public. And whatever. We were married! I was looking forward to showing off my gorgeous ring, my gorgeous hubby, and my incipient baby bump. Isn't it just the best Mansfield miracle that Will Hooks and I ended up together after all this time? I was thrilled to be able to present everyone with our picture-perfect family at our first important reunion.

Then I got the phone call. From fucking Ashley Dix, of all the goddamned fucking people in all the goddamned fucking world. That demon-spawn voice never changed, but even she didn't sound happy to tell me this news. "Um, Kat? Have you heard? From Beanie? Did Beanie call you? About Derek? Beanie found him, Kat. She found him in bed, this morning? She's really upset. She didn't know he was going to die. Like, Derek and speedballs? Did you know?" I hung up on her, unable, unwilling to process whatever the fuck it was she was saying to me. Dots called thirty seconds later.

Derek had been found dead in his bed by another one of our classmates, Ashley's BFF Beanie. Dead? I just saw him a few months ago. Ugh, Derek was sleeping with Beanie Harriman! Gross. What? Dead? What? Twenty-eight years old and dead of a massive coronary? Twenty-eight? Forget now showing off my newlywed status at reunion, I wasn't even sure I could go. I wasn't sure I could face the questions. Really wasn't sure I could face Beanie Harriman. *She wouldn't show up, would she?* I focused on hating her instead of allowing myself to grieve for Derek. I couldn't let that kind of grief take me away from my family. Disgust over his bad taste was much safer.

The phone kept ringing. "Any heart disease in the family?" Why did people keep calling me to ask me these things? Like I would know. I didn't fucking know. Maybe. His mom died when she was fairly young. Maybe it was a congenital weakness. Maybe it wasn't his fault. Maybe he had a heart defect, not a drug problem. No, wait, his mom died in a car accident. I knew that.

I didn't know if he had any heart problems in the past, but I knew that Derek had just given himself a heart attack, a massive, fatal heart attack. Just shy of his twenty-ninth birthday. Just a little bit older than Brian was. He did so much cocaine and so much heroin mixed together that his heart gave out, a week before our tenth reunion. And he was sleeping with Beanie Harriman, *fucking gross.*

I had all these pregnancy-brain ideas about what our meeting at reunion would be like. He'd see me across the quad. He'd walk over with that saunter that's supposed to look like he wasn't in any hurry. I'd see that grin, that unforgettable grin. I can hear his voice saying "Hey." I'd say "Hey" back. I imagined him telling me all about AA and NA and how he'd really gotten his shit together this time, and since he was gonna be in New York again anyway, maybe he'd stop by to see me. I'd put out my hand to stop him, and say, "That would be really nice, but Will and I are married, and I just don't think it would be a good idea." Then I'd turn and walk away and leave him standing there, knowing just how much he lost when he chose drugs over me.

Instead, he went and died, and I feel robbed. He never got to tell me at our tenth that he'd changed. He never got to see me at our twentieth, still looking mighty damn good. Still married to Will with our beautiful girl at our side and our two gigantic golden retrievers at home. And even though I never wanted him to ask, Derek never got to see my baby's pictures and wonder.

Derek's been dead for nearly fifteen years now. I'm sure I probably wouldn't think about him hardly at all if it were possible to see him. But it isn't, so sometimes I do.

When I heard that Derek died, I briefly considered thinking about asking for a DNA test. And yes, I do know how crass that sounds. But if you found a winning lottery ticket lying in the street, you'd think about cashing it in too. I probably could have done it without letting Will know. Just in case the baby had a claim on Derek's estate. I briefly thought about calling his dad and telling him that I might be carrying the only grandchild he would ever have. Derek was an only child, and as far as I had heard he didn't father any children. All that Wilkeson money would eventually belong to my baby. I was a newly wedded, newly pregnant, hormonal, crazy mess. So yes, I thought about it. But I didn't do it.

Because I couldn't do that to Will, or to us, or to my baby. We were so much better off with everything the way it was. With everything settled. Before I even met her, I knew this was the one truth I would always hold to. Will was her dad, no matter what else.

It's not like having all that money ever did Derek any fucking good. All it gave him was the unlimited freedom to wreck his life. And my baby will be more than fine with her family's old money, even if it is split five ways. I let the image of all the Wilkeson millions pass right on out of my head. I saw what that man did to his son. Nothing was worth letting him anywhere near my child. I would protect my baby no matter what.

Derek's dad passed away recently and left a large chunk of cash to build a new state-of-the-art athletic center at Mansfield in Derek's name. Every prep school in the area will spend the next five years trying to raise money to compete. The Derek Wilkeson Athletic Center is going to be quite the thing. We'll have an Olympic-size pool, six squash courts, a fencing center, and even heated seat cushions for the VIP seats in the new hockey rink.

At our twenty-fifth, I'll have to go to the dedication. I'm the chair of the reunion committee. I'll probably even have to give a thank-you speech. It would be weird for me not to. People would notice. People would wonder. But there is no way I'll be able to sit through that dedication without welling up over the waste of Derek's short life. I'm sure I won't be the only one. There are plenty of people who remember Derek as the sweet, messed-up California boy he was. It won't be weird. No one will think anything untoward about a few extra tears.

At least his dad left the money for a place Derek would have liked, not a library or classrooms or something like that. He'd like to know his name comes up every time the kids are talking about sports. Honestly, though, they should have taken at least some of the money and built a rehab center in town. It's not like he was the last Mansfield kid who needed help. Heated seats in the rink? Really? But a rehab center would mean admitting that a problem exists. Which will never happen. Because everything is supposed to look perfect from the outside looking in.

There are times on the bad days when I wonder what would have happened if he knew about the baby. Would he have lived, gotten better, and come after us? I know not telling him was the right thing, because he was too fucked-up to be near a baby. Way too fucked-up to be near my baby. I stand by every decision I made when I found out I was pregnant. I was right to let the good man who had always loved and taken care of me love and take care of us both.

Even if here we are now.

I am exhausted and overwhelmed. I am just so damn tired. I don't want to have to try so hard anymore. I have been trying to be perfect for one boy or another since I was fourteen years old and I don't want to anymore. I'm sick of thinking only about what other people see when they look at me. I'm sick of being this tired. I want to be happy. I want to not have to care about what other people think.

Home Again

One Week Ago

After fixing my makeup with baby wipes and the kit from my purse so I don't drive home looking like a crazy person, I drive home thinking that the biggest problem in my life is what is going to happen with Will and me. I've had enough with the pretending. My plan is to go home, confront Will, and see what he says. It is time to stand up for myself. Time to take control of my life.

With Bree gone, much of the joy from my house is gone too. When I made my decision, Will got everything he ever wanted out of life. But he doesn't seem at all happy about it right now. On some level, I knew when I made that decision that all I really wanted out of life was to be able to have a normal, happy life with Derek. And I knew I may as well have just wanted the ability to sprout wings and fly.

I took the right path, the only path, and I know most people would see it as an easy one. But there is no way I am willing for Will and me to now be these pathetic people. He can't be the affair guy. I can't be the unfulfilled housewife. It's just too horrible. Too cliché. Pathetic. So unfun.

Will won't put up a fight, I know that. If I say get out, that is what he'll do. He's feeling guilty about cheating on me. He already bought me the guilt car. He'll give me a more than fair settlement and move on, if I tell him that's what I want. He will throw enough money at the problem until it goes away. He would never want to look like the bad guy. And he'll still be a great father to Bree. He will do whatever I say I want. He always does.

The problem is, I don't know what I want.

My panic returns. *What if I'm wrong? What if it doesn't matter what I want this time? What if he no longer wants me? What if I'm no longer pretty enough?* The one constant of my life has been that Will has always wanted me, even long after he'd won me. But what if I'm not good enough now that I'm no longer a pretty young thing? Despite it being common knowledge and all that men improve with age, he really isn't better looking now than the thirtysomething I married either. His hair is a little thinner and his middle is a little thicker. But no one would think of consigning him to the garbage heap because he's hit his mid-forties.

It is too terrifying to have to think that I might not actually know what he will say after I tell him I know about his affair. I think he will say it was a mistake. I think he will want to stay married, but I'm not sure. Will he be relieved to have it all out in the open and tell me he is throwing me over for a trophy wife? Worse, could he expect me to go along, look the other way, and be the Little Wifey, running the house while he runs around, like his mom always did? Because there is no way I'm doing that.

Whatever is to come, I need to stop pretending I didn't know.

When I get to the house, his Audi is already tucked into its spot in the garage, so I know he is home. I take three deep cleansing breaths as I walk past it and knock on the wooden doorframe for luck. I enter the basement from the garage, as ready as I am going to get. I walk up the stairs, put my purse on my desk next to my computer, turn off my cell, and yell up the stairs, "Will?" He must have just gotten out of the shower. He comes downstairs in sweatpants with wet hair.

He confesses almost before I say I know. He saw the look on my face when he came downstairs, and I knew he knew what I was going to say. He grabs a beer from the fridge and sits on the kitchen counter and lets me say it. He runs his hand through his blond curls and I can see the thinning spot at the top of his head. *Have we really known each other since he was sixteen?* His replies come in a staccato beat.

"This secret felt awful," he says.

"I never meant to hurt you," he says.

"I don't even know how it happened," he says.

"I love you. I want you. All I've ever wanted was you," he says.

Then, "Can you forgive me? Can you try? Can we try?"

I am in yet another heap of tears. I'd lost count on the day. "I don't know, Will. But I know I want to try. I love you."

He exhales hard, as if all the breath is leaving his body. "You never say that, you know."

"Don't be ridiculous, Will. Of course I do."

"Nah, Kat, you really don't. You say 'love ya, bye,' to end a conversation. You end emails and cards to me and everyone else with love and xxoo. On our anniversary, you talk about how lucky you are to have such great love in your life. But what you never do is just look at me and say, 'Will, I love you.' When I say it to you, you smile and preen, flip your hair, and bump me with your head, like that's supposed to be a stand-in for the words."

And then, just under his breath, he says, "Princess Diana, right? There were always three of us in the marriage, so that made it rather difficult ..."

"What?"

Then he gets off the counter and says it louder, directly to me, in a plummy English accent: "There were always three of us in the marriage, so that made it rather difficult ..."

"What the fuck does that mean? You mean your assistant?"

He actually snorts. "Kayleigh? Seriously, Kat?" Will puts his hands on my upper arms and looks directly into my eyes. "No, Kat, I mean Derek."

"Derek? Who? What? Are you joking? Derek? The Derek who has been dead for fifteen years? That Derek? What could he possibly have to do with this? With us?"

"For real, Kat? You really want the truth out of me? Fine. Dead or not, Derek has been with us every moment of every day since the day you two met. I was there that day, remember me? I was there every time he broke your heart. Even back in school, I was there, hoping you would finally turn to me. That you would someday feel that way about me. Even dead, every time you hear his name, you get a half-smile and turn your head almost like you expect to see him coming around the corner. The thing with Kayleigh happened because she acts like that when she sees me. And you were too busy making sure everything looked perfect around here that you forgot to even pretend to look like you felt like that about me." Will picks up my chin and forces me to meet his eyes.

"Do you know how many years I have waited to see that look on your face over me? Can you imagine what I feel like, when I have to stand there while people ask you questions about him? Still? After all these years? Like I'm not even there? Like you still belong to him and I'm still just waiting around and carrying your books? Hoping for my chance? Even though I'm your goddamned husband?" He drains the beer and puts the bottle in the sink.

"Do you know that I tried to stop Mansfield from naming that stupid new athletic center for him? I called my dad and asked for the money to override their donation. I humiliated myself in front of my own father to try and beat a dead guy. To make sure I didn't have to hear people talking about him." Will's caustic laugh turns into an anguished cry, and he looks down at the floor.

"But the board's compromise was that it should be the Hooks-Wilkeson Center and that would have been even worse. So I tabled it."

"Oh, Will, Jesus." I see the deep hurt in his eyes, and I know that for all the wrong he has done in our marriage, I have caused at least as much damage. "I can't— I didn't— I don't—" I sob too, as I try to get out the words.

"Let me finish, Kat. Look, I know I fucked up with Kayleigh. But this was the only time I ever cheated on you, I swear. This has never happened before, and it will never happen again. I'm not that guy. I'm not my dad. I know you aren't my mom. And if you want, then Kayleigh's gone. I'll fire her first thing in the morning." Will looks back at me again and I can see the tears shining up his eyes. "I have no problem telling her to go. But Kat, if we want to do this, if we want to try to make this marriage work, you have to let Derek go too. I can't do this anymore. I can't spend the rest of my life waiting for you to get over him. Dead or not, no matter how many horrible things he did to you and to other people, he has been my competition for my wife since we were schoolboys. I'm forty-four years old, Kat. I can't live like this for the rest of my life. I can't live with feeling your regret."

"Oh, Will. My god, Willie. I am so sorry. I never thought— I never meant— I didn't know. I am so sorry, Will. I love you." I put my arms around his waist and hugged him as tightly as I could. I pulled my head back and looked up into his eyes. "I do love you, Will Hooks. I married you. Long before Derek died, I chose you. He asked me to meet up with him that night, before I said I would move in, not only to catch up, but because he thought he could get me back. He thought he could convince me to dump you and move out to California with him. That was how I knew what I really wanted was you. I picked you then and I would pick you now, even if he was still alive. He was never any competition for you. He was a childish infatuation, but I love you. He invited me to meet him again for brunch the next day, to try one more time to convince me to leave you and go off with him. I turned him down again. I didn't tell you then because I guess I felt sorry for him and sad for him too." I tell Will about the last time I saw Derek, at Odessa. And about how mad Derek was at me for choosing Will over him. I tell him the honest truth, that when I was really given the choice and forced to make it, I had chosen him. I said no to Derek, and I said yes to Will.

Will kisses me harder than he has in years. And then we are pulling each other's clothes off, and he hoists me up on the kitchen counter, and we are making love right there in the kitchen with all the lights on.

Can I forgive him for cheating on me? Yeah, I think I can. Can he forgive me? He says he has. Will we stay married? I don't know. I think so. We've been emotionally closed off from each other and living in our own parallel universes for a very long time. But we've been married for a long time. We have a life together. We have a child. We're a family. You don't just throw that away. Our parents went through all kinds of better and worse, and they all stayed married. We do love each other, Will and I, and we do want each other to be happy. Can we be happy together? We don't know yet. But for the first time in a long time, we are trying to tell the truth to each other. We decide to tell Bree in person together over Parents' Weekend.

As promised, Will fires his assistant the next day. Sends her off with a nice settlement and stellar letters of recommendation. I make us appointments with a family therapist, both together and alone. We're trying to spend some time, just the two of us. Trying to remember what we like about each other. Having dinner. Talking. Listening. Making love in every room of the house. I went to his last hockey game. We play tennis together. We're both reading the same book. We're signed up to take a photography class together this fall. I have promised myself that I will remember to make goo-goo eyes at him across the studio table.

Then this happens with Bree. While I'm home alone because Will has to be away on another business trip. When I'm so wrapped up with him, and us, that I forget to worry about her.

Now

So on top of dealing with my perfect marriage not being so perfect, this morning I find my perfect child in the hospital with alcohol poisoning. This week has been a doozy. Before that terrifying phone call, I thought without Bree to mother every day, I needed something else to do with my life, something that was just for me. And maybe I do need that as well. But I've still got lots of mothering to do.

This perfection thing isn't working for any of us. And now I see it hurting Bree too. I need to keep her safe more than I need to look like my life is perfect. I can deal with everything else except the idea that she got hurt because I didn't speak up before something bad happened. Even though my gut was telling me something bad would happen. I didn't listen because I had gotten so used to punishing myself for making one bad important life decision by refusing to make any important life decisions ever again.

I've outsourced all decisions to Will for the last fifteen years and spent my time making sure everything about our life looked perfect to the outside world. Today, I handle everything decisively, all on my own. I make the decisions I think are best for Bree, and I don't care what other people think. Maybe it is a blessing that he has to be away. I need to regain the faith in myself that I used to have. The faith I gave away. The thing I did get right driving home last week was that it is time for me to decide what path I want my life to take and stop just going along. I was never meant to be just a pretty flower waving whichever way the wind blows. I was meant to be happy. I deserve to be happy.

As soon as Bree is released, we'll drive back home. She will come home for a week to recover. Then she can go back to Mansfield if we decide together that is what's best for her. I've taken care of all of the details with the Hulk. Bree will not be booted. Nothing goes on her permanent record. None of those girls will get into any trouble. Bree had an allergic reaction to something she ate, went into anaphylactic shock, and needed to go to the hospital. Her friends are heroes for getting help. End of story.

Of course, the kids at Mansfield will all know the truth. They always do. But that is the official lie.

I will no longer allow Bree to feel pressured to do what she is expected to instead of what is good for her. If she needs more time, if she needs some help, she can do that at home. We will talk to a doctor. We will figure it out and decide together as a family what is best. But I will not ignore my gut feelings ever again. If I am not convinced she should go back, then she isn't going. I'm the Mama, and we can have all these discussions, but I have the final say. If I get an inkling that she's going because she thinks that is what she is supposed to do, then she's not going.

I want her life to be happy, not perfect. It's way past time for us all to be happy.

Once she comes home and has some time to settle in, Will and I will sit down with her and tell her the truth about what is going on with us. That we're working on our marriage and that we don't know what will happen in the future. But we love each other, and we love her. We are trying. We are being completely honest with each other.

Except for the one truth that will always remain mine alone.

1/25/2023

Made in the USA
Columbia, SC
26 December 2022

75048284R00167